The Guru Who Came Down *from the* Mountain

ALSO BY ROSHEN DALAL

The Puffin History of India, Vol I (1997)
The Puffin History of India, Vol II (2003)
The Puffin History of the World, Vol I (2013)
The Puffin History of the World, Vol II (2014)
The Religions of India: A Concise Guide to Nine Major Faiths (2006)
Hinduism: An Alphabetical Guide (2010)
The Compact Timeline History of the World (2010)
The Vedas: An Introduction to Hinduism's Sacred Texts (2014)
India at 70: Snapshots Since Independence (2017)

The Guru Who Came Down *from the* Mountain

A Novel

Roshen Dalal

SPEAKING TIGER

SPEAKING TIGER PUBLISHING PVT. LTD
4381/4, Ansari Road, Daryaganj
New Delhi 110002

Published in India by Speaking Tiger in paperback 2018

ISBN: 978-93-86702-74-6
eISBN: 978-93-86702-75-3

10 9 8 7 6 5 4 3 2 1

Typeset in Garamond Premier Pro by SÜRYA, New Delhi
Printed at Thomson Press India Ltd.

For Ardeshir

CONTENTS

1. The Truth Is Revealed

Nityananda

Everything changed after I heard the news. I thought my heart and mind were always stilled in meditation, but there is no stillness in me now. My heart aches, my stomach churns, my eyes burn with tears. I tell myself, be a witness, the Self is perpetually pure, observe, there is a lesson in all this, but right now I have lost my hold. And so, I have come here, to this cave of ours near Gangotri, to stare at the waters of the river, to feel the coldness of the ice on the mountains, and to quieten my heart and restore my peace. I must do this before I see him. The love of a disciple for his guru is eternal, is unconditional. It must be so, I must make it so. Diana and Sophie are with him already, looking after him, comforting him, but I, the seniormost, have fallen short.

What bothers me is the innocent people I have betrayed. I stood up for him in court, I vowed there was no truth in any of the allegations. I was close to him, I said, one of his main disciples, and I knew for a fact he had never forced himself on any women, on any of his female disciples, never slept with them, never fathered any children. He was an ascetic, celibate from birth. When the reports first reached me in the ashram I dismissed them, supported Dev, and called them 'hysterical women' as he had done. There was Gudiya who was discredited in court, still in her teens—she was pregnant, and she killed herself... Then there were Lydia, Serina, and so many others. And that was not all—I recollected the accusations of drug-dealing, of guns and weapons, of murders, deaths. Were those also true? My heart sinks—what have I done? I thought I was a man of god, I thought I had almost reached the goal. Now these words hammer in my head: *What have I done? What have I done? How can I meet the eyes of those who trusted me?*

I take deep breaths to calm myself. The moon rises over the trees. I sit in meditation, and fix my gaze between my eyebrows. My training cannot let me down. I must be calm and I will.

***

Our cave had a few provisions, a table, a straw mat and some blankets, and I went inside to sleep. I woke in the morning while it was still dark, and walked down to Gangotri. It was early April of the year 2000 and the Gangotri Temple was still closed, the Goddess Ganga in her winter abode at Mukhba. She would return with much fanfare by the end of the month, carried in a procession, accompanied by chants and music.

I had a wash and a cup of tea, and waited for some form of transport. There were fewer buses at this time of the year, but an army jeep was going down to Uttarkashi, and I got a lift. Taking a bus from there I reached Rishikesh in the late evening and found my son Nachiketa waiting at the bus stop.

'What are you doing here, Nachiketa?' I asked.

Nachiketa and I had returned from the US a few days ago. We had travelled from Delhi to Rishikesh together, but from there I had proceeded to Gangotri, telling him to take our luggage and wait for me at the ashram.

'Swamiji wants to see you urgently,' he said.

'I'll go tomorrow.'

'Why not now? I'll take your bag to the ashram and wait for you there. It will just take you half an hour.'

After the long journey, I was tired. But I liked Nachiketa's suggestion, it would be good to get over that first meeting. I handed my small bag to him and walked to Dev's house, which was quite close by. Dev had moved there about a year ago, after he had been found innocent in the case filed by Serina. I hadn't met him since, I had remained immersed in my teaching schedule and in running my ashram in Wisconsin.

***

I reached his room and stood in the doorway watching him. He was lying in bed, his face exhausted, thin and pale. I had a brief recollection of how I had seen him last, he wasn't tall as I am, but his years of yoga exercises had made him lithe and strong. What a transformation had taken place! I steeled my heart to feel no sympathy. I used my intellect to discard the reverential awe I had always felt for him. He was a fake, he had ruined thousands of people. I was no longer his disciple.

He opened his eyes and looked at me. 'Ah, Nitya,' he said. 'You have come. Come here, come near me.' He held out his hand. I took a few steps forward, but ignored his hand. He let it fall on his chest, and was silent.

'You wanted to see me,' I said. My voice was cold, I didn't want to be in the same room as him.

'Why don't you come closer,' he said, 'are you afraid of my disease?'

'It's not your disease I abhor,' I said, 'it's *you*.'

'High-sounding words and oh-so-righteous as usual,' he replied. 'So what are you accusing me of?'

'Do you still deny all those accusations Serina and others made against you?'

'No, Nitya. I won't deny everything now. I'm on my deathbed. But still I need your sympathy, and not all the accusations were correct. Haven't we always had a good understanding? Haven't I helped you, transformed you, cured you of the depression you were in when you joined me? Can you forget or deny all that?'

'I believed in you,' I said. 'And you deceived me. You made me an accomplice in your nefarious deeds.'

'Can't you talk normally, Nitya? What's the use of all these words? A son does not deny his father, even if he has done wrong.'

'I am not your son.'

'My last days are here, can't you forgive me? Is it such a sin to make love to a few women?'

If that was all, I wouldn't have been so upset, but this one revelation, that Dev was dying of AIDS, had led to a flood of doubt. Dev had always affirmed that he had taken sannyas at a young age. If that was a lie, what in his life was true? He said that not all the accusations were correct, but that did not mean that all of them were untrue—had he slept with underage girls, and with his own disciples, some of them, so the rumours went, young boys? That is what bothered me, along with the fact that I had believed him to be celibate, as every true guru must be. It did not matter to me whether they were women or men, but sex with those who looked up to one as god, was a terrible betrayal. There was a lot I wanted to say to him, to pour out all I had heard against him, but something held me back. A realization was dawning on me that I was trying to put all the blame on him, when I too was responsible.

Hadn't there been indications of what he was like almost from the day I first met him? Gudiya's case came to mind, it took place soon after I joined him. Young Gudiya lived in the ashram, and was just around fourteen years old, but somehow, had become pregnant. The ashram doctor, Appaswamy, accused Dev of enticing her to sleep with him, even of raping her, but the case fell through as the girl herself refused to support Appaswamy's accusations. In court, Gudiya would not look at Dev or answer any questions. Others said the doctor was responsible, and was using Gudiya in an attempt to oust Dev and take over the ashram. For a few moments then I had doubted Dev, but as Appaswamy fled to India and was never heard of again, it seemed to me he must be responsible. After this, though, I had heard many more stories of Dev's culpability. Why was I now pretending I knew nothing? Another voice in me protested, *I'm innocent, I truly did not know.* But I *should* have known. I had to face the bleak fact that it had suited me not to know. I had to look into myself, at my own blindness and refusal to see.

I was tired. 'What did you want me for?' I asked, in a more normal tone.

'When I'm dead,' he said, 'will you take me to the ashram and place me in samadhi? Will you cremate me? What will you do with this husk that remains?'

'I haven't thought about it,' I said, which was true. But how could he ever be placed in samadhi? A guru or yogi in samadhi was meant to emanate peace to all who came there, to worship or meditate at the site.

'Whatever you do, Nitya,' he said, 'I want all the correct rites performed. And I want the gurukul boys to pray and chant for me.'

'I'll think about it,' I said, 'and now I'll proceed to the ashram, I've come to you straight from Gangotri.'

He waved his hand dismissively, and I left the room.

I walked to the ashram, with memories of my first days with him reviving in my mind. I drank a cup of tea, and joined Nachiketa for a simple dinner prepared by the ashram cook. Then I slept. I was relieved to be back in a bed after days of sleeping on a mat in the cave, but still, I had a restless night.

***

The memories remained with me the next day. It was many years ago, my first meeting with Dev. I was married then, I was living a contented life. I'd completed my PhD and was teaching ancient Indian history in Ved Narayan College in Delhi. Though I'd had an arranged marriage, we were happy together. My wife, Kusum, was caring, helpful, and a support to me in every way. Our son had just been born, and we named him Sudhakar.

Someone invited me to a seminar organized by the disciples of Swami Shankarananda, and I was persuaded to go by a friend of mine. He told me that Shankarananda was a great swami with a huge following, and had an ashram in Rishikesh, near my hometown, Dehradun. That made me mildly interested in him. It was a day-long seminar with various speakers on food, health, and leading a good life. They advocated drinking only herbal teas and eating only boiled vegetarian food, performing simple exercises in fresh air, and being positive, among other things. There are any number of such speakers today, but in those days—in the mid-1980s—these ideas were not as widespread. In the course of the seminar, there was a tea break and then a lunch break. Though chai was served, their food principles had been followed in the lunch, which consisted only of boiled vegetables, with very little salt and some odd seasoning. I found it inedible, and wanted to leave. My friend stopped me. 'Wait,' he said. 'Swamiji himself will speak in the afternoon. You must hear him.' Another hour passed. I was bored, half asleep and hungry. When at last Shankarananda spoke, I was quite impressed by him, he spoke about how he never went to temples, as the best temple was in one's own heart. Even so, I had no intention of joining him at the time, but a year and a half later, Kusum died.

It was a huge shock to me, as she was only ill for a week. She had had a high fever but the doctor and I both thought it was just a bout of flu. Perhaps it was, but it developed into pneumonia, and despite frantic efforts to save her, she did not survive. A deep depression gripped me after her death, as well as the fear of losing my young son. Then, by chance, there was another meeting with Swami Shankarananda. He was invited by the principal of my college to give a talk to the students of Sanskrit and of ancient history. After the talk, I met him and something led me to tell him about Kusum's death and my subsequent depression. I explained that my depression was heightened by the fact that I felt responsible: I should have taken her to a doctor on time, I should have been able to save her. Shankarananda assured me that I was not responsible in any way. Every person's life and death was determined by their own karma, he said. His eyes held mine with a depth of compassion and I felt peace wash over me like a wave, as if a huge burden had been lifted. He added that right discrimination and the path of truth led to freedom from suffering and an identification with the divine, with

Brahman, the source of all creation, the ultimate goal. Of course, I had read about the eternal Brahman, unborn, beyond touch, beyond sound. I felt that perhaps with Shankarananda, I would actually get a glimpse of it. In those few moments, a kind of yearning grew in my heart. When he suggested I join him and teach in one of his own institutes in the US, I agreed. It seemed like fate, as if it was leading me in the right direction. Also, I definitely needed a change, and somehow, with that decision, I gained a new purpose in life. I believed I would be able to help others, forget my own sorrows, and at the same time share my knowledge of India and its past. As soon as I agreed to join him, Shankarananda asked me to call him by the name Dev, a name that all his friends used.

I wondered if this was his original name, but I did not ask him at that time. I felt privileged and special to get to call him Dev, till I realized that almost everyone, except the very young, or the very new, or those relatively unknown to him, did so. It was one of the things I liked about him, his informality, and the fact that he usually wore ordinary clothes, gerua or saffron robes being confined to special occasions or gatherings of swamis.

Initially, I spent some time in Dev's ashram in Rishikesh, but he soon sent me to the US, making me the head of one of his newest ashrams near Oshkosh in Wisconsin. A teaching institute was attached with courses accredited to the nearby university. I was able to teach ancient Indian history to students far more interested in the subject than those in the college in Delhi. And I earned a huge amount of money compared to what I was earning in India. After about two years with him, I told Dev I wanted to take sannyas, and he agreed. After all I did not want to marry again. My pleasure and joy in life was to lose myself in study, research and teaching. In Shankarananda's protected world, I felt free to do so. I was renamed Swami Nityananda Giri and was respected and looked up to as a teacher, even more than before.

With my base in Wisconsin, I travelled to other parts of the world, and to India, giving talks on ancient texts. I was grateful to Dev, I thought the world of him then. Copying his informal style, I asked most people to call me Nitya, and rarely wore gerua. But I wanted a break with the past, and did not use or reveal my original name, Prem, to most people. And I myself renamed my son Nachiketa. I did not send Nachiketa to school. I did think about a boarding school, but the idea didn't appeal to me. He had already lost his mother, and if I sent him away from me, he would almost lose his father as well. There was an element of fear too in me, what if something happened to him when he was far away from me? And wouldn't sending him to a boarding school be an abdication of my responsibility? As a result, Nachiketa was my constant companion, he travelled everywhere with me. Perhaps he was more educated than other children his age. When we were in Rishikesh he studied Sanskrit at the nearby gurukul. His English and Hindi were good, and he knew some French and Spanish. He knew basic maths, whatever was needed in daily life. And I used to teach him in my own way, tell him about books, read to him, and narrate stories from the ancient past. I thought of Nachiketa like a sort of future Buddha. He would grow up in a protected environment, he would study, understand and contemplate. Like the Nachiketa of the *Katha Upanishad*, he would ask the right questions, and ultimately he would be enlightened. He would take over and run Dev's ashram at Rishikesh, or perhaps all his ashrams and institutes.

Now I see I was ambitious for my son, just like any other father. And I was in retreat from the world, buried in ancient texts and books. I did not see the truth regarding Dev, because I did not want to see it.

***

That evening, I decided to visit Dev again. I wanted to ask him what had made him like this. Was it just power that had gone to his head? Had he once been different? I wanted some sort of explanation, or something that would convince me that he wasn't a bad person. On hearing that he had AIDS, without asking him anything, I had more or less jumped to the conclusion that every negative story and rumour I had heard about him was true. Perhaps it wasn't so, perhaps, as he had said, not all the accusations were correct, perhaps I had overreacted. But another part of me knew why I had been so quick to believe the worst about him. It was only a reaffirmation of what I already knew, but refused to acknowledge. Gudiya, the other women, shouldn't I have taken those stories more seriously? And then there was Jeff who confided in me and told me that drugs were being sold in Dev's main ashram near Sparks, Nevada—I refused to believe him, or even to investigate. Jeff was one of my own students in Oshkosh. A friend of his was in the Sparks ashram, and evidently told him that he was upset about something. Jeff went to visit him, and on his return, came to meet me, telling me that his friend had told him that a staff member there, the psychiatrist in fact, was persuading people to buy drugs from him. It would cure all their problems, they were told. It did raise a doubt in me, I asked Dev about it, but when he said it was nonsense, I believed him. Several years later, one of the residents informed me that Mark, Dev's bodyguard and constant companion, was importing and selling guns and ammunition. I had never liked Mark, there was something about him that made me uncomfortable, yet I just kept quiet and let it slide. Now, I told myself, there may have been mitigating circumstances, perhaps everything was not true, and if so my own guilt too would be reduced. When I reached his house, Diana stopped me outside his room. 'He's not at all well,' she said. 'And your meeting with him yesterday deeply disturbed him. I don't think you should see him today.'

'He and I have things to discuss, Diana,' I said. 'It was on his request that I came here yesterday. Why don't you ask him if he would like to see me, instead of making decisions for him?'

I wasn't usually so assertive. Diana looked at me, surprised, but went in to ask him. She was back a minute later. 'He wants to see you,' she said, 'but don't tire him.' When I went to his room, he turned towards me with the trusting look of a sick child gazing at its mother. I was touched, but did not want to waste time on sympathy. He did not have long to live, and I had to know the truth.

I got to the point straight away. 'Dev,' I said, 'I didn't want to bother you, but it's important for me to know something about your life. How did you come to be a swami, and to what extent are all the negative stories about you valid? What made you do all that you did? I don't think your earlier account of your life, of living with a swami from your young days, is true.'

'I wanted to tell you myself,' he said. 'I don't have the

energy to talk much, but I have written down part of my story. I planned to give it to you yesterday, but you were not in a good mood.' He handed me some sheets of paper. I saw the pages had his handwriting on them. I looked at him. 'Read them,' he said. 'It is not a justification, but perhaps some sort of an explanation. This is as much as I could write down. I will write more later. I hope that after reading it you will understand me better. Come back when you have read it—I'm very tired today.'

I left him then, told Diana to go to him, and walked back to the ashram. The next morning, I sat down at my desk, and began to read what Dev had written. This first part, which I give below, began with his present situation, but was mainly an account of his early life and marriage.

2. As Death Approaches

Dev's Story

I know I am dying. Sophie and Diana have come from the US to look after me, my Indian disciples are too shocked. I don't know how long I've got, my body is gaunt and emaciated, my hair is falling, there are patches on my skin. I pull myself out of bed at times and stand at the window, holding on to the frame to prevent myself falling, gazing at the mountains, those mountains that I love so much, changing colour with the seasons, with the hours of the day, blue, purple, green, grey. If I'm lucky, if the day is clear, if there are no clouds, behind them in the distance I catch a glimpse of the snow-covered peaks.

I am fortunate to be in my own house that I had bought so many years ago. And my mind is still clear and sharp, unaffected by this disease they all seem to fear so much. I trust it will stay so till the end; in some ways I've been disciplined through most of my life, with my mental exercises, pranayama and asanas. And now I begin to write down my last thoughts, to assess my life, to look back. Diana offered me a laptop, but I've never used a computer, I've always had others to do everything for me. So, she has given me a clipboard and a few pens, and placed a stack of paper on the table near me.

To be honest, I have not written anything much in my life, apart from some poetry. My best poems are on the woman of my dreams, not Gita, who was once my wife, not any of the other women I knew, not even the intelligent and beautiful Sharada, but the perfect woman I never found. Perhaps after my death I'll see her, standing on the other shore, her arms outstretched, waiting, waiting for me. But at night when I sleep I get terrible dreams, and it makes me wonder, what does the other side hold for me? What will happen after I am dead?

It troubles me that Nitya, the disciple to whom I feel closest, the one I love so much, has not come to see me. He supported me all those years, when so many allegations were levelled against me, when I had to appear to defend myself in court, he was my staunch friend. But he believed me then, and now I know, hearing of this disease, he is shocked. Perhaps he asks himself why he accepted me as his guru, why he was so fervent a disciple. He will search his conscience for the answer, he will meditate, but in the end he will come to me, he will not be able to deny to himself the benefits he has gained from me, both materially and otherwise. He is an honest man.

I look back at the first time I met Nitya, it was when he attended my seminar, though Nitya of course was a name I gave him later. On that first occasion, I saw him in the audience. My eyes kept straying back to his face, his refined features, his expression calm and composed. During the tea-break, when he walked across the room, I saw that he was a head taller than most of the people there. I asked about him and was told that he was Prem Rawat, a teacher in a college. Rawat? Then he was from my own Garhwal region! Right then I hoped that he would one day join me. I had thousands of disciples and the seniormost headed my various ashrams. But among them, I did not have a single friend. I saw in a flash, a kind of vision, that Prem could be both a disciple and a friend.

Then, a year later, I met him again. He was no longer that calm, serene person he had been. His face was darkened by sorrow, he looked thin and stooped. Seeing this change in him, I knew that the time was right. I learnt that he too had lost his wife, that he had a son he would have to bring up on his own. I persuaded him to leave his job and teach at one of my ashrams, it wasn't very difficult. After he joined me, we spent some time together in Rishikesh. Then I sent him to teach in my new ashram in Oshkosh. Over the years we did become friends. We had so many discussions on spirituality, the true path, and the ancient texts, I counted on him to clarify my thoughts, I used his wisdom in my speeches.

Now Diana has come, to wash my hands and face and settle me down for the night. She tells me I must sleep.

As I drift into sleep I think with affection of Diana. She is still the efficient cheerful person she has always been. She's a little plump, and has dark brown hair tied in a bun. She grew it long for me, because I like it that way, it makes her look almost Indian. Her eyes are brown too, her mouth wide and pale. And she's short, hardly five feet two. I like that too, because I'm short myself, and I've never been comfortable with women who tower over me. As for Sophie—well Sophie hasn't been with me long. These days she looks stern, doesn't talk, and leaves the room as soon as she can.

***

I slept an uneasy sleep and in the morning before I woke, I had a dream. In the dream I heard a noise on the balcony and I got up and went out to see what it was. A small white horse stood there, about two feet high, eating the leaves of one of the plants. But there were strings or ropes bound around it, as if it had been tied up, and somehow had broken loose and come here. I brought a pair of scissors and wanted to cut all the strings, to free it from its wrappings, but then it raised its head and looked at me, and I was afraid.

I woke feeling disturbed and confused. It was a beautiful little horse, why hadn't I been able to set it free?

Diana came along, and as she sponged me with hot water from a basin, I thought about the horse. I'd been good at interpreting dreams once, and now I saw that the horse was my spiritual self. It could have grown to its full size, developed wings like Pegasus, and flown through the sky. But it was stunted, and in addition, bound, tied up in string. But at least it had returned to me.

I must find it again, I thought, I must release it. There was still time before I died. I had to look back on my life and see where I had gone wrong. And what I had done right. I believed, in the balance, I had also done a lot of good.

***

My family were sheep- and goat-herders, as well as traders. We lived high up in the Himalayan mountains on the northern border of India, in the small village of Jadang. Nearby was the larger village of Nelung. Before Independence this was part of the state of Tehri Garhwal, one of the many Indian states not directly under the British. In these villages, at a height of 3,400 metres, snows were heavy in winter, hence we used to move down to the plains with our herds for six months of the year.

Tibetans call us Rongpas, and we use this name for ourselves too. We are also known as Jads, as Jadang, just five kilometres from the Tibetan border, is near the Jadang gaad, one of the gaads or streams forming the Jad Ganga, a river also known as the Jahnavi. The valleys of these gaads lead into Tibet. Thag la and Tsang chok la in the Tirpani gaad valley, were the passes normally used by us Jads and our Tibetan counterparts.

Lower down, at Bhairon Ghati, the Jad Ganga and the Gangotri river join together, forming the Bhagirathi. When the Alakananda joins the Bhagirathi, the combined river becomes the Ganga, most sacred of all our rivers, flowing swiftly down to the plains and then across northern India, before entering the sea, carrying with it the bones and ashes of the millions cremated on its banks.

My ancestors must have migrated here long, long ago, either from the plains or from neighbouring hill regions. We like to believe we are Rajput in origin, though we speak our own, unique, Jad language. Lying in bed, I remembered the beautiful village and region of my childhood.

Among the places the Jad flows near is Lanka in the Bhairon valley. Was this perhaps the true Lanka of the Ramayana? I have often thought it was a more plausible location for a series of events that must have taken place in the Stone Age, if tradition is to be believed. There is even Janak Tal, a beautiful pristine blue lake, in the Jadang gaad valley. The local legend is that King Janaka spent time here in prayer and meditation. And of course, Lakshmana-siddha, near Dehradun, is said to be where Lakshmana practiced austerities, while Rama did so right here in Rishikesh. Strangely enough, they did this to atone for the sin of killing Ravana.

My region is linked not just with Ramayana legends, but with those of the Mahabharata too. The Pandavas are said to have lived and roamed in this area and are believed to be born at Pandukeshwar, between Joshimath and Badrinath. There are many other places around here associated with them, and numerous stories. They walked through this area on their way to heaven, when one after the other all the Pandavas except Yudhishthira fell down dead. Yudhishthira proceeded onwards with his dog, refusing to enter heaven without the faithful animal, until the problem was resolved when the dog turned into the god Dharma. On an earlier occasion, Bhima, the third Pandava married Hidimba in the mountains, and had a son named Ghatotkacha. We consider Hidimba a local woman, and in our region Ghatotkacha is not known, but their children are Babika and Babiki, a boy and a girl. Our local story is that the two children were grazing their rhinoceros, when the Pandavas appeared, and despite the children's pleas and tears, the Pandavas killed the animal. Only later did they discover that they were Bhima's children, and regretted what they had done. My father said that Babika and Babiki were like us, as we too cared deeply for the animals we grazed.

***

I was born in Bagori, a small village in Tehri Garhwal, around 1945–46. It wasn't known as Bagori in those days, but was part of the village of Sukhi. My mother was never quite sure of the date, but it was one or two years before India became independent.

Bagori, at a height of 2,409 metres, about a thousand metres below Jadang, was along the route of our annual migration. It was on one of these journeys that I was born. We would start from Jadang and proceed to Bagori near Harsil, a place we called Haniya, a distance of about

31 kilometres. Harsil was well known as the residence of Frederick Wilson (1816–1883), who had married a local woman, minted his own coins, and built a suspension bridge over the Jad Ganga. He also amassed money through logging, the denudation of our mountain forests began in his time. From Harsil we proceeded to Uttarkashi, Dunda, Dharasu and then to Chor-Pani. Chor-Pani is near Rishikesh, and was at that time a forested area, where we set up temporary huts, though we usually preferred to stay at Dunda, as we did not like mixing with people of the plains.

In my young days, our annual move to warmer regions would commence in September, while the return journey would begin at the end of February, after Losar, the Tibetan new year, which was one of our main festivals. All our herds went with us. Both men and women carried pots and pans, blankets, and some food-grains on their backs. Women would also carry small children, and thus I began travelling on my mother's back when just a couple of weeks old. Our large and strong dogs guarded us and the herds. On the journeys we often ate only mandua rotis with onion and salt. Mandua, a type of millet, is very nutritious. We erected simple tents, or slept under the open sky, or under rock overhangs.

There are extensive bugyals or meadows near Jadang and these were good grazing grounds, but when we returned from our annual migration, the animals would be taken to graze in higher pastures, where there was even more luxuriant, juicy grass. Eating from these grasslands, the sheep and goats developed coats that yielded long, fine wool. In the forests slightly lower down, grew kharshu, birch and juniper trees, as well as shrubs of various kinds. Small streams flowed from the Jadang gaad, with icy water in which we children sometimes bathed, though not too often. A little way away, clear spring water flowed down the rocks, and we collected this for drinking and cooking. Springs were sacred, and only a clean vessel could be used to collect this water.

As soon as the snows melted and the mountain passes opened, the barter trade with Tibet would begin, after consulting an astrologer for an auspicious date to start the treacherous journey. Salt, borax and wool from Tibet and gur, rice, wheat, oil, cloth and shoes from the plains, along with local herbs, dried mushrooms and amaranth were among the various goods we traded. Most of these were transported in bags on the backs of our herds of sheep, though occasionally mules were hired. Sometimes we got chorgai (mountain cows), yaks and small mountain horses from Tibet. After crossing the border, Jad men stayed with Tibetan families, while coming from the other side, Tibetan traders, whom we referred to as 'mitra', or 'friend', stayed in our homes. In Uttarkashi, on our side of the border, we sold the goods for money. There were traders who dealt in musk, hides and horns, these had a high value, but my father refused to do so. He said he did not want to benefit from dead animals. He said that killing animals unnecessarily was wrong, and would repeat the story of Babika and Babiki, who cried when their animal was killed.

We lived a simple life. My mother worked hard, cooking, collecting water and fuel, washing the utensils and clothes, growing a few crops, spinning the wool of our sheep, and knitting warm clothes and blankets, though weaving was the work of another caste. Food too was simple, including chacha, or butter-tea, which we often drank to gain energy or warmth, sattu, mixed millet flour, cheena or barley, and baadi, a dish I still like. Baadi is just salt and mandua flour cooked in boiling water till it thickens, eaten with ghee and gur, but it brings back nostalgia for my village and my childhood. Later our diet changed and we ate more rajma and potatoes, along with rice. My mother made a lovely dish from potato skins, which were roasted on the fire and then ground. Today everyone advocates green vegetables and fruit, I used to too, in my days as a guru, but as a child I don't recollect having any. Not much grew in our region, and supplies from outside hardly ever came. We never killed our animals for meat, and nor did we usually drink their milk. If an animal died a natural death, people of our group would cook and eat it, and sometimes those who were sick, or the young children, drank a little goat's milk.

Though girls and boys were to some extent equal in our society, they had different roles. In those days we had no schools, and boys learned to work with their fathers, while girls helped their mothers. Small boys could not accompany their fathers either to the high pastures, nor on cross-border trade, so as a young child I had a lot of freedom. In addition, my mother was quite indulgent towards me as I was the only boy and the youngest, and also because she had almost lost me when I was born. I had three older sisters, two were already married before my birth, the third was twelve years old, and she looked after me like a second mother. Till I was six or seven years old, I ran and played the whole day, particularly when we lived in the winter months at Dunda. I grew strong, taller than the other children, who saw me as their leader, and I would organize both their games and their mischief. But something changed in me around the age of seven. This change began when my mother told me the story of how I got my name.

***

Now that I am dying, it's time to tell the truth. I used to say that as a child I would meditate and recite sacred chants without being taught. That a swami came and took me away to the mountains, that my father gave me up with reluctance, but could not refuse a holy man. I told stories of how I grew up with the swami, what he taught me, his strictness, his training, the miracles I experienced. These stories came to me so spontaneously, that perhaps I was a creative genius of sorts, or perhaps, I convinced myself, all these things were true, but had taken place in another life. The reality is different, though I did have an early association with a guru.

My mother told me my birth was unexpected. I was premature and very weak, not expected to live. Our group waited at Bagori for her to recover, and for me to gain a little strength, but, she said, I seemed to be fading. Then a sannyasi on his way to Gangotri, passed by. He touched my head, and said that I had a great future. I would live and be strong, and even be a holy man like him. With the permission of my parents, he named me Devdarshan, one who has the vision of god. My mother said I rapidly gained strength, and within a week was almost like a normal baby.

After I heard about this, for some reason, I hoped he would come and take me with him. I am not sure why I thought that, because till then I had been quite happy. Whenever I could, I escaped, and wandered around by myself. The other children tried to be friendly, but I did not want them any more, I was always alone. In my solitary walks and climbs, I had a strange sense of joy, and a glimpse of something glorious and grand, which I could not put into words, or even into thoughts. I felt that somehow I was different, destined for a great future.

The sannyasi never returned, but about a year after I had separated myself from the other children, I met an Englishman in Dunda. In the villages we were cut off from news, there wasn't even a radio in those days. But of course by that time we knew about India's struggle for independence, and that this had been achieved in 1947. And we knew that though our maharaja did not want it, we had been integrated with the rest of India. Soon we would have schools and better development. And the English, the villains, had been thrown out of India after 1947. Then what was this Englishman doing here? We did not know then that there were many of them who loved India and stayed on, some in towns and some in villages, and many who were loved by the people here.

The Englishman, I didn't know his name at that time, lived in a small hut like ours. He made his own mandua roti on a wood fire just like any of us. And as he had no wife to do it for him, he collected the wood from the forest himself. When I went for my solitary walks, I often saw him walking surefooted with long strides, or just sitting on a rock and staring into space. His hair was dark, almost black, and his skin was somewhat like ours. After seeing me a few times, he asked me my name. He had learnt a little Garhwali, which we knew as it was the language of the region, though not our own. I could understand what he said, though his accent sounded strange. 'Debu', I told him, as that was my pet name, and he said his name was Mr Robinson, and made me repeat it, till I got it almost right. Then he took out something from his pocket, a paper packet that he opened. In it there were flat, square pieces of something brown that he began eating, and gave me two pieces too. I tried it, it tasted strange. It was my first experience of a biscuit.

Thus started our friendship. In those winter months, I spent as much time as I could with him, and he began to teach me the English alphabet, how to speak a few sentences, and even how to read. Summer approached and it was time for us to return to Jadang. Mr Robinson did not seem to know that we were Jads, nor of our annual migrations, and when I told him, he looked surprised, thoughtful, sad.

The next day he went to my father and told him that I was a bright boy, and he would like to send me to a good school in Nainital. Nainital was far away, said my father, but Mr Robinson said he had once been a teacher in a school there, he knew the principal and he would ask him to take me in. My father said he'd think about it; he and my mother discussed it for several days, on the whole they thought it was a good opportunity. So it was decided I should go to St Mark's Boys' School, and I was happy, though apprehensive. Mr Robinson told me about Nainital. It was in the mountains too, and not that far away. There was a big lake there, and the local people spoke Kumaoni, which was not very different from the Garhwali language. But, said Mr Robinson, in school I would be speaking English and learning English. And if I studied well, I could go to college and get a good job.

I also remember that I didn't have a second name, a surname, at that time. Mr Robinson added my father's first name, 'Mangal', to mine, thus I became Devdarshan Mangal. Though my date of birth was not known, this too was required for school, and the date 6 March 1945 was chosen. Letters went to and fro, lists came of what I would need, but things were not finalized until we returned the following year after our winter migration to Jadang. Then, in 1954, Mr Robinson himself took me to Nainital, equipping me with uniforms, books and everything else. As I entered the tall school gates with him, I found everything very strange at first. There were so many boys there, big and small! I'd never seen anything like it. And all wearing the same sort of odd clothes that I too had to wear. Mr Robinson took me to the principal's room, a man even more strangely dressed, all in white, whom I was supposed to call 'Father'. I already knew what father meant, how could I call him that when I had my own? He was expecting us, Mr Robinson introduced me, and 'Father' said he would take care of me. As Mr Robinson turned to leave I had a mixture of confused emotions, a sudden wave of affection for him, along with fear and panic. I wanted to rush to him, hug him, and beg him to take me back with him. He must have sensed something of this, as he patted me on the back, and told me to be a brave boy. 'This is your start to a better life,' he said as he left. It is true, school was the beginning of a better life—though not a great one.

I slowly got used to the school, participated in all the activities, and made some friends. I was given special tuition to catch up with the other students of my age, and it did not take me long. I was on the whole an average student, but very good at games and sports. And somehow, I developed a love and passion for English literature, and specially for Shakespeare. I didn't quite understand why at that time, but later it seemed to me that all the essential questions and philosophies of life are contained in his works. Initially it was his language that entranced me, and again evoked in me a longing for something, I was not sure what. A part of me still remained distant and aloof from my surroundings. I went for long walks whenever I was allowed to, and as I walked up and down the mountains, along narrow pathways, surrounded by trees, I felt at peace. After these walks, at night I often had wonderful dreams, and saw golden lights, dark blue skies and sparkling stars. In these dreams my heart would be filled with joy, and I was more sure than ever that I was destined for something great.

But I could see that though I'd come a long way from being a simple mountain boy, studying in St Marks wasn't going to lead me very far. If I did well, I may have become a schoolteacher instead of a herdsman and trader, but was that any less common a destiny? Some of the boys spoke of government jobs, joining the civil service, or of joining their fathers in business. It wasn't for me, I knew, and it all left me feeling even more restless and dissatisfied.

I kept my thoughts to myself. I saw Mr Robinson and my parents and sisters in the holidays. My family and friends all looked up to me, and certainly I felt different from them, but it was not enough. After some years Mr Robinson returned to England. He wrote a couple of books on his life in Dunda, which were quite well received. We exchanged regular letters and he continued to pay all my expenses. I passed out of school with a high second class, that is, with average marks. But my English teacher, Mr David, told me: 'You are the best student I have ever had, in my thirty years of teaching.' I was both honoured and flattered by that, especially as there were many Anglo-Indian boys in the school, whose first language was English.

Mr Robinson urged me to go to college, and paid for my

college course and stay in a hostel. Now I was in Dehradun, closer to my home town, and studied English literature. It wasn't a great college, as the classes and lectures were mainly conducted in Hindi, though the books, exams and tests were in English. I was used to living with other boys, but because of my time in St Marks, I faced some problems in the hostel. Of course, I knew Hindi, Garhwali, and some Kumaoni, along with my own Jad language, but in school we were forced to speak only in English, and I had got used to this. When I saw the reaction of the boys in the hostel, and faced their hostility, I switched over to speaking in Hindi, but my English was streets ahead of theirs, and they were envious. They also seemed bigger, stronger, and older than me, and I wondered if I would be able to continue there. There was a day student I made friends with, Deepak, and he suggested I could live with him and his family on payment, but I understood it would cost far more than the hostel. I thought of making a request to Mr Robinson, but my problems were solved when two of the toughest boys in the hostel changed their approach. For our first monthly test, they asked me, rather roughly, for my notes. When I shared these with them without any protest, they became my friends, as they saw my uses—they probably felt that I was their best hope for passing tests and exams. Three years passed, and I received a BA degree. I had the highest marks not only in the college but in the whole of Dehradun. The teachers were very happy with my results, it gave them credit too. I wondered what to do next, but they suggested a one-year teacher's training, that would get me a job in a school. There was no problem getting admission, and after a year, I got my teaching degree and easily got a job in a school as an English teacher. Back in my village, all thought I was a lucky fellow, educated and with a good status, but I remained unhappy. I didn't know what I wanted, but this wasn't it.

By that time, a lot had changed for us. Jadang and Nelung were lost to us, and Bagori, my birthplace, had become our permanent summer residence. Our original villages were occupied by the army in the late 1950s, when the Chinese were increasing their control over Tibet, and beginning their incursions into India. The Dalai Lama fled Tibet and reached India in 1959. The Indo–China war took place in 1962, and we had to stop trading with Tibet too. After our community left Jadang forever, at Bagori, they began to celebrate a new festival called Panoh, just before they left for Dunda in September, when the cold would begin to set in. Panoh was a reenactment of the legendary visit of the Pandavas. Two pumpkins represented the rhino, and in the enactment it was 'killed', while two children representing Babika and Babiki, wept. Then a goat representing Duryodhana was sacrificed, though Jads would never perform this sacrifice, it was done by a person of a different caste. I was not there at the time, but my father complained to me about it, he never liked these new elements, and the killing involved. As Jads, we always had our own local deities, along with Tibetan Buddhist and Hindu beliefs. When we lived in Jadang, we believed these nature spirits, of the sun, forests, mountains and streams lived among us, we never confined them in images and temples. At the entrance to Bagori, is our main deity, Me-Perang, who guards and protects us, represented by a bamboo pole, topped by a red scarf. Cut off from Tibet, Hindu influence began to increase and Me-Perang soon joined other local deities in their pilgrimage to Gangotri, an entirely new development. I was one of the first Jads to get an education, but soon there was a primary school that moved along the migratory route, and a secondary school at Dunda. Many Jads now leave the area for education and work.

***

On my visits to Bagori, my father sensed my unhappiness, and thought what I needed was a wife. In school and in college, I'd joked with my friends about girls, but something held me back from meeting or talking to them. Some of them approached me themselves, but I did my best to avoid them. When my college friends began to think me strange, I invented a childhood love, back in Jadang or in Bagori. 'But she is a village girl,' they said, 'and you are educated.' I told them that out of love for me, she too was trying to get an education.

In fact, I knew no one, and did not like any of the girls my father suggested for me. How could I ever be happy with an uneducated village girl? 'You are living in Dehradun,' said my father. 'Find one for yourself, we will accept her, whoever she is.' His attitude was far advanced for the times and more so for the backward region where we lived. Though in our community, parents often did consult their children while arranging their marriages, many marriages took place at a very young age, and a free choice was rare. But I was not able to follow his advice. I was too shy, and too withdrawn. Time passed, and I continued to live a solitary life. Despite my success as a teacher, I was depressed and lonely.

I was almost twenty-five years old, when my father felt he had at last found a match for me.

It so happened that there was a girl from Nakuri, a village near Dunda, who was educated, who had completed her school and college despite the odds against her, and done her teacher's training in Dehradun. And she was even teaching Sanskrit in a girls' school there. Apparently, like me, she had a patron who paid for her education and persuaded her parents to let her study. Her patron was a retired brigadier, a well-known mountaineer, who had lost his only daughter in an accident. Now my father approached him with a proposal of marriage for me, though she was not a Jad, and was almost my age, my father felt it might work. Among Jads only the man's family can make a request for marriage, though it is often the other way around in the plains. 'If you don't like her, we won't go ahead,' he said to me. 'Just meet her and see what you feel.' Perhaps he knew that the idea did appeal to me. She would be like me, from a village nearby, yet educated. She would know Garhwali, if not the Jad language, and was not a stranger from the town. She was a teacher—perhaps we could open a school together. Thus I dreamed, before meeting her.

Though we were both in Dehradun, the meeting took place in Bagori. Gita was brought to our small home there, by her parents and her patron. I saw her face, and my heart sang. She looked beautiful to me. Her light brown eyes glowed in her oval face, her skin was creamy and clear. Two long black plaits hung down on either side of her face, entwined with colourful ribbons. She looked up at me, and then lowered her eyes shyly, under long eyelashes. Some of those golden lights and flashing stars seemed to shine in my heart and mind again. I said, 'Yes,' and my parents were pleased. The marriage details were worked out, and on one happy day in May 1970 we were married. I was twenty-five and Gita was twenty-four. It was much too late for a hill girl to marry, but being educated it had been difficult to find a match for her. And in the plains,

I guessed she was shy, just like me, and did not speak to too many people.

***

Now it's 9 p.m. and Diana wants me to get some rest. I've been writing all day, though of course in between Sophie and Diana have been attending on me, with lunch, tea and biscuits, dinner, a sponge of the face and hands...I eat very little, and sometimes they feed me with their own hands, as a mother would a child. I don't remember my mother doing it though. Hill children are taught to be independent, and until this final illness, I was a good eater.

Diana sat beside me this evening, holding my hand. Together we gazed out of the window, watching the tree tops turn dark, and breathing in the cool air that pervaded the room. She is kind.

***

Nityananda

There was more to read, but this is as far as I got today. What was most intriguing was to read what he had written about me. What was it he saw in me, something even I was unaware of? I was many years younger than Dev. I had joined him only in 1988, when he had already been a guru for quite some time, and gradually, we did become friends. He was my guru, I admired and respected him, he had reached out to me when I was depressed and despairing. Thanks to him, I had a new and different life, and slowly, the pain of Kusum's death receded. In the ashram there were many people to help me with my young son, and he too thrived.

3. And Then, a Tragedy

Dev's Story

I had a nasty dream last night. I dreamt that somebody, a man whose name I can't remember, had died and been buried a while ago. Now four unknown people had come to me and were asking me to give them boiling water to pour on his grave. I protested, I didn't like the idea, it made me feel queasy. The man was dead. Let him be in peace, boiling water would deface his body, I said. They did not listen to me, and began to heat the water themselves. I woke, my heart hammering, feeling sick.

What did the dream mean? And why did it disturb me? I had fallen asleep thinking of Gita, remembering those few good years. I don't normally look back on them, for it pains me to think about those days, my confusion, and the end of all my dreams. Gita was dead, yes, long ago, and had I been trying, not just to efface her memory, but to deface it? But the body in the dream was that of a man. Is the dream about me? A predictive dream? When I am dead and gone, will people deface my memory? And why were there four men?

A new thought comes to me, a new fear. When swamis of our sect die, we aren't burnt, we are buried, but not in a coffin. We sit in padmasana, the lotus posture, and a samadhi, a sacred place, is built around us. The power we had, the sacredness, remains at that spot, and disciples come there to commune with the guru, to get his blessing. But will Nitya and the others place me in samadhi, now that I have AIDS? Or will they consign me to the flames, like an ordinary mortal? Even then the son must light the fire, and as I have no son, at least none that I have acknowledged, will Nitya do it for me, will he at least be my son, if not my disciple? Last night's dream has generated these fears. And there is more to them than just what will happen to my body. A greater fear which is always present, is what will happen after my death? I wish Nitya would come soon.

I could hardly eat any breakfast this morning, but I could not confide my concerns to Diana and Sophie. For one, despite being so close to me, they don't fully understand our Indian way of life. And besides, I don't want them to know I am afraid, I want them to continue to respect me, to think of me as their guru. I had told Diana I must have got AIDS from a visit to a dentist in India. Perhaps she believes me? It is unlikely, as Diana knows about many of my affairs. She's never been judgemental though.

Isn't it ironical that four years ago, I finally gave up sex, took to celibacy for the first time after establishing my own ashram, and being acknowledged as a guru. And then a year later, when constant fatigue and frequent fevers led me to a doctor, I was diagnosed with AIDS. The seeds of it must have lain dormant in me for years, from where and when they came, I cannot say. I knew so many women, and even a few men. I gave up sex after I won the court case filed by Serina. I gave it up in gratitude, in a vow I made to god, a being whom I'd never worshipped before, hardly even thought about, though I could convince my disciples not only that I knew god but even that I was god, had achieved that divine union described in all our texts. Serina accused me of exploiting her when she was still underage, a child, and nothing would get her to take back her accusations, not friendly talks by senior ashram members, not offers of money, nor threats. In fact, I still feel I was not at fault in Serina's case. It's true she was only fifteen, but I wasn't interested in her at all. There had been an earlier case regarding Gudiya, but as I assured Nitya at the time, that had no truth in it. I had never looked upon her as anything but a daughter. Gudiya, as far as I knew, had been attracted to a young man, a Chinese-American, who came to the ashram for a course, and succumbed to his charms. She may not have known much about how one gets pregnant and must have approached Appaswamy when she felt unwell. He saw it as his big chance to remove me from the scene, and persuaded her to accuse me. He must have told her that this would solve all her problems; perhaps he even promised her marriage. I could have explained all this, but when Gudiya saw me in court, she was unable to make those false accusations, the case was dismissed. With Serina, things were different. She was almost six feet tall, and well-built. Her mother had brought her to the ashram in Sparks, as she said the girl was only interested in athletics, and was failing in school. She was a good cross-country runner and had won several competitions, but without completing school she had a poor future. The mother, Paula, said she had already taken her to a psychiatrist, as she believed that refusing to study was a deliberate protest, but it hadn't helped. She hoped that a course in yoga would lead Serina to focus and concentrate. Paula added that her husband had a flourishing business, and implied that a big donation would come our way if the course helped Serina.

As I said, I was not interested in the girl. I like mature women, especially those who are feminine, and ideally, shorter than me. It was Serina who made an appointment with me, saying that she needed to discuss something. Hoping for that big donation, I was willing to give her some time. But when she came to see me, she literally threw herself at me. I was taken aback, but did not resist, after all, any type of sex was pleasurable for me. That was the only sexual encounter with Serina, but then the accusations began. I had the family investigated, and understood it was a plot to get money from me, their business was failing. Instead of taking the money offered, they sued me for a million dollars for breach of trust, and accused me of rape.

As if that wasn't bad enough, encouraged by her stand, some others spoke of my giving them drugs, and even of my making money by importing and selling huge consignments of drugs, and of dealing in arms. That was only partly true, as Mark, my friend and bodyguard, was in charge of both the drug consignments and the arms deals, but of course I knew about them, sometimes used drugs myself, and gave them away free to special students. I said it was to liberate them from their conditioning, and to help them to meditate, but it was, on the contrary, to bind them to me and to increase Mark's profits. I received a portion of those, and along with donations from the foolish and the wealthy, they helped to sustain my travels and my ashrams and to buy all kinds of luxuries. But why should I admit it and go to prison for years? Wasn't I benefitting the world by running those ashrams? Nitya gave evidence for me in court, and affirmed my innocence in all spheres, claiming I was celibate, had taken holy vows, was a spiritual person, in fact fully enlightened. Nitya is an honest sort, and I've always valued him. His trust in me, his respect, meant more to me than that of any of my other disciples, and I did not want to disillusion him. Very early on I sent him to look after the ashram in Wisconsin, and kept Mark away from there. I didn't allow Nitya to spend much time with me, to reduce the likelihood of his finding out, though even so, there were enough indications of what was happening in our centre at Nevada, and in all the other ashrams except the one he headed. Yes, it was not just I who was involved in sex and drugs, the ashram heads were part of the drug racket, and getting money from it. Whether or not they had sex with their disciples was up to them, but participating in the drug network was a must. Of course, they were carefully coached in this by Mark. Not every student had to be enticed with drugs. A psychologist assessed each visitor and resident in the ashrams, and depending on the profile, a tentative approach was made. As for arms dealing, that too was Mark's sphere. I had no involvement in it, except, of course, a share in the profits.

Nitya's the sort to judge and condemn and he would not have remained silent had he known the truth, so if he defended me, he must have believed in my innocence. There had been others as honest and straightforward as Nitya who had become my disciples, but I had never let them remain with me. I had either made their lives miserable with unreasonable demands, or had allowed Mark to threaten them. Yet I had treated Nitya differently, and as I tried to think why, I realized it was because he was different. There may have been others as honest, but I had not met anyone like him, his shining purity attracted me more than the most precious of jewels. Nitya was what I could have been, and what I longed to be. Power and wealth were what I had wanted all these years, and drugs and guns had given them to me. But now, as each passing day brought me closer to the end of my life, the thought grew in me, consumed me, that this was not the legacy I wanted to leave behind. I tried to keep Nitya far from me, yet I wished I could make him my successor. He would put a stop to all the illegal activities in the ashram, remove the current heads and bring in new and honest people. People who would be gurus in the true sense, make the ashrams into the havens of peace and purity that an ashram should be. *This* was the legacy that I wanted to leave, that only Nitya could build for me. But I hesitated. Would he succeed, or would it lead to a threat to his own life? I knew the present ashram heads would put up a stiff resistance, and I knew that they, and Mark, would stop at nothing to prevent their lucrative business from being made to shut down. I did not want to put Nitya at risk for the sake of my own desire to achieve in death what I had not been able to accomplish in my lifetime.

Diana, who has been my personal secretary for years, and occasionally my sexual partner, not only knew all about my affair with Serina and with other women, but even about the drug consignments and Mark's arms deals. Yet she supported me. And so did the others, Vidyananda, the head of my ashram in Italy, Aparna, Mamta, all those American women I'd renamed with Indian names, and all of whom I'd slept with—they all denied that there could have been any truth in the charges, all said the 'evidence' must have been planted. Mark conveniently disappeared, a lot could be blamed on him, I claimed I had no knowledge of what he was doing. Of course, I secretly met Mark later, he always remained loyal to me.

Frankly, I'd been terrified. So I prayed to god almost for the first time in my life, made a bargain, and god acquitted me—that is, s/he saw to it that all those who knew of my guilt supported me and confirmed that Serina was hysterical, emotional, and had been visiting a psychiatrist for years, which of course she had been, though in court she claimed it was because of me. A few threats from Mark and promises of wealth and high posts in the ashram from me for the others, helped in getting their support. I requested Sharada to give evidence for me, but she refused, she stayed away from it all, and no one referred to her. It was an agonizing wait while the jury went in to debate and decide on my guilt or innocence. They returned in less than an hour, with the verdict 'not guilty'.

Yes, if I look back, I was a happy man the day the judgement came, I was convinced god existed. I kept my part of the bargain by giving up sex, and was sure he would keep his. Though soon after that I was diagnosed with AIDS, I didn't complain, and I never spoke to god again. Anything was better than my languishing in prison for years, my reputation destroyed. And it was not the first time I avoided prison, but that I will write about later.

After the case and the AIDS diagnosis, I decided to return to my homeland and to move into my own house. Long ago I had set up an ashram in Rishikesh, and a few years later I bought a house nearby. On my visits to India I always stayed in the ashram for a few days or weeks, the house was kept open for visitors and special guests. It is the first time I am living in it.

***

I asked Diana to send word to Nitya. To tell him he must come and see me soon. Once again I began thinking of Sharada, I wondered if I could get her to come and see me, but I doubted it. When Sharada joined me, she was deeply depressed, after twenty years of marriage followed by a divorce. There was one child who had died of cancer. She blamed herself for everything that was wrong in her life. I sent her to the Nevada ashram to work in the book-publishing department, and being a fine artist, she illustrated some of our books and designed the book covers. In the conversations we had I saw she was both sensitive and intelligent. I tried to get close to her, but no matter what I said, she would not consent to physical closeness, and remained withdrawn and uncommunicative. She was egoistic, I said, she needed the guru's touch, but she saw through me, and in the end I gave up. And one day, she just left the ashram. I tried to keep in touch with her, but it was always I who made the effort—quite strange for me, because I was the guru, so much in demand. At times I felt Sharada was the only woman I admired, in the same way that I admired Nitya, and that if she had responded to my advances, if she had loved me as I sometimes thought I loved her, I would have been saved, transformed, purified. Perhaps my feelings were totally irrational, and of course, it had been some years since Sharada had left the ashram.

***

I'll get on with my story. After Gita and I were married we returned to Dehradun and rented a small three-roomed cottage for ourselves. Till then I had been staying in a single room, while Gita was living with relatives. With both of us employed in schools, we were well off, and we furnished and decorated our home with care. My family expected Gita to stop working after our marriage, but I let her continue. I liked to feel that though we worked in different schools and taught different subjects, we were both essentially doing the same thing. Thus, even when I was away from her, I always felt close to her, imagining her in similar situations, in the class, in the staff-room. I said I saw golden stars when I first met her, and this feeling of glorious joy continued through the early years of our marriage. There was nothing outwardly unusual about our lives, there were the daily problems of cleaning, cooking, of leaking roofs from the incessant rain, getting repairs done, of completing school corrections and preparations on time, rising early and rushing off to the bus stop, where we caught school buses going in different directions. All along, though, I was filled with a kind of ecstasy. Earlier, I had had great dreams, but had suffered terribly from loneliness and despair. In those years before my marriage to Gita, somehow I had made just one friend, Deepak, whom as I mentioned earlier, I had met in college. He accepted me, my silences, my English-speaking ways, and my aversion to joining in the boisterous fun of my other college mates. But even so, we were not really close, it was not as if I confided in him. Mr Robinson had done something great for me, but at the same time he had made me an alien. At some level, I cared deeply for my parents and sisters, but I couldn't really talk to them. I had nothing in common with others in my village. Even when I became a schoolteacher, my colleagues never quite saw me as one of them. Perhaps it was my English that set me apart, the fact that I spoke more fluently and was more comfortable in that language, while out of the classroom all the other teachers would communicate in Hindi. Or perhaps it was my nature, more solitary and quiet than theirs. Now with Gita, I felt every dream was at rest, every part of me and my life was fulfilled by my marriage. I had nothing more to yearn for, for nothing could be greater or more worthwhile than the love we shared. I was sure that Gita felt the same. We were wonderfully compatible physically, it was the first time for me, as I'm sure it was for her, and we explored and discovered each other's bodies with delighted anticipation. I, who had so much sex later on, with so many people, don't even like to use that word in connection with her. We shared a sacred, divine, wondrous love, which went far beyond physical touch. That's how I saw it, at least, and I tried, inspired by all the literature I read, to write down my feelings, but I tore up all my attempts, as I failed to convey what I felt, as I think I fail even now.

We had three years of this bliss before a cloud entered my life. Even then it wasn't the usual kind of cloud that blights a marriage, for Gita was an unusual person. Somehow, when writing of her, I cannot give her shape and form, she remains a mystical dream-like figure. I remember, she wouldn't call me 'Dev' or even my pet name 'Debu', but chose her own name for me, 'Manu'. She used to keep a picture of me among the gods in her puja corner, that was the degree to which she loved and respected me. 'You are my god,' she used to say. Some women never call their husbands by their name, but we were educated, we dispensed with all that, it was just that she chose a special name for me. I know I'm prevaricating because I don't want to write down what happened. But now I'm coming to the end of my life, I must try to make sense of it all.

Three years passed, but Gita did not get pregnant. My family had been raising questions from the end of the first year, but I hadn't bothered so far. Now, even my colleagues had started to make comments, to suggest that something was wrong. After all, Gita was growing older, and so was

I. I too began to feel that a child or two would be the completion of the perfection we shared. Gita herself never seemed to miss having a child. If her friends or relatives had questioned her, as they must have done, she did not tell me. One day, when we were sitting on the porch holding hands, peaceful in the evening light, I said to her, 'Wouldn't it be good if we had a child? Let's both go to a doctor and find out what's wrong.' I wanted to show her that I didn't blame her, I wasn't one of those backward men who thought the woman was always at fault. Her grip on my hand tightened but a shadow crossed her face. 'No, Manu,' she replied, 'I don't want a child. I never want a child'.

'But why?' I asked.

She remained silent. A new thought came to me. Perhaps she was practising some form of birth control, and hadn't told me about it? I knew she wouldn't hide anything from me, and yet the first doubt of her now arose. For hadn't she hidden this from me, that she did not want a child? Why had she not told me, I asked her, and then, was she... was she doing anything to prevent a child? 'No, Manu,' she said, 'I have done nothing except pray to god, that no child will be born.'

'Why?' I asked again, but she did not answer.

We continued to sit there holding hands, we had dinner and went to bed as usual. That night she told me a story. She asked me if I knew the story of Pururava and Urvashi. 'No,' I said, 'I've never heard of them.' I guessed it was a story from the Puranas or some other part of Sanskrit literature that she had specialized in. After all, she was the Sanskrit scholar. In fact, I haven't mentioned it yet, but everyone looked up to me in the school, considering me the final word in English literature. I knew I wasn't, but I did have a good memory and a love for what I read, and as a result I knew almost all of Shakespeare's plays and sonnets by heart. I knew a lot of Walter Scott too, and Macaulay, and large sections of the Bible. At that moment of time I felt that Sanskrit literature was somewhat inferior, beneath me. Neither of us could imagine then, that one day I'd almost set aside Shakespeare, and be an expert in Sanskrit and the ancient texts.

Resting her head on my shoulder, Gita told me this story. Pururava himself was a strange sort. He was the son of a god, the planet Budha (Mercury) who himself was the son of a god, Soma. His mother was Ila, but Ila was someone who was alternately a man and a woman. Thus, Pururava wasn't an ordinary mortal, but Urvashi was an apsara, a celestial nymph. They fell in love and married, but there were certain rules laid down for Pururava. Though they could live together and have sex, he was never to show himself to her naked, that is, all their lovemaking had to be in the dark. The gandharvas, who were singers and musicians, the heavenly consorts of the apsaras, were angry that a nymph of heaven had decided to marry someone not of their own kind, and therefore they conceived an ingenious plot through which she saw him in a flash of lightning. Urvashi disappeared and was lost to him, but by a long and arduous series of events, they were reunited, and he became a celestial being like her. My Gita said to me, 'I am like Urvashi, though in different circumstances. If we have a child, I will vanish. And unlike Pururava and Urvashi, we will never be reunited.' She quoted two lines from Sanskrit to me, and translated them: 'I have passed like the first of dawns; I am like the wind that cannot be caught.'

'You are not a celestial being, Gita,' I said. 'You were born in Nakuri, a village not far from my birthplace. So I don't know what you are talking about.' To tone down the harshness in my voice, I then told her the story of Psyche, not exactly similar, but with some parallels. 'See Gita,' I consoled her, 'such myths exist in all cultures. And they all have happy endings, so what is there to worry about?' Telling each other stories in the dark, I felt closer to her than ever before.

But Gita was not consoled. 'Don't ask me to have a child, Manu,' she insisted. 'Then we will always be happy.'

'All right,' I said, smothering my thoughts and feelings. And we slept.

***

I couldn't write more yesterday, because Sophie brought Nachiketa to see me. She drove to the ashram to look for Nitya in the hope that he might be there, but found only Nachiketa.

Nachiketa, almost fifteen years old, is Nitya's son, very sober and serious, but loving too. He travels with Nitya, but I had heard that they returned to India a few days ago. He is already quite a scholar. Whenever he is in our Rishikesh ashram, he spends a lot of time sitting in meditation under the great banyan tree there, or wandering along the banks of the Ganga, singing bhajans. He often seems rapt in ecstasy, and speaks of divine visions. But I wonder—is it real, or does he pretend, like so many of us? Does he already see that he has a better future as a guru than as a teacher or a businessman? That he'll have more power and money?

As he entered he touched my feet, even as I continued to lie in bed, and stood before me, respectful, reverential. I had no appetite for small talk, and said to him straightaway, 'Nachiketa, I want your father, do you know where he is?'

'Yes, Swamiji,' he responded, 'he is in Gangotri, at our retreat there.' Our small cave retreat was beyond Gangotri, closer to Gaumukh, considered the origin of the river Ganga, from the icy Gangotri glacier, though I had always thought the sources of our own Jad Ganga, should be considered the true origin of this greatest of rivers. The retreat could not be reached except on foot, the terrain was rough, and there was no clear path.

'Bring him to me as soon as he arrives in Rishikesh,' I said. 'Tell him I must see him, if only for fifteen minutes. Then he can leave again if he wants.'

'Yes, Swamiji,' said the boy and stood there looking at me. I was touched by his wise and gentle gaze, and I thought of confiding in him. 'I am dying, Nachiketa,' I said. 'I want to know in what manner your father will perform my last rites.' Even as I said this I asked myself why this was so important to me. How did it matter, when nothing of me would remain, only an empty body, a shell? Perhaps towards the end of one's life, traditions and superstitions become stronger. Somewhere in me I believed that without the correct rituals, my soul would wander unappeased, would traverse dark spaces, would never find rest.

'Well, Swamiji,' Nachiketa was already speaking as my mind wandered. 'You know the answer already. Sometimes holy men are cremated, but you know that in our sect they are placed in samadhi.'

'You are wise, Nachiketa,' I said. 'Your namesake visited the house of the god of death, Yama, and learnt the truth about life and death. I will tell you my own truth. I have a dreaded disease. I have AIDS. Will your father agree to place me in samadhi?'

'Some die of cancer, some of AIDS, others die a natural death. Death is the same for all, so how does it matter?' replied Nachiketa, speaking like one who had truly visited Yama. 'But I will ask him to come and see you,' he added, as he looked at my face and glimpsed my fear and disturbance. He took my wasted hand in his and said, 'What do you fear, Swamiji? Your illness has made you weak. You know the inner light is always the same beyond all disease. It is you who taught me these words from the Bhagavad Gita.'

And he recited:

'As a person removes his old clothes and puts on new ones, the embodied Self leaves the worn out body and enters one that is new.

'Weapons cannot hurt it, fire can never burn it, water does not moisten it, winds do not dry it. The Self cannot be cut, burnt, wet or dried. It is eternal, all-pervading, never-changing, immovable, and ancient.

'It is unmanifest, beyond thought and beyond change. Knowing this to be true, you should not grieve.'

It was as if he was the guru and I the child. What could I tell him? I knew those words and so many more like them. But how could I confess, even now, that I who had taught those words, inspired so many by them, how could I explain that they had never meant anything to me? Words, these are just words, but death is approaching and I see only darkness ahead, and some menace in the darkness that makes me afraid. If only my dream woman was waiting for me there! She would be better for me than any light.

I remained silent, keeping my thoughts to myself, and Nachiketa looked at me gently and then left the room.

***

I had a restless, disturbed sleep last night. My chest hurts. And this brings about a compulsion in me, to write more, to finish the story of my life before I die.

I must continue with my story of Gita, for that was the starting point of a different life. After that talk about a child, my happiness was somewhat dimmed. I said nothing to her, our lives remained the same, but I did not feel the same joy, the same completion.

At that time I was teaching *A Midsummer Night's Dream*, and lying in bed at night, feeling somewhat distant and alienated, even though Gita was near me, some of its words resounded in my head. I felt like Lysander who in the forest said: 'One turf shall serve as pillow for us both; One heart, one bed, two bosoms and one troth.' But Hermia replied, 'Nay good Lysander; for my sake, my dear, Lie further off yet, do not lie so near.' In my half-dream I heard Hermia's words again and again in Gita's voice: 'Lie further off yet, do not lie so near.' Gradually I began to hear them in my waking hours too. Was I going mad? I tried to watch my mind, to control it, but instead of calming down, new words came into my head, this time from Robert Louis Stevenson's 'Ticonderoga': 'It sings in my sleeping ears, it hums in my waking head.' Yes, that's how it was, those words kept singing in my head. 'Lie further off yet, lie further off yet...' It is so many years since I thought of those days, but now, once again they return to me. I was over-reacting, I knew that, but I could not stop myself.

Gita felt the change in me and knew what the matter was. She tried everything to please me, was extra loving, cooked fancy food, gave me small presents, said wonderful things to me, but my heart remained sad.

At times I asked myself why I could not be grateful

and happy for what I had—a good job, a pleasant house, a wonderful, loving wife. The answer came to me one day, something I knew all along, but had been suppressing. Gita did not love me. That was the reason why she did not want to have a child. And perhaps, perhaps she loved someone else? She had lived in Dehradun before we were married. Could she have met someone, been in love, but been forced by her parents to have an arranged marriage with me? Could she perhaps, even have had sex with someone else? I remembered that first time between us, so wondrous for me, Gita didn't bleed or have any pain. I knew from my reading that that wasn't essential, but still...

I could not bring myself to spy on her, but as the doubts grew in my heart, I had to ask her. 'Do you love someone else, Gita? Is that why you will not have a child with me?' Three months had passed since she had told me the story of Pururava and Urvashi. I held her hand as I asked the question, but I could not look at her. She was silent, and when I raised my eyes to her face, it was pale. 'Well, Gita,' I said, 'won't you answer my question?'

'I do love someone, Manu,' she said in a faint voice. 'But it's not what you think. It's not a real person. It is someone who often appeared to me in dreams, both by night and in the day.'

'Tell me about him,' I said, feeling quite calm, and slightly superior. Dreams were no threat to me, surely. Of course, I hadn't seen my own dream woman then, that would come later.

'His name is Varun,' Gita continued. 'He is tall and slim and his face shines with an inner glow. He appeared to me first when I was thirteen years old. He told me I had been married to him for many lives in the past. But in this life, for some reason he was unable to explain, he could not take his birth in the world to be with me. He wanted that I should die young to be with him, but his Elders told him to let me be. He did not wish me to marry. As soon as I saw him in my dream I fell in love with him. He was like the god Krishna, so glorious and handsome. He appeared to me almost every day until I was eighteen years old. Whenever I was alone, he would come to me. We walked and talked together, we shared everything. On my eighteenth birthday, he told me he had to go away for a while. I should not forget him, he would always love me, and one day he would come to me again. I didn't forget him, but as one year passed and a second, I told myself perhaps these were childish imaginings. I felt very alone, for with him as a companion, I had not sought others. I could not tell the old brigadier who had paid for my education about my love, would he have believed me? He brought me several marriage proposals, but I refused to consider them. Many years passed without a glimpse of Varun and when the brigadier suggested I marry you, I agreed. But the very day after our wedding Varun appeared to me again. Now I did not know whether to be happy or sad. But he consoled me. "We'll be together in other lives," he said, "not this one. The Elders wanted you to be married, and to this particular man. Be happy with him, but do not have a child. If you do, you will have to leave him. And nor will you be able to return to me immediately. I am giving you this warning because I know things you cannot know. I will teach you two mantras now, keep them secret. The first will prevent childbirth. The second will bring me to you, but only if it is an emergency, and that mantra can only be used once. This separation is necessary for us now, but one day we will be united in eternity."

'I asked him, "Who are the Elders? How do you know all this?"

'"I cannot tell you any more," he said and he vanished.'

'And you have not seen him since?'

'No.'

I believed her that day. I told her I believed her and we were at peace for the evening, but by the morning I had even more doubts and confusions. What did I believe? That there was another world, a different dimension? That there were 'Elders' who guided our lives? Or that she spoke the truth as she saw it, about her own fantasies? Or not even that. Perhaps she had deliberately invented it all, using fragments of what she had read in Sanskrit texts, invented it to hide a different truth. She loved someone else, a flesh-and-blood person, she wanted to leave me one day and marry him, and that is why she would not have a child by me.

I went off to school as usual, not revealing my thoughts to her, but all day they preyed on my mind, and by the time I returned in the evening, I was righteously angry. Why was she trying to make a fool of me? How could I have been so childish as to believe her? I was home before her, walking up and down in the garden. She came home, greeted me affectionately, and after a wash, entered the kitchen to make tea and some snack, as she usually did. I waited a few minutes, took deep breaths to keep calm, and went in after her. She looked up at me smiling, strands of hair straggling across her face. The besan had been mixed to make pakoras, she was chopping onions and potatoes. She was as usual, my lovely Gita, how could she have been deceiving me? But still, my anger hadn't left me, and I spoke in a harsh tone. 'Tell me those secret mantras of yours, Gita, if they exist,' I said. I'd never spoken to her in that way before. She stood still, and looked at me, astonished. Tears filled her eyes. I couldn't bear to see her like that, my anger melted. I took her in my arms, she laid her head against my chest, and love flowed between us. I vowed never to hurt her again, to forget about children, to forget Varun and the mantras, to be happy as we once were, to be grateful for whatever we had. I kept to my vow, though somewhere within me, doubts still lurked which I suppressed, and refused to express even in my own thoughts.

Almost four months passed before I noticed some changes in Gita, sensed some difference in her body. What was it? Intuition told me a child was growing within her, but Gita had said nothing, and I too kept my thoughts to myself. A few days later she told me. My happiness was tentative, cautious. Why had she concealed it so long? Pretended she still had her monthly periods? She sensed my unasked questions. 'I thought I'd lose the child, but now I'm confident that he will be born.'

'He?'

'Yes, I'm sure the child will be a boy.' I looked at her, confusions and questions still within me. 'I stopped saying the mantra,' she added. I wanted to ask about Varun, but I could not do so. At that moment, I was sure that whatever she had told me earlier were just fantasies, the fantasies of a sensitive, imaginative girl, growing up in a rigid society. Now she was a woman, soon to have a child, the fantasies were in the past, something we could both forget. The reality of our relationship had led her to drop them. I felt strong and confident, I had been right to wait, to be patient and tolerant. She was mine now, she belonged to me, the imaginary Varun was gone.

Did she want her mother to come and stay with her for

a while, I asked. No, she said, we were city people now, and her mother was a village woman with village superstitions. The changes in her body that she must have noticed from the very first month, had obviously convinced Gita she was pregnant, but now I felt she should see a good doctor. I suggested it, and was taken aback when Gita told me she had already found one. 'I confirmed my pregnancy with her,' she said. How could she do that without consulting me? 'My colleagues in school recommended her,' she continued. 'She's very good. Her name is Dr Shanti.' Colleagues in school? So everyone knew about her pregnancy before me? I was upset, but, 'I'd like to meet her too,' was all I said.

We went to see her a few days later. She seemed efficient and reassuring, yet though I couldn't quite understand why, I was uncomfortable. Dr Shanti's smooth manner—I felt somehow that it was false, that there was something else behind it that was being concealed. Were there some problems in the pregnancy that she did not want to express in front of Gita? I worried over it at night, and the next day I told Gita that I had some extra work in school, left without waiting for the school bus, and went to see Dr Shanti on my own. It was quite early in the morning, but she was nice enough, and even gave me a cup of tea. Once again, she reassured me that all was well, yet she wouldn't look straight at me. Could Gita have told her all those fantasies? Indirectly I tried to ask her, 'We've been married almost four years,' I said to her, 'yet Gita did not conceive earlier. What could be the reason for this?' At that she looked directly at me, an expression in her eyes I could not understand. Was she angry? Amused at some ignorance of mine? That's what it seemed to me, a mixture of anger and amusement. But she only said, 'It often happens,

Mr Mangal. The first child takes long to come.' I could think of nothing more to say. I left her then, and walked to my school, reaching late. I was preoccupied all day, the students irritated me, I couldn't focus on teaching. On the way home in the school bus, I tried to calm down. I told myself that I too had succumbed to fantasies, to unreal thoughts without any basis. There was nothing to fear. I was determined to set aside my apprehensions, and by the time I arrived home, I had succeeded.

***

I insisted that Gita take six months' leave when the ninth month began. She could resume work after the baby was born, I said. I felt protective and decisive, at the same time aware that I was a modern, understanding husband, who would never stop his wife from working. We'd get a woman to look after the child when she went back to school. I'd already begun to plan the future.

Gita's pregnancy was smooth, she seemed to have no problems, but she was a bit moody. That was only natural, I told myself. In the middle of October, the ninth month, Gita complained of pains early in the morning. There were few phones at that time in our town. I got hold of a tonga and took her straight to the nursing home and then went to call Dr Shanti. She said she would come soon and was there within half an hour. Everything seemed to go smoothly, and at 9 a.m., my son was born. Dr Shanti came to tell me. 'Both are fine,' she said, 'no problems at all. An easy birth.' She took me in to see them. Gita held my hand, and I peered at my red-faced son, who blinked and it seemed he smiled, as if he recognized me...I was amused at my own thoughts, I was again getting as fanciful as Gita, but I was so happy and so relieved. Gita asked me to bring a few things from home, and I said I would, still gazing lovingly at them both. 'Let her rest now,' said Dr Shanti. 'You can come back in a few hours.'

I'd been up since before dawn, and had had four hours of anxiety, and not even a cup of tea in the morning. Now I went down the stairs with a jaunty step, to the canteen in the basement for a hot cup and something to eat before I made my way home. I was absolutely euphoric. I'd bring flowers when I returned, I'd cut some wild roses from our own garden, I planned, and I'd buy sweets for everyone in the nursing home. We'd name the boy Santosh, peace. Or perhaps Ashish, blessing. Sitting with my cup of tea, my reveries of the future, how he would grow, take his first step, which school we would send him to, his brothers and sisters to come, I was suddenly aware of Dr Shanti standing in front of me. I smiled at her.

'I'm sorry, Mr Mangal,' she said.

'That's all right,' I replied, still in my dreams. What could disturb my happiness now? Then I noticed the expression on her face. 'What is it?' I jumped to my feet as a sudden fear gripped me. 'Please come,' she said, her voice a shaky whisper, and I followed her, straight into Gita's room. Gita... her eyes were closed, she appeared to be sleeping peacefully, yet there was a difference, her skin looked pale, bluish. I touched her cheek, it was cold, I reached for her hand, it seemed limp. My eyes then went to my son. He too seemed to be sleeping, his face even redder than before. I looked at Dr Shanti uncomprehendingly. 'They're gone,' she said. 'They're in another world now.' Dead? Were they dead? I caught hold of Gita and shook her. I still remember that feeling, her body flopping against me. Perhaps I screamed or called out, I don't know, the succeeding hours were a blur.

The next I remember, I was lying in bed at home. A colleague of mine, Naresh, was leaning over me. He was asking me something, I couldn't hear. 'Devdarshan, Devdarshan...' he was saying. My colleagues rarely called me Debu or Dev. I hadn't encouraged it, I wasn't that friendly with them. I heard some sentences, 'Bodies should be given to the police...post mortem, you must ask for a post mortem...untimely death...' I roused myself. 'No!' I said, 'No.' I couldn't bear to think of my beloved Gita being cut open. And my little son. It was Varun who had taken them, Varun in whom I had never believed. In my deranged state at that time, I was convinced of this. Even later, when I tried to think rationally, I couldn't think of any other explanation.

Naresh was holding out a cup of tea. I drank it, the hot liquid and sugary sweetness stirring my body to life again. I got up and moved into the other room. It was full of people, old friends and acquaintances gathered together to offer support. Deepak, Ramesh, Imran, their wives, even Deepak's mother was there. I saw the principal of my school and various colleagues. I still hardly knew what was happening, as people came up to me, hugged me and held my hand, many with tears in their eyes. It surprised me. I hadn't been close to anyone, except perhaps Deepak, and even he, I hadn't had much contact with recently. I had neglected them all after my marriage to Gita, still now they had come to help me. After a while Deepak and Naresh took me into the other room. 'I think you need to have a post mortem, Devdarshan,' Naresh was saying that dreaded word again. 'It does not look right to us,' he added.

'I already said no,' I replied. 'I don't want it. Just let them be in peace.'

They stood looking at me, not sure what to say. 'Where are they?' I said. 'Bring them home.'

'The hospital did not want to release them,' said Naresh, 'until they heard from you. The head doctor was suspicious...'

'Why should he be?'

'You see, Dev,' said Deepak, 'you probably did not know, but...' Naresh put a hand on his arm and he stopped speaking.

'Did not know what?' I asked, and I wondered, was she ill in some way? Had she and Dr Shanti both concealed it from me? I knew Deepak's mother was the maths teacher in the school where Gita taught. What was it that they knew and I didn't? 'Nothing, Devdarshan.' It was Naresh who answered. 'The deaths looked suspicious, that's what Deepak was saying.' Suspicious? They did not know about Varun. Varun had got them, I was sure of it. But I wasn't going to share those supernatural fantasies with them. 'Just bring them home,' I said.

There were some delays. The police had already been informed. I had to sign some forms. My friends ran to and fro between me, the hospital and the police station. Even so it was the next morning before the bodies, tied in white shrouds, entered the house. I could not bear to look at them. By then my parents, Gita's parents, and many relatives had arrived. The old brigadier, Gita's patron, was there, tears running down his face. He came up to me, put his arm around me in a tentative hug, squeezed my hand. Gita's mother, I thought she would blame me, but instead she kept saying, 'My Gita was so lucky, so lucky, a happy life, no sorrows, she was fortunate.' Her younger sister was weeping though. My mother along with Gita's mother and sisters, took my dear ones into the inner room, and gave Gita her last bath, and dressed her, made her ready for her final departure from this world according to her own customs, which were different from our Jad rites. Then they brought her into the front room, arrayed in her red wedding sari, sindoor in her hair, a woman considered fortunate to die before her husband. Yes, it's true, they are the lucky ones, to never have to suffer the desolate fate of a widow. My little darling was near her, wrapped in a white cloth. Gita was placed on the bier, and we began the walk to the cremation ground. I remember the women crying and screaming as they watched us depart, these days women too go to the cremation, but it wasn't the custom then. I did not feel anything much at the time, I had been drenched in grief but now I was calm, somewhat blank. 'Ram Nam sat hai, Ram Nam sat hai,' chanted the little procession, though I walked quietly. I had tried carrying one end of the bier but I stumbled, and Deepak, ever at my side, took over. My father carried my little darling, my unknown son. My little one could not be cremated, children never are, we would have to bury him, and we went to the burial site, while others proceeded to the cremation ground to get the pyre ready. I kissed my dear son, and as he was laid in a hastily dug pit, I thought my heart was breaking. A memory came to me of a picture I had seen in a newspaper which had brought me to tears, a father going to the grave of his newly dead young daughter, and placing a bar of chocolate on her small grave. I lost my composure, tears began to flow, and I had to be supported as we proceeded to the cremation ground. The cremation pyre was still being built, it took a long time, some of the wood was soggy and wet from the recent rains, more dry wood had to be found, the priest recited prayers, somehow I found the strength to circle and light the pyre. The flames rose, I sat down at the side, tears blinding me. Some time passed, I am not sure how much, most people had left, just a few friends remained, and Deepak came and told me it was time to leave, we could return to collect the ashes later.

How could I go back to that house without Gita? But I had to, there was no option. According to tradition, no fire would be lit in the house for four days, and neighbours and friends sent food, though it was several days before I could bring myself to eat, and lived on sugary tea. Gita's family and mine did not have much appetite either. White sheets were spread on the floor for mourners to sit, visitors came every day. On the third day we collected the ashes and set off for Haridwar, there they were emptied in the river, and carried by the swift current, a part of them would perhaps one day reach the far distant sea. Then the chautha, the fourth-day prayers, after which fewer people came. My parents stayed with me till the tehravi, the thirteenth-day prayers, held because Gita's family wanted it. Then they left, because I asked them to. I wanted to be on my own, to think and feel, to look back on the past, to try and understand what had happened. I told them I was all right, that I had to get back to work and prepare for my classes. I needed to concentrate on that, I said. They remained sad, but I knew from some stray talk that I had overheard, that my mother was already asking around, thinking of another girl for me.

***

I was alone now, but I could not bring myself to go back to work. I walked up and down, through the empty house and garden. I let the flowers wither and die and the lawn turn to weed. As I walked, I alternated between deep sorrow and perhaps an even deeper anger. I felt the anger emanate from the centre of my heart in dark flashes, so powerful that it seemed it would consume everything before me. I remembered one of Gita's stories, how the god Shiva had burnt Kama, the god of love, to ashes with his anger. Shiva's anger came through his third eye, mine was fiercer and deeper, for it was from the heart. I felt mine was strong enough to literally burn someone up. But whom? Who was I angry with? Wasn't it with Gita herself, and wasn't she already burnt? Somehow life had tricked me. I still couldn't totally believe Gita's fantasy of Varun. But then how had they both died just after the baby was born? Was my suspicion of Gita being ill in some way, correct? Or was there negligence on the part of Dr Shanti? Strangely, she had not come, either for the funeral or to see me and offer condolences. Perhaps I should have had that post mortem. But it would have been terrible to have the bodies cut and sliced open. And it wouldn't bring them back. My thoughts went round in circles as I walked aimlessly, emptiness, silence, and desolation around me.

The house was unkempt, the disarray growing every day. I bathed every morning, the cold water refreshing me after my restless nights, I looked for fresh clothes to wear, but could not get around to washing those I had discarded. I didn't cook either, though I brewed endless cups of tea, which I drank black, without milk or sugar, something unheard of in those days, only because there were packets of tea in the house, but I had run out of sugar, and could not be bothered to buy either that or milk which I would have to boil. Gita had always taken care of everything.

Sometimes I went to the nearby dhaba and brought back some parathas to eat, or some buns and biscuits that I had with my tea. There were visits from my friends, Deepak particularly, but I didn't want to see anyone. Usually I put a lock on the front door and entered from the back, so that people would think I had gone out.

About three months passed like this. One day, when I was standing outside in the neglected, overgrown garden, the principal of my school, Mr Gosain, walked in. He had come many times before, he said, but I hadn't been at home. He looked at the garden, at my own haggard state. Without my inviting him, he walked into the house and surveyed the chaos. He turned to me. 'Devdarshan,' he said, 'won't you come back to work? It's time to forget, to move on. It will do you good to have a routine again. The children are fond of you, and you know how you love teaching, particularly your beloved Shakespeare. For the annual function we want to put on a production of *A Midsummer Night's Dream*. Won't you come back now?'

Shakespeare! Yes, I had even forgotten him, forgotten the other poets that I had loved, the verses that were otherwise always pouring through my head. But without even thinking I replied to him, the words coming from some deep space within me. 'I can't do that,' I said. 'I can never come back. I will waste my life in forgetting, when what I need is to gain an understanding of life, death, rebirth, the truth of what lies beyond this world.'

Only as I spoke, did I realize that my thoughts had not been going around in circles without any purpose. Through the wanderings of my mind, I had found an aim, and even as I voiced my aim, my heart lightened. My principal seemed to see in my face something of what I felt. 'In that case,

Dev, I will not try to dissuade you,' he said. 'In fact, if you like, I will give you the name of an ashram beyond Almora. I myself stayed there for a while. You may like it better than other ashrams, as it has few rules, and a vast library. You can go there, study, meditate, and practise yoga, read whatever you like, and perhaps you will find some peace, or even discover the truth. I'll keep your job for you for one year. Then you can let me know what you want to do.' I'd never known Mr Gosain to be so kind and understanding. He had always been stern and strict, making allowances for no one. Perhaps I could have looked for other options, or different ashrams, but I didn't have the energy or will, I was grateful, I agreed. Mr Gosain then sat down and wrote a letter to the head of the ashram. 'He is an Italian,' he said. 'His name is Enzo.'

'Italian? How can he be a guru then?'

'He doesn't claim to be a guru, though there can be a guru from any country. But he runs the ashram. There are spiritual discussions every day, and an ancient yogi lives in a cave in the nearby mountains. He comes to the ashram and teaches specialized techniques to those who want to learn.'

'What sort of techniques?'

'Yoga techniques...control of the mind; control of the body. For instance, I learnt from him how to switch off my thoughts and be calm in the worst situation.'

It definitely sounded attractive to me. I had almost lost my sanity with my incessant thoughts.

After Mr Gosain left, I felt life flow through me again with a new sense of purpose. I soaked some of my dirty clothes in soap and water, and began sweeping and mopping the house. If I were to go to an ashram, I should purify myself first, leave a clean house behind. I wouldn't give it up for a while though, I could afford to keep paying the small rent from my savings.

I spent the next week washing, cleaning, dusting, arranging, putting things away neatly in cupboards and trunks. I polished our old kerosene stove, bought a few vegetables and some atta, and cooked a simple meal for the first time in months. I had grown very thin. When everything was cleaned up, I looked into the mirror and wondered if I should get a haircut, my hair was straggling over my ears. 'Let it be,' I said to myself. 'It will be suitable for life in an ashram.' Perhaps in that moment, I already knew that I would soon make a new life for myself.

Finally, I went to see Mr Gosain. I asked if he would do me one more favour, if he would use my savings to pay my bills and send me money when I needed it. He agreed, and we went to my bank together, where I authorized him to draw money from my account. That essential task done, I pushed all thoughts aside, and got ready for a new beginning.

4. In Search of the Past

Nityananda

I read through what Dev had written twice over. I was intrigued to read about his childhood. I too was a Garhwali, but I had been born in Dehradun, not in the high mountains. My ancestors were from Pauri, what was formerly British Garhwal, adjacent to the state of Tehri Garhwal from where Dev came. Though from almost the same region, I knew little about the Jads. As for the stories Dev used to tell everyone, about being born in Gangotri and adopted soon after by a swami, I had never quite believed them. I didn't know that he had been married, and I wasn't sure what to make of it. He was trying to justify his actions, but had he succeeded in doing so? Was the death of his wife and child, and the grief that overtook him, sufficient reason for all he did? Or were there more reasons that he would reveal later? I began to wonder if he had conspired somehow in her death, but was concealing it from me, just as he had concealed so much else.

I went to meet him to find out if he had written any more. He said he had not finished the next section. I asked him which school he had taught in, and the name of the school where Gita had worked, and he told me that he worked in the JW School, while Gita taught in the Nita Devi Pathshala. I had a vague idea that I may be able to discover more about her. Then I posed a question about something that I had found most puzzling.

'Do you mean to say that all your life you've believed in

the existence of Varun, and that Gita died through divine intervention?'

'Not always. I doubted it at times, but what else was I to believe? The facts supported it.'

'No, Dev, I don't think so. There has to be another explanation.'

'I thought you were a spiritual person, steeped in thoughts of the other world.'

'Perhaps, but for things like this, there is always a rational explanation. It must have been a natural death, Dev. All sorts of things go wrong in childbirth.'

'But I still remember how they looked. So calm and peaceful. And Dr Shanti herself couldn't figure out what was wrong.'

'You should have had a post mortem done then. For all you know it was murder or suicide.'

'Nitya! That's not possible.'

'Why? Didn't you say yourself you suspected her of having an affair, or of having had one before your marriage? Whatever it was, I don't believe there were any supernatural causes.'

No, I couldn't believe that nonsense. Being a spiritual person doesn't mean suspending belief in natural laws. Of course, I don't deny miracles can happen, but all practical causes should be explored, before jumping to conclusions about supernatural ones.

'But—murder—no one murders for such reasons. And suicide—I don't know. She had decided to have a child, after all. And would she have killed our baby, after she had made that decision?'

'Perhaps it wasn't your baby.'

'Nitya, why are you saying these things to me? It's cruelty. I'm going to die, so let me die in peace.'

'Well, Dev,' I said, suddenly throwing caution and restraint to the winds, and feeling once again distant from him, 'you decided to tell me your story. And perhaps you are no stranger to murder yourself.'

'What are you saying, Nitya?' His face, if it was possible, turned even more pallid.

'There were rumours I ignored, just as I ignored those about your women. What happened to Lydia? And what about Sarita?'

'When Lydia was shot in Chicago, I was in India. And when Sarita died in India, I was in the US.'

'Yes, but what about Mark your "marksman"? Wasn't he directed by you?'

'No, Nitya, no. I don't know what you're talking about.'

By this time I was angry, flushed and upset, both with him and myself. I'd come to listen to him and had even thought of helping him in his last days, instead here I was accusing him of murder, for which I had no actual proof. Dev was by now pale and sweating, lying against the pillows, struggling for breath. I almost thought I had murdered him with all my talk, or at least hastened his end, but still, I could not apologize for what I had said. I just said, 'Rest a while, Dev, we'll talk later,' and left the room, calling to Sophie and Diana to go to him.

I felt a pulse throbbing in my head and knew I had to calm down, to sort things out in my mind, but just for a while I needed to stop thinking. I went out of the gate, turned left down the road, reached the riverbank and walked in the grass near the river. The sky was overcast, the river muddy. White egrets hopped aside as I walked, a cold wind blew, and I took deep breaths, focusing on a mantra to clear my mind. 'So-ham, so-ham,' I breathed, in and out.

I remembered how often we had walked along this path, Dev and I. Whenever he stayed at the ashram, we would set out every evening with the 'charity bag,' an airbag filled with about twenty thousand rupees in hundred-rupee notes. The local people would have heard of his visit, and knew the routine, they would be waiting along the way. As we walked, villagers would drop to the ground at his feet and beseech him, 'Swamiji...I have to get my daughter married...I have no money...'; 'Swamiji...my child is sick. I have to take him to hospital.' There were requests of all kinds, and Dev would dip into the bag I held open for him and give a handful of notes to anyone who asked for help. When the bag was emptied, we'd return to the ashram, a peaceful walk, since all the villagers would have gone back home, as they knew money was not distributed on the return journey. By then it would be dark, the swift flowing river somehow seeming more sluggish, its sound softer, merging into the silence of the night. At times the moon shone, reflected in the dark river, the trees rustled their leaves. I thought so highly of Dev then, I was filled with the satisfaction, the largeness of heart, that every philanthropist must feel. But were we truly doing something good? I am not so sure now. Were we changing their lives in any way, by these random handouts? Was there something better we could have done, with Rs 20,000 every day? Dev was in fact buying their gratitude, their reverence and affection. The villagers did not know where the money came from. They did not know that in a small side room at the ashram lived Mrs Mehta, wife of a rich industrialist. Plain, thin, and nondescript, her husband had fallen in love with someone else, but he did not want a divorce, that would be too much of a scandal. He allowed his wife to live in the ashram, donated money to it, and in addition, transferred a large sum of money to a local bank account for her. Because of his donations to the ashram, Mrs Mehta lived in that side room for most of the year, free of charge. She had no children, but at times she did visit her husband's home in Mumbai. Occasionally, she went to our retreat in Gangotri. She did not spend any money on herself, and so for the two or three weeks a year that Dev visited, she would draw out the money her husband put in the bank for her, and use it to fill his 'charity bag'. Now I begin to wonder, was she too one of his women? I know she adored him, he gave her meaningless life a focus, but was there nothing more? She would have come to serve Dev in his illness, but she is ill herself, her husband has put her in an expensive nursing home in Pune. She has terminal cancer.

After his visit to the ashram, which would be for about one week at a time, Dev would leave again, either back to his ashram in Nevada, or for Florida or Switzerland or Germany or Italy, or somewhere else in the world, giving lectures, acquiring more devotees, adored and admired by all. No, not by all, there were always some who accused him, but at that time I believed none of the accusations.

I notice I am avoiding referring to Dev as 'Swamiji'. Though on his own insistence, I never called him that to his face, I used to so reverently refer to him as 'Swamiji' to others. Now it seems to me, he is no swami. I'm digressing, I'm letting my mind wander, because I don't want to think of the conversation we had today, of the anger that arose in me. Mark was said to have killed two people, and some suggested even more, but I had doubted the truth of this, and even if there was some truth in it, I never believed Dev had anything to do with it. But today, I more or less accused him of it myself. As I said earlier, I've begun to doubt everything about him.

I thought back to the stories I had heard about Lydia and Sarita, two people who died in mysterious circumstances after opposing Dev. I was not anywhere near them or Dev at the time, yet the stories had trickled in through the underground network of gossip, and in addition, I and others had earlier received a letter from Lydia. Initially I had believed what Bidyut, the head of the Sparks ashram at the time, told me. His version was that Lydia was attracted to Dev, but falsely accused him of sexual molestation when he rejected her. Lydia had created a scene in the ashram and on one of Dev's visits, had shouted at him in front of other ashram residents. Dev responded by telling her she was 'a stupid, foolish, woman', before walking away. The next day he left the ashram for a talk he was giving in Romania. Two days later, Lydia too left, returning to her home in Chicago. But she continued to accuse him in letters to teachers and heads of his ashrams. I did not pay much attention to the letter I received—actually such letters were not unusual. I believed that many women became his followers because of the emptiness in their own lives, not because of a genuine spiritual quest. Not just women, but men too—that was among the reasons why I myself had joined him. Next, I heard that Lydia was in therapy, and I hoped that she would forget the past and find some peace. Around three months later, while Lydia was dining in a Chicago restaurant with a friend, she was shot dead by a masked man, who made a quick getaway in the confusion that followed. He was never identified or caught. Was Mark involved? That was the rumour I later heard, but it seemed unlikely to me then. By that time Lydia was not only in therapy, but in a new relationship, she had moved on.

As for Sarita, I knew even less about the issues involved. It seemed that once when Dev had visited Sri Lanka, she became his follower and donated land and money to him, to build an ashram there. When nothing had been built for several years, she wanted her property returned. Evidently, Dev did not respond to her letters and requests, and she came to India, reaching his ashram in Rishikesh, only to find that he was not there. She decided to stay on in Rishikesh, as he used to return there every few months. Two months later, while crossing the road, she was killed in a hit-and-run case. Neither the driver nor the vehicle was ever located. When I heard about this, I just thought it was an unfortunate accident, though a year later I had a twinge of doubt when I learnt that the land had been sold. But I set my doubts aside, I believed in Dev.

I hated these dark thoughts that passed through my mind and pushed them away.

The cool breeze refreshed me as I walked along. A few people passed by, greeting me. One stopped to ask about Swamiji. I again began to think about his story of Gita. I couldn't imagine how he ever believed that nonsense, it was too irrational. I had heard of Dr Shanti, she had a good reputation, I think she still saw patients though she would be over seventy. Perhaps I could go and visit her, ask her what happened. Would she remember anything at all? Dev said he had married in 1970, and Gita had died in October1974. Now it was 2000, almost twenty-six years had passed, she'd be unlikely to recollect anything that happened so long ago. Of course, Dev had retained the memory, it was important to him, it shaped his life, but to her Gita must have been just one of her many patients. Still, I could try. These were my thoughts along the way, and by the time I reached the ashram, my head had somewhat cleared. I wandered in the garden a while, before going inside. Nachiketa was sitting under the great banyan tree, meditating, his eyes shut, his face calm and peaceful. What did he think? What did he feel? Was I bringing him up the right way? He was always serene, spiritual and meditative. A sort of impatience filled me and I went and stood before him. He opened his eyes. Uncharacteristically, I began to criticize him. 'You don't care about anything, Nachiketa. You are just sitting there, absorbed in your dreams.'

'I am in meditation, not dreams.'

'The world could fall around you and you wouldn't be bothered.'

'But Baba, I thought that was the purpose of meditation. Didn't you tell me that when I was younger? "Sit, Nachiketa, never mind what happens around you. Let the world fall down, don't open your eyes." And didn't you tell me that that was how the Buddha gained enlightenment? And you read the Bhagavad Gita to me, "Sit by yourself and watch, as nature performs her tasks..."'.

I looked at him. He seemed agitated, disturbed, unlike himself, and I knew my own confusions, reflected in my behaviour, were disturbing him too. It's true I had taught him to meditate like that. But now it is as if I have forgotten all that I learnt and taught. Happiness, it seems to me, comes in forgetting, in not remembering, in not caring. Perhaps meditation is one way to do that.

I sat down next to him, and after a while I said, 'Everything I believed in seems wrong to me now, Nachiketa. Perhaps one cannot reach an understanding by reading texts, by meditating. People have done all this for centuries. They escape from the world, but the world doesn't change.

Suffering, misery and evil remain. We sit meditating, we find inner peace, and we just don't care about what is happening.' Nachiketa was struggling to express a thought. 'Baba,' he said. 'There is a moment in meditation, it comes rarely, but it does come. The moment of pure love. That is not a non-caring state.' Yes, that was true! I remember those moments, suffused with the white light of love, embracing the whole world. But did those moments do any good? Could they, or should they, be translated into action?

I couldn't think any longer. I held his hand for a minute and then went inside. Lying on the bed, closing my eyes, a new worry came to me. Nachiketa was just a child, and here I was burdening him with all this. He should be free, he should run and play, indulge in pranks like other children... Pranks and Nachiketa! It was such an absurd thought, I began to smile as I drifted off to sleep.

As I slept I thought briefly of Sharada. I had always liked her, I found her totally different from the rest of the women in the ashram. There was something aloof and dignified about her. I wondered if I could contact her and get her to visit Dev. That would enable me, too, to meet her again.

***

I went to see Dr Shanti today. I hoped that by meeting her I would get more insight into Gita's death, and my doubt about Dev's possible involvement in it would be answered. I took the ashram van and drove down to Dehradun, but I didn't get to see her in the morning. Her waiting room was full of patients, mostly women, some accompanied by their husbands. Obviously, despite her age, she was still a popular doctor. I looked a bit strange, a lone man going to see a gynaecologist. I asked the receptionist when I could meet her, I wanted some information, I said. 'Are you a policeman?' asked the comfortable-looking woman, wearing a name tag that read SAVITA NEGI. What made her ask that? I was sure I didn't look like one. Were there some enquiries being made about Dr Shanti? Was there another suspicious case? My mind was full of questions, but I just said I wanted to meet her on behalf of a friend, regarding a patient she had treated some years ago. The receptionist told me to return in the evening, after 7 p.m. What was I to do till then? It was only twelve in the morning. Should I return to the ashram and drive back again in the evening? It wasn't very far, but it was more than an hour's drive each way. The roads were bumpy, and if I went to the ashram, I wasn't sure if I'd have the incentive to return. Perhaps I could visit one of my old friends in the city instead. I'd had some good friends in my college days, and I'd kept in touch until I joined Dev. Now my life was at a turning point again, and maybe it was time to revive old contacts. I thought of one of my best friends, Vijay, whom I knew was still in Dehradun. Unlike many of my other friends, he'd never left to take up a job elsewhere, but had joined his father's business. I knew where he stayed, or at least where he used to stay, but it was over ten years since I had met him. Could I just walk in on him after all these years? Well, why not? I knew he would welcome me. This was India, after all, not the US, where everyone was so formal. And not just India, but small-town India, where the old values were retained, and friends and guests were always welcome.

According to the Puranas, a householder was to wait outside his house in the evenings for a guest to come by, and see to it that the guest was welcomed and fed, before eating himself. Not too many read the Puranas these days, and I doubt if anyone consciously follows their precepts, but some things had been unconsciously imbibed. The guest was to be treated like god, I too had been taught that in my young days. Still, I was slightly hesitant. I thought, instead of going straight to their house, I'd drive to his father's office first. Vijay was sure to be there too, and then if he wanted he could invite me home.

The office was seven or eight kilometres away, a little beyond Jakhan. I turned the van around and drove towards Ghanta Ghar, and then began the drive up Rajpur Road. The traffic still wasn't too fast these days, apart from some speeding Delhi tourists and youngsters on motorbikes. I thought of Dev's story and a memory came back to me. Dev had mentioned that Deepak's mother used to work in the school where Gita taught, and I knew Vijay's mother too had been employed in Nita Devi Pathshala. Perhaps I'd get some information on Gita, if I could meet his mother. After crossing Dilaram Bazar, the air was clearer, the congestion on both sides of the road diminished. It was a long time since I had come this way. Driving slowly, I was happy to see that despite the new shopping complexes, the tall trees lining the road were still intact. I came across a sign that I remembered had been there even in my student days. It said, 'Every policeman is a citizen in uniform, every citizen is a policeman without uniform,' so I suppose I could have told the receptionist, 'Yes, I'm a policeman out of uniform.' And after all, wasn't I seeking information like a policeman? I was convinced there was something suspicious about Gita's death, and here I was, trying to unravel the mystery after all these years. Perhaps I had missed my calling.

Another sign, one I had not seen before: 'Drinking and driving take you straight to the grave. Happy journey.' This made me laugh—I was feeling refreshed, forgetting for a while my own confusions and anguish, and even my search for an answer to an old puzzle. This was May 2000, at the height of the struggle for a separate hill state named Uttarakhand, to be carved out of Uttar Pradesh, and a sign a little further on, saying, 'Independent state of UK,' was amusing. I wondered what a visitor from the United Kingdom would make of it.

Just past Jakhan I turned right into a small lane, and drove into the office compound. I remembered it well, but more rooms seemed to have been added to the old building. I went inside and was stopped by a receptionist, a young woman in a stylish salwar kameez, and long painted nails. This was a new addition—there hadn't been a receptionist in the old days. I asked for Vijay. 'He's not in town,' she said, hardly looking at me. She didn't volunteer any more information, or ask why I wanted to see him. I stood there for a few minutes, at a loss. Just then Vijay's father came out of the inner room. I rose to greet him, and after a while he recognized me. 'Very good to see you, Prem,' he said. It was a long time since anyone had called me by my original name, and it gave me a start. 'Vijay is not here,' he added, 'but I cannot let you go back like this. I was just going home, and my wife will be happy to see you again. You must come and share our simple meal.'

I said I would follow him in my own vehicle, and we went outside. Of course I'd come in the ashram van, and the name 'Shankarananda Ashram' was written on the side. 'I've heard of the ashram,' he said. 'Are you visiting or living there?'

'I work there,' was all I said in response. He got into the car and I followed him in the van. The house was not far way, located down a steep winding road. Mr Bharadwaj called to his wife from outside, saying, 'Look whom I've brought with me!' Mrs Bharadwaj came out and greeted me warmly, she had no difficulty in recognizing me. She saw the name of the ashram on the van and said, 'I heard Swami Shankarananda is ill...'

'Yes,' I said. I did not volunteer any further information, and perhaps there was something in my tone that stopped her from asking.

Inside, their servant immediately brought me a glass of cold nimbu-pani, a welcome refreshment. Lunch was almost ready, said Mrs Bharadwaj, as she plied me with questions. Where had I been all this time? Why was I in the ashram van? What was I doing? I did not want to hide anything from them. I told them I had become Shankarananda's disciple some time ago, and had taken sannyas soon after that. I had a son named Nachiketa who lived with me in the ashram. I had come to town today to meet Dr Shanti, but I had an appointment for the evening, and so I thought I'd look up Vijay instead of driving back and forth.

Mr Bharadwaj could not contain himself. 'So you believe this Shankarananda is a good man?' he asked.

'I did believe it once,' I replied. 'Now I have some doubts, I do not know.'

'You know he ordered the killing of Madhav Kumar who accused him of appropriating his land?'

'I don't think that's correct,' I responded, but immediately asked myself why I was still defending him. Old habits take long to die. 'It may not be true,' I said in a milder tone, while within me anxiety grew, wondering if this was yet another death he was responsible for. Vijay's mother saw I was a little uncomfortable. 'What took you to Dr Shanti?' she asked, and added, 'I hope I'm not being too inquisitive. Perhaps someone in the ashram requires her.'

'No,' I said, happy that she had brought up the topic herself. 'I wanted to inquire about a very old case of hers. There was a young woman who died long ago in childbirth, in fact I think you knew her. I wanted to find out something about her sudden death. Her name was Gita Mangal.'

'Gita!' she exclaimed. 'Of course, I knew her. I remember the incident, there was a lot of talk at the time, but what is your interest in it?'

'I'll tell you later,' I said, 'if you can tell me what kind of talk there was.'

'Well,' she said, 'after all these years perhaps I shouldn't say it, but the rumour was that Dr Shanti killed the mother with a lethal injection and smothered the child. In fact, the nurse insisted she had seen her giving the injection and later suffocating the baby, but Shanti accused her of doing it instead, and the whole thing was hushed up.'

I'd had suspicions that something was amiss, but I hadn't expected this.

'But why?' I asked. 'Why should she want to kill Gita?'

'Everyone knew that Shanti's husband, Ajit, and Gita were having an affair before she married Mangal. It continued after her marriage too. Ajit used to be the sports teacher in school. I guess he always felt inferior to his doctor wife. She wouldn't even use his surname, referring to herself by her first name, Shanti. And Gita was lost and lonely when she first came here from her village. She stayed with some distant relatives who surely didn't want her there. Ajit was twice her age, he became her confidant and father figure, and then one thing led to another.'

'Shanti's husband? Where is he now?'

'He too died in mysterious circumstances, soon after Gita's death. A heart attack, it was said, but no one knew the truth.'

'But...if that was the case why did Gita choose Dr Shanti as her doctor? How could she trust her?'

'Gita later confided in me,' said Mrs Bharadwaj. 'One day Shanti came upon the two of them together in her house in the afternoon. After all, where else could they meet? They couldn't even talk much in school without creating a scandal. And he could hardly visit her relatives' house. When Shanti found them they were only talking, and according to Gita till that point they had no physical relationship. But oddly enough, Shanti encouraged them. Instead of creating a scene she befriended Gita. She said she would give Ajit a divorce, and help them get married. The closeness between Ajit and Gita increased, but Shanti kept putting off a divorce. She convinced them that the scandal would affect all their careers, and they may have to leave the town. But she said she did not mind their friendship. She said her feelings for Ajit had long since died, they were not compatible, but she had remained in the marriage to maintain a respectable façade in a small town like Dehradun. Gita's family was desperate for her to get married. She refused offers of uneducated men from her village, and many refused her because she was too educated. She was almost twenty-four years old when the proposal came from Devdarshan Mangal's family, and it seemed like a perfect match. And Shanti even encouraged Gita to marry, so that her relationship with Ajit could continue without anyone being suspicious. She said she was trying to start her practice in Chandigarh, and that would be the right time for both couples to get divorced.'

'But after she married did Gita want a divorce?'

'On the whole she did, though she was confused. That is when she began to confide in me. I tried to convince her to forget the past and accept her marriage with Devdarshan. Gita said Manu, as she called him, genuinely loved her. She liked him, but she loved Ajit. He expected their relationship to continue, and Shanti still did not seem to object. For several years Gita refrained from getting pregnant, thinking that ultimately she would be divorcing Devdarshan. She asked Dr Shanti for help, and she fitted her with a Copper T or whatever there was in those days to prevent pregnancy. But something happened, it failed. It was natural for her to consult Dr Shanti when she got pregnant.'

'But...if Shanti didn't mind initially then why later?'

'No, Prem, my guess is she always minded, and that she bided her time, waiting for her revenge.'

'Maybe it wasn't like that,' said Mr Bharadwaj. 'Maybe she hadn't minded initially and jealousy grew later and reached a height, especially when she saw her with a baby, as Shanti never had a child. Maybe she hadn't planned it so cold-bloodedly.'

'But Dr Shanti—she's still practicing. She has so many patients.'

'She accused the nurse and sent her away. The nurse had come to me before she left because I had accompanied Gita on some of her visits to the doctor. The nurse was unaware of the affair. I did not tell her either. I and a few others knew about it, but soon all talk about it died down.'

'But you don't have any evidence against Shanti except for the word of the nurse. Perhaps the nurse *was* responsible?'

'What motive could the nurse have? And in fact she was

ready to go with me to the police. After she came to me I told my husband the whole story. He even went to the SP and told him the nurse's story, and what we suspected. But the SP said the doctor had already given a statement of wrong treatment and negligence against the nurse, who was lucky she hadn't been arrested. When my husband told him about the affair, he said he could not act on rumours. He said if Gita's husband came to him and filed an FIR he would investigate again.'

Mr Bharadwaj then took up the story. 'By then Gita had been cremated. We both went to see Devdarshan Mangal, though I had never met him before. My wife too had not gone when Gita died as she had high fever that day. We offered our condolences, but could do nothing more. The man was in a deranged state, wild with grief, he seemed to have lost his reason. We did not feel we could tell him of our suspicions. It was clear he had loved Gita—how could we have added to his sorrow with the story of her treachery? Later we heard he had left here, no one knows where he went or whether he is still alive.'

Mrs Bharadwaj could not restrain her curiosity any longer. 'Why are you interested in Gita after so long?' she asked.

'Devdarshan Mangal is now on his deathbed,' I replied. 'He told me a funny story about his wife, and believed she died of supernatural causes. I wanted to discover the truth, and thought Dr Shanti would throw some light on it. I did not know I would find out so easily.'

'No,' said Mr Bharadwaj. 'We do not know the truth. We know the nurse's story, and we know that Dr Shanti contradicted her story. We know that Gita had a long-term relationship with Ajit, and we know all the rumours and talk that prevailed at that time. We don't know for sure that Shanti had anything to do with the deaths. Perhaps the truth will never be known.'

'You said Devdarshan was on his deathbed,' said Mrs Bharadwaj. 'Where is he? Has he come to Shankarananda's ashram in his last days?'

'He is Swami Shankarananda.'

'What!' both cried out together, shocked.

'Yes,' I said. 'He turned from the world because of his sorrows, though he never knew all this.'

'And will you tell him anything of this?' asked Mrs Bharadwaj.

'I don't know. I think I will meet Dr Shanti. And perhaps, if possible, the nurse.'

'He started out with sorrow, but he then became a crook,' said Mr Bharadwaj, reflectively.

How was it that someone living in Dehradun, where I thought Dev was revered, someone who had no connection with him, was calling him a crook? What did people know about him, what were the rumours? He had already mentioned the death of Madhav Kumar. I decided to probe him a little more about it. As he hesitated, Mrs Bharadwaj said that they were good friends with Madhav Kumar's wife, and though the police took no notice of her complaint, she was sure that he had been murdered. Madhav had farmland in an area where Shankarananda wanted to build a new ashram, but he refused to sell it. One day Madhav went missing and a few days later his body was found at a distant location, he seemed to have been run over, and the police called it an accident. But he could never have gone there himself, his wife had said. He could not drive, there were no easy transport facilities, and he would never go so far without informing her. While they were busy looking for him, and after they found him and were engulfed in grief, their land had been occupied. When they complained to the police, fake registration papers were produced. And that was not all. Some of Madhav's neighbours' land too had been appropriated in the same way, though without any other murders.

Then Mr Bharadwaj took up the story. He said that five of his friends had invested in a new deposit scheme apparently floated by the well-known Sarina Company. But when they tried to get the interest on their investment, they discovered that Sarina was not involved in it. Members of Shankarananda's ashram had used Sarina as a front and taken all the money. A considerable amount of money had been lost.

All this was new to me. Did Dev know about it, or was this being done without his knowledge, after he had become ill? I would ask him about it. I told the couple that I would try and find out who in the ashram was behind these crooked ventures.

'Come, let us have lunch,' said Mrs Bharadwaj. 'Here we are talking away and you must be hungry.'

Lunch was a simple but tasty meal of two sabzis, dal, raita and roti with sooji halwa for dessert.

Mrs Bharadwaj began asking me about Nachiketa. I told her how I had kept him with me since his mother died, had never sent him to school. I said I had thought he would have a life free from imperfections and would travel on a spiritual path, but now I did not know if I had done right or wrong in protecting him from the world. Or, I found myself confiding, if I had done it out of my own fears.

'I'm sure he'll be fine,' she comforted me, with a motherly smile. Then she went on to confide her own problems regarding Vijay. He wasn't married, she said. Some years ago he was passionately in love, but the young woman he cared for went in for an arranged marriage. Her parents hadn't liked Vijay, because—she paused a bit before blurting it out—Vijay had a bit of an alcohol problem. He drank too much. And after his rejection, it became worse.

'He doesn't do much in the business,' said Mr Bharadwaj who was a wholesale dealer in saris, and now, he confided, had expanded to include readymade clothes. 'But I've sent him on a business trip to Varanasi to select saris from there, hoping he'll gradually take on more responsibility. You must come when he's back, he would be very happy to meet you again, and maybe you could help him too.' Yes, I said, I would definitely come.

After lunch, coffee was served. Mrs Bharadwaj suggested I rest in the guest room, until it was time for my appointment with Dr Shanti. I could join them for tea before that, she said. I agreed, and she led me to a large bedroom, with a double bed, a desk and a TV. I lay down, tired, thinking about relationships, about love, rejected love, failed love and the effect it had on our lives. Weren't we all, Dev, Vijay, and I, in a sense in the same situation, suffering from loss?

I began to think about my wife, Kusum. She was a good person. I can't say I was passionately in love, I was depressed by her death, but did not become deranged or take to alcohol. My main anxiety and worry was regarding our small son. I truly missed her, and the way she took care of everything, making no demands, leaving me free to read, write, teach, and spend time with my students. The house was always neat and clean, the food well-cooked, Nachiketa perfectly cared for, at least that's how it seemed to me. I usually had my head buried in a book, and I would absentmindedly eat the parathas she served me in the morning, drink the tea that followed, and leave for work. I was rarely home for lunch, but for dinner there were always two or three sabzis, fresh hot phulkas, dal made differently every day, and then kheer or some other sweet. Nachiketa, or Sudhakar as we called him then, would come to me fresh from a bath, he would already have been fed, and would play on his own while we had dinner. Kusum was always cheerful, she welcomed anyone I brought home along with me for a meal—who wouldn't be happy with a person like that? It's not that I would have minded if she had been different, wanted to work, or wanted me to help her in the house, but Kusum just focused on the home and made life easy for me. I never heard my son cry while she was alive. I do not like to remember the days after her death, when Sudhakar's wails seemed incessant, and he refused to eat. I left him with my sister for a month, and then employed a woman to take care of him, but until I joined Dev, he remained dull and depressed.

I drifted into sleep, and was woken by someone knocking on the door. It was Mr Bharadwaj, suggesting I get up and join them for a cup of tea. It was almost 5.30 in the evening. I felt refreshed after my sleep, and tea was a relaxed affair, with pakoras and cake. I asked Mrs Bharadwaj if she remembered the name of the nurse. It turned out she not only had her name, but even her address, written on a page torn from a small notebook. 'She gave this to me when she left,' said Mrs Bharadwaj as I copied it down. 'All these years, I kept it in my drawer in an old purse. Sometimes I thought of throwing it away, but I had believed her story. I hoped some day justice would be done. Perhaps I was just waiting for someone like you. But I don't know what has happened to her, or if she is even at the same address—it was so long ago.'

'I don't know if there is any chance of justice,' I said, 'but I will try to meet them both.'

The nurse's name was Renu Rawat, Rawat was a common surname in this region, it was mine too. She had provided an address in Doiwala. I thanked them for their hospitality, promised to visit again, and left around 6.45, reaching Dr Shanti's clinic by 7. I already knew part of the story, but I thought I would pretend that I knew nothing. When I reached there, I spoke to the receptionist, reminding her that she had asked me to return at 7 p.m. She spoke on the phone and said Dr Shanti was ready to see me.

I went into her room, and saw a frail, white-haired old lady. She looked at me without speaking, and I introduced myself. I said I was sorry to trouble her, but a young woman under her care had died in childbirth in 1974. Her husband, now on his deathbed, believed she died of supernatural causes. I wondered if she remembered the case and could shed any light on it.

Dr Shanti said she had many cases, and that was a long time ago. She asked for the name of the woman, and when I said Gita Mangal, she frowned, looked at her desk for a while, and said she did have a vague memory, because Gita was the only patient she had who died of eclampsia soon after delivery. She then explained that eclampsia led to convulsions and organ failure. I asked about the baby, and she said she could not remember—she thought the baby had lived.

There was nothing more to be said, and I left after telling her that no, the baby too had died.

Once again, she said she did not remember.

Now I had several different theories regarding Gita's death. Death by eclampsia seemed possible, but then why had Dr Shanti not said so at the time, why had she accused the nurse, and why had the nurse claimed that she had seen Dr Shanti giving Gita an injection and smothering the baby?

I was inclined to believe that Shanti had killed both mother and child, but there was no real proof.

As I drove back in the fading light, I thought I would make a short stop at Doiwala, at least check whether anyone lived at that address. Doiwala is just about twenty kilometres beyond Dehradun, on the route to Rishikesh, where our ashram was. I reached the main Doiwala market and asked for directions at a teashop. Only a few thousand people live in Doiwala, and the teashop owner said he knew the house, but no one lived there. When I asked why, he said he did not know, but the house had been locked for years. He pointed out the way, and I drove up to the house. It was deserted, the garden overgrown and the house almost covered with creepers and plants. I knocked on the door of the nearest house, which was across a small road. A middle-aged woman tentatively opened the door a crack. I apologized and explained I was looking for the nurse Renu Rawat. 'She died long ago,' the woman said, 'and her family moved away. The house has remained empty ever since, people consider it unlucky, and no one wants to live here. I don't know much, I was not here at that time. I heard she died from some poison. Varmaji, the chemist on the main road knows more about it.' I thanked her and left, hoping the chemist was still open. It was now past 9 p.m., and I arrived at the shop as he was pulling down the shutters. When I stopped the car and got out, he looked fearful, but calmed down when I spoke to him. I explained what

I wanted, and he said he remembered the case, but asked why I wanted to know. I told him that an old friend who was on his deathbed wanted to get in touch. He seemed to accept the explanation.

'Renu was taking some medication for early onset arthritis. Some of the pills in her bottle of medication contained poison, that was revealed after she died. The police questioned me, but the pills were not from my shop, they were from the hospital where she used to work. She had just recently left the hospital after facing some problems there. The family said she was murdered and accused some doctor in the hospital, but the police declared it was suicide,' he said.

'How could it be suicide if there was poison in her medication?'

'She was a nurse. The police concluded she put it there herself to throw suspicion on a doctor who had accused her in the death of a patient.'

'Where is the family now?'

'I don't know. Renu had a younger brother, and he and her parents moved away soon after.'

He had nothing more to tell me, and was impatient to go home.

It was past ten when I reached the ashram. The door to Nachiketa's room was shut, he must have been asleep. There was dinner in the kitchen, but instead I made myself a cheese sandwich, thinking over what I had learnt as I ate it. Based on Mrs Bharadwaj's story, Dr Shanti seemed responsible for all the deaths—Mrs Bharadwaj was unaware that Renu Rawat too was dead. After so many years, it may not be possible to prove anything. I would tell Dev all I had learned, I decided. Perhaps it would pain him, but as he was seeking to understand his life, it may help him to do so. I would also ask him if he knew anything about the accusations Mr Bharadwaj had made. If Dev too had been involved in these murders or money collections, perhaps he would now admit it, or I may be able to tell from his reactions to my account.

I did not sleep well, and the next morning I drove over to see him, and told him everything I had found out about Gita, including what Dr Shanti had said. I left it to him to draw his own conclusions. He discounted Shanti's version of eclampsia. He thought Mrs Bharadwaj's story was true. 'Somewhere in my heart I always knew this, Nitya,' he said, 'though I had no idea who she was having an affair with. I wish she had confided in me, had not told me those fanciful stories.'

'Yes,' I said, 'that would have been better'. He did not show any signs of guilt or confusion, still, I asked him that if in his heart he 'always knew this', perhaps his account had not been quite true. Had he conspired with Dr Shanti in Gita's death? He did not respond with anger, but assured me that he had nothing to do with her death. Once she had got pregnant, he had not doubted her at all, it was only when she had said she did not want a child that he had initial doubts. It was years later, he said, that he again began wondering if she had loved someone else.

He seemed convincing, but still, I wasn't sure what to believe.

He was still thinking, going over what I had said to him, when I narrated to him all that Mr Bharadwaj had said. This seemed to be a shock to him—I was convinced by his reaction that he knew nothing of it. He said he had no plans for another ashram in that area, and asked me if I could find out who was responsible, both for the takeover of Madhav's land, and for the fake finance scheme. Not many people had stayed in the ashram over the past year, and in his house there were only Diana and Sophie, so who could have been involved in all that? I asked him if he remembered who had visited and stayed in the ashram, and he said Vidyananda, the head of his ashram in Italy, and Mark had visited. Then he handed over another stack of papers, the second part of his story.

Driving home, I thought over how I could find out more about the people involved, and what could be done regarding Dr Shanti. I decided to phone Mrs Bharadwaj and tell her what I had learned, and also ask her if she could tell me something about the people involved in the land acquisition and financial deals. I got through to her on the phone after I returned to the ashram and first told her what I had discovered about the nurse. She was shocked and promised to request her husband to take it up again with the police, even though it had all happened so long ago. She did not know who had been involved in the other matters, but would try and find out from Madhav's wife and the friends who had made the investments.

5. Leaving the Shadows Behind

Dev's Story

As I left I looked back at the shuttered house, where I had been so happy, at the arid, overgrown garden, that was once full of flowers. There was a pang in my heart, a grief, then Puck's words returned to my mind to console me: 'If we shadows have offended, Think but this and all is mended—That you have but slumbered here, while these visions did appear.' Yes, as I set off in the early morning, the air crisp and clear, my life so far seemed like a dream, a sleep filled with visions. I was embarking on a new path, and I would totally forget Gita, her absurd stories, her strange death.

Yet the past never leaves one. I could have found happiness with another woman, but I caused every woman I met sorrow, because in myself I had stored first the pain of Gita's death, and then the hurt caused by others. Sharada, particularly Sharada comes to my mind, as I wrote earlier, no matter what I tried, she refused to sleep with me, and that is why she haunts me still. She was the only woman who ever rejected me. That doesn't mean I slept with every woman I met, far from it, but I expected that once I chose a woman, she would see it as an honour. But Sharada didn't see it that way. She said that when she left her husband, she was finished with men and relationships forever. She joined me, she said, only because she thought I was an ascetic.

I never did become an ascetic though I pretended to be one. I was different in my younger days, I believed in sex only within marriage, and was celibate till I married Gita. Once I had known sex with Gita, there were more desires in me, but they were never out of control. It was after I reached the US, and the events that I will describe later, that I began to yearn for women, to be near them, to hear them, smell them, feel them, and more and more I longed for sex.

But I am digressing, rushing ahead with my story. I remember that morning, it was the 26th of February 1975, when I set off, chanting Puck's words like a mantra in my mind. I had to first reach Almora, not too far from Nainital, the place where I had been to school. I had just a small bag with me, and I had put some money in an inner shirt pocket. I reached the bus stand in Dehradun and was told there was a landslide and two broken bridges along the direct route to Almora. I took a bus to Delhi. Of course, there was a breakdown along the way, and though I'd started at 6 a.m., it was 5 p.m. before I reached Delhi. I didn't want to stay there, looked around for a bus to Almora, and found one leaving at 8 p.m. It would be travelling at night through the hill roads, was it safe? Well, how did it matter? If I died I would join Gita, I thought. Then with a shudder I brought myself back to reality. Gita was with Varun, I was on my own now. I wouldn't die, I would change my life, be totally different, and never feel pain again. Yes, though through the coming years I had a lot of sorrow and fear, I never did feel that sort of helpless pain in all those years, but now sick, and on my deathbed, I feel it once again.

I dozed in the night bus. We reached Almora in the morning. From there I had to walk, the ashram was about twenty-five kilometres away, and there was no motorable road in those days. I went first to the hotel Mr Gosain had recommended, for a wash and breakfast and to get a guide for the journey. I discovered it wasn't exactly a hotel, but a large house, with a couple of extra rooms that were let out. Girija Kumar, his wife and four daughters, lived there. Each room had a bathroom, and when a bucket of hot water was brought, I had a quick bath. The weather was cold, but at least there was no snow. A steaming hot cup of tea, along with puris and aloo were served to me. I looked at it, and remembering how Gita used to often serve me like that, I felt tears coming into my eyes. 'No!' I told myself sternly. Pushing Gita out of my mind, I savoured my meal.

'It's a long and tiring walk to the ashram,' said Girija Kumar. 'Rest here today, and start early morning tomorrow. There are uphill and downhill paths, it will take you two days, and you'll have to camp on the hillside the first night. You'll need a guide, and I have arranged one.' I agreed, and spent the day strolling in the crisp sunshine, eating delicacies that Mrs Kumar prepared. I slept well at night. Girija woke me with a cup of tea at five in the morning, and Bholu, the guide, and I set off at 5.30. It was still dark. Bholu carried some thick blankets, and the food Mrs Kumar had packed for our journey. They had refused any payment, insisting I was their guest, Mr Gosain's friend. Bholu added my small bag to his load, for he could see I wasn't in very good shape. He asked if he should hire a pony or mule for me to ride on, but I said no. After all, I had grown up in the mountains, and I had always been strong. I'd thrown off my grief and depression, I'd soon regain my strength.

I was weaker than I thought, and we had to make frequent stops. Still, over the rugged and sometimes nonexistent pathways, we did cover about half the journey the first day. At midday we sat down on a rocky outcrop, and ate a paratha each. There was a flask of hot tea, and that revived me. In the evening, when the sun had already set, but its last rays were still red in the sky, we reached a small shelter, just a roof over four pillars, and Bholu said we'd spend the night there. It was an old and crumbling structure set against a rock.

Bholu put down his load. We ate a couple more parathas each, of the large number packed by Mrs Kumar. We'd been speaking in Hindi along the way, but now I spoke to Bholu in Kumaoni that I'd picked up when I was in school in Nainital, and he immediately became more friendly. He told me a bit about his life. His own village was not far from the ashram, he said. 'I suppose you'll pay a visit there too?' Yes, he said. He would go there, though he never felt good in his village. He was one of twins, but for some reason his parents always favoured his brother. He ran away when he was twelve years old, and initially carried loads in Almora, but then started working as a guide whenever he could. 'Sometimes foreigners come, and they pay well,' he said. I began to wonder how much I should pay him, and he seemed to read my thoughts. 'I won't take money from you, you are one of us,' he said. Then he told me of his sadness, that because of his estrangement from his parents, they were not even ready to arrange his marriage. 'You can choose someone yourself,' I said. He was indignant. 'Our girls are not like that,' he said. 'They follow our traditions.' I pondered over what he had said, his mix of independence and tradition. Each person had sorrows, confusions, of their own. Perhaps one day I'd be in a position to help people like him. Meanwhile he had gone towards a thicket of trees, and after a while returned with a bundle of twigs and dry leaves. He lit them, and gazing into its crackling flames, the small fire made me feel warm and peaceful. As the fire died down, we each spread a plastic sheet with a blanket on top on the ground, covered ourselves with two more blankets, and slept.

I woke early, it was still dark. I thought I heard a rustling of leaves, a low growl. A chill went through me. Wasn't this leopard country, and weren't some of them known to be maneaters? I was crazy to have come on this journey, why hadn't I thought of this before? And why hadn't we lit a bigger fire that would last longer and keep the animals away? My long spell of grief had made me lose my common sense. Bholu woke a second later, and sat up. Fishing a powerful torch out of his sleeping bag he shone it, and as I too struggled to sit, and followed the beam of the torch, I saw the leopard, standing just a few paces away. I looked at that beautiful creature with a mixture of fear and wonder. Were these to be the last moments of my life? Bholu was out of his nest of blankets. What followed left me amazed. Turning the beam away from the animal, he walked towards it, and muttered something. The leopard looked at him for a few seconds, then quietly walked away.

'Are you a magician, Bholu?' I asked. 'What did you say?'

'Let's get up, it's morning,' was all he replied. And indeed, it was dawn, the dark clear sky with its bright stars was beginning to lighten, with the first rays of morning light reaching it through distant space.

Had I seen Bholu talk to a leopard? I wanted to question him, but as I saw the tops of the tall trees beginning to glow with the gentle rays of the sun, my heart and mind became quiet, for a few moments I was totally at peace. As my mind started up again, like an engine that can never rest for long, I asked myself why, in my grief and depression, I hadn't gone to the mountains before. Having grown up in them, I know people living there feel pain and sorrow just as much as those in the plains. Yet somehow, when one reached there from a life in a city, the quietness and stillness seeped into one. Thoughts slowed down, they couldn't rush ahead at the same pace. It was as if they were chilled and calmed by the clear cold air.

Bholu had been making tea on another twig fire. He brought me a cup and told me that further on there was a stream where we could wash. I thanked him as I sipped the warming brew. Soon, after a wash, we were ready to start. Bholu packed up and loaded himself with the bags, but I insisted on taking one this time, as we started walking uphill once again.

The rest of the journey was uneventful. I had difficulty catching my breath on the tough climb and didn't try to talk. Bholu too didn't say much, though he took my bag from me. After lunch he told me the ashram was now not far away, just outside Hansa village. We would reach there soon. We arrived around 5 p.m., as darkness was descending again. It was the 28th of February, the last day of the month. Why am I writing all this, instead of the more essential details of my story, when I have so little time left? But perhaps this too is important, perhaps every detail is, to reach an understanding of the life I lived. Was I responsible for all I did, or was I just a product of my circumstances? Was there a higher power guiding my life, and if so, was this power good or bad?

I'm tired out, I must rest awhile.

***

It's early morning, I'm awake before dawn. I dreamt of snowy mountains, of walking in a snow storm as I used to when I was young. In my dream I felt the soft flakes and tasted the icy lightness on my tongue. What does it mean? My end is near? Well of course my end is near, and I must hurry up with my story.

***

The ashram consisted of a large old building with a few small newer-looking cottages nearby. There was quite a bit of land enclosed in a ramshackle fence, and later I saw there were sheds and storerooms at the back. As we entered the open gate, we were met by a young man, a foreigner, around twenty years old. I explained who I was, and he introduced himself as Edward, gave me a wide smile, took my bag, and asked me to follow him. Bholu did not want to stop, he said his village was not far away, and if he carried on he'd reach before night. He brushed off my offers of payment and said he would come to meet me after a few days. Edward guided me to my room through a doorway at the side of the building. The room was neat and clean, but very small, hardly eight feet square, a cubicle with wooden partitioned walls. There was a charpai with a thin mattress, covered with a thick woven sheet, and two or three rough blankets neatly folded at the foot of the bed. A small table was near the bed, and a lantern stood on it. A few pegs were screwed into the wall opposite. Pointing out a tin trunk under the bed where I was to store my belongings, Edward left. I put my few clothes in the trunk, hung my towel on one of the pegs, put my soap, mug and other toiletries on the table and then sat down on the bed. I wanted to just lie down and rest, but I needed a wash first, and wondered where the bathroom was.

In a few minutes another man came in. 'I'm Enzo,' he introduced himself. So here was the head of the ashram. He looked about forty-five, but was balding, with wisps of white-blonde hair on his head, and pale, washed-out, blue eyes. Despite this, his skin was brown, I thought it seemed darker than mine. He was stocky and short, a few inches over five feet, and thus on the whole did not look very different from the local people. I was just slightly taller than him. Blue eyes of course, aren't common here, but there are many with light brown or hazel eyes. I later discovered that blue eyes aren't that common for Italians either, but several northern Italians do have them.

'You must be tired,' he continued. 'I've asked Cynthia to bring you some soup. Then you can rest, or even have an early night if you like. If you have the energy, Cynthia will show you the ashram, and the fields behind where we grow some crops. We have a few goats too, for milk. And there's a good library, if you'd like to read something.' Meanwhile he opened the petromax lantern and lit it, turning the wick up, as it was already quite dark in the room. I asked about a wash, and he showed me a large bathroom down the corridor which had buckets filled with water, and beyond in a courtyard, some dry latrines, deep pits with wooden boards above them. In Dehradun we had a flush system in our house, linked to a sewage tank in the back garden, but how could one expect it here, where there was no electricity, plumbing or water pipes. In Bagori we didn't have bathrooms, and still don't have them today. We just used some part of the open land, and bathed in the river.

Water was drawn from a rainwater tank, Enzo said, and filled in the bathroom. The tank had a percolation system, which cleaned and purified the water. Water for drinking and cooking was taken from springs, he continued.

As we returned to the room, a young woman entered, wearing some kind of blue work clothes and carrying a tray on which there was a large covered bowl. She was short and slim, with dark brown hair and piercing deep blue eyes, very different from Enzo's washed-out look. She had a wonderful smile, and a rather cheeky grin. There was something about her, her cheerfulness, her eyes, that made my spirits lift, my tiredness left me. She put the tray on the table, gave me a friendly wave, and left without a word. Did Enzo notice the change in me? I think so. He smiled and left too, saying, 'I'll see you in the morning.'

The soup was thick and warm, it seemed a mixture of vegetables of all kinds. I drank it and then went to the bathroom. After a quick bath in the icy water from one of the buckets in the bathroom, I changed into a fresh kurta and pyjama, and returning to the room, turned down the lantern and lay on the bed. I had no energy to do anything more, certainly not to wander around the ashram or visit the library.

A razai had been brought and placed on the bed. As I covered myself with it, warmth seeped through my body, for a minute I had a vision of short dark brown hair and bright blue eyes, and then I slept.

I woke early next morning as the dawn light filtered through the windows. A moment of confusion, then I knew where I was. I felt fresh, alive, and new, my entire past at least temporarily forgotten. I looked out of the window and then opened the door, went down a short passage and stood outside. The air was cold, heavy with dew. We were already on a mountain, at a height of around 2,500 metres but the even higher mountains all around were a dark, deep blue. The still-grey sky was turning lighter. I thought to myself, how could Gita matter, here was this world, so beautiful, so perfect. But just as I thought that, her memory returned, and pain dimmed my senses once again.

There was a hand on my shoulder, I turned around to find Enzo standing there. 'Mr Gosain told me you want to discover the meaning of life and death. Get ready for the day and then we will begin.'

Begin? Begin what, I wondered.

Enzo replied as if I had spoken. 'The journey of the discovery is long,' he said. 'How much you proceed is up to you. I can give you some tools to get you started.'

I could not help myself. I asked Enzo almost rudely: 'Have you discovered the meaning?' He stood silent, looking abstracted.

Then he said, 'I have some hints. I have gone part of the way. I can't say I have discovered it, but I can point you in the right direction. All the sages say reality is an illusion. We think we live in a real world, and that is how we delude ourselves. So to start with, forget about god. Forget the past. Forget the future. Try to discover what you enjoy doing, and pursue it. Live life to its fullest. Enjoy yourself in every way.'

This was not what I expected. Was this a guru? He was telling me to forget about god. To do whatever I liked. I was disappointed. But then as I turned to go inside to bathe and change, I had a moment of joy, of great liberation. Enjoy yourself? I had never heard that before. No, I did not come from a society in which enjoyment was encouraged. Of course, in the boarding school in which I grew up, there were occasional pleasures, furtive bouts of laughter, but I could not fully participate even in these. We were always told to be sober and responsible, to study hard, to be neat and clean. Later, in my college days, my fellow students were rather wild, sneaking out to drink alcohol and smoke, I don't know if they were enjoying themselves, or just trying to escape from the stifling atmosphere in which perhaps we all lived. I had had happy moments with Gita, but even that happiness was part of a life of responsibility and dignity. Perhaps the only true freedom and enjoyment I had, was when I lost myself in the words of Shakespeare.

I went inside and once again had a bath in the frozen cold water. I had bathed in icy streams in my village hence it did not bother me. When I had finished and got dressed, I found Cynthia waiting outside my room. 'You've missed the morning meditation,' she said, 'but come and have breakfast.' I learnt that the morning meditation began every day at 5 a.m., when it was still dark. But there was no compulsion to attend it, said Cynthia. Sometimes only one or two people came.

For breakfast there was hot coffee and some sort of nutty bread. In fact, I had never drunk coffee before. We always had tea. Coffee was something people drank down south. And why was there bread? I didn't like bread. Why couldn't we have parathas or even plain rotis? A memory of Gita surfaced again, and of the delicious breakfasts she used to make. Aloo parathas, gobi parathas, muli parathas, puris on Sundays and holidays, and sometimes extremely elaborate breakfasts, a sort of brunch, of chole and kulcha followed by warm, freshly made jalebis. I would help by mixing the jalebi batter and making a hole in the half coconut shell that she would use to dribble the batter into the hot oil...I saw her face again as if she were in front of me, and a shaft of pain along with dark anger arose again. I shook my head and tried to free myself of these thoughts.

Thinking all this I hadn't paid much attention to the people around me. Now, after helping myself from a side table, I settled down in a chair along a long rectangular table, and saw that other residents were doing the same. There were just about ten people apart from me. I had already met Enzo, Edward and Cynthia. And all of them, except possibly one person, who could have been from our northeast, were foreigners. As everyone sat down and began to eat, there were friendly smiles and introductions—Peter, Francois, Alicia, Petra...and the one I thought could possibly be an Indian, was a Japanese named Ono.

Why were they all foreigners? Why were there no other Indians? Were they here legally? Could they be spies? For a few confused moments, I felt I had to defend my country against them, a kind of nationalism and pride arose in me. I think I had felt this way only once before during the Indo–China war, when I was in my last year of school. Soon I calmed down and began to eat. The bread was quite good. I needed more sugar in the coffee but it wasn't bad either. And hadn't Mr Gosain recommended this place and been here himself? Why was I getting paranoid thoughts?

Around the table there was some desultory conversation. The warmth of the coffee seeped into me. I relaxed.

After breakfast we all washed our own plates, mugs and spoons, and placed them in a rack. Enzo told me that the bread was made right there in the ashram, baked in clay ovens. He explained that the ashram did not employ servants or helpers, everyone joined in to do all the work that was required. Duties changed every week, and there was a weekly meeting to decide who would do what. He said that as I hadn't been there for the meeting, he was assigning me the task for the first week—I had to keep the grounds clean, sweeping up leaves and placing them in compost pits. If there was still time after that was done, there was weeding and digging in the garden. I liked the concept of doing one's own work, of the equality it implied, but still, resentment rose in me. Had I been given these menial tasks because I was an Indian? Enzo seemed to read my thoughts. He explained: 'We do all the work in turns. You will soon learn to do everything here, and to bake bread and cook too.'

He went on to say he was sure I had managed a good wash after my journey, but hot water was provided on Sundays and everyone bathed once a week. I stared at him in astonishment. Once a week? In my worst days of depression after Gita's death I hadn't missed my early morning bath using a bucket of cold water. Could it be that these foreigners bathed only once a week? Something led me not to put my astonishment into words. I just said that I had already had two baths, and I did not need hot water. Enzo laughed. 'I half expected that,' he said. 'I know, you Indians are like that'.

There was a divide between us. He said, 'You Indians,' I thought, 'These foreigners.' Throughout my life I found that no matter how much one tried to integrate, to talk of oneness and unity, this cultural divide always existed, along with at least a slight feeling of superiority on both sides. And one of the things I attained as a guru was to ensure that foreigners could not assert their sense of superiority. I tried my best to get them to feel inferior, and I think I succeeded.

There was another way in which 'we Indians' differed, at least middle-class Indians. This was a difference I wasn't proud of. Most of us looked down on manual work as inferior. I didn't mind doing it, but my first reaction had been somewhat the same.

Enzo then briefly explained the daily schedule. After the early morning meditation, there was time to get dressed, followed by breakfast, about an hour's work, and some free time. A study class began at 10 a.m. This included a lecture and discussion and could go on for some time. After that we could spend time in the library. Lunch was at 12.30, and after some free time, we had to resume work from 3 to 6 p.m. Then there was a light evening meal, a discussion, and meditation at 8 p.m. Of course, as there was no electricity, it would be good if we turned off our petromax lanterns and slept by 9 p.m. Nothing was compulsory, he said, except the daily work, because without that the ashram could not function.

After breakfast, I went into the grounds and began to sweep up the leaves, load them in a basket, and carry them to the compost pit. Enzo offered me a rake, something I had never seen before, and which I found quite inefficient. I asked for a jharu instead, and managed better with that. Sweeping done, I sat outside on the verandah for a while. Everyone else seemed busy, and there was no one around.

6. Reading the Ancient Texts

Dev's Story

Just before 10 a.m., I went inside the building and began looking for the class. I saw two or three people converging at a room and moved towards it. Inside it looked like a regular classroom with a teacher's table in front, and desks and chairs. There were smiles and a few friendly waves as I sat down in one of the chairs. Only two of the people I had met at breakfast were there, but there were two others. I had hardly been there a few moments when Enzo came in, and stood in front of the teacher's table. 'Let us begin,' he said, and everyone began to chant,

'Om sah navavatu...'

The whole chant was in Sanskrit, and I learnt the meaning only later.

'May He (the Lord) protect us.
May He bless us with the bliss of knowledge.
Let us make an effort together.
May we study well together.
May we never quarrel.
Om Peace Peace Peace.'

As soon as I heard the chanting I began to get irritated. Of course, I wasn't an expert in Sanskrit, though I had picked up some from Gita, and like most others—my colleagues and friends—I knew some commonly used Sanskrit chants, such as the Gayatri mantra. Their accents and pronunciation were atrocious. And that included Enzo's. Once again, I wondered, what were these people doing here? Why couldn't they search for spirituality in their own countries? I remained silent, and Enzo said to me, 'You'll soon learn the words,' irritating me even further.

After a few moments I said, 'Yes, I could learn the words in a few minutes. And I could teach you to pronounce them correctly.' I thought Enzo at least would be annoyed by my response, but that was not the case. He smiled and said, 'We have started this chanting only recently. None of us know Sanskrit. We'd greatly appreciate it if you taught us to pronounce the words correctly. And next you could start teaching us a few more chants.' I agreed and thus from the second day of my stay there I too became a teacher—in a small way at first, but gradually, I took on a bigger role.

In that first class, Enzo began to discuss the *Katha Upanishad*. This Upanishad deals directly with the central question then in my mind—what happens after death? Its story centres around a boy named Nachiketa. Nachiketa was unhappy with his father, who he felt had made an unworthy offering to the gods, a gift of barren cows. 'To whom will you give me?' he repeatedly asked his father, knowing he was precious and loved. In anger his father replied, 'I give you to Mrityu, Death.' And so Nachiketa, the dutiful son, went off to the abode of Yama, god of death, but Yama wasn't home. Nachiketa waited for him for three days, and when Yama returned, he apologized, for a guest must always be treated with honour. Then Yama granted him three boons, as Nachiketa had waited for three days. Through these boons, Nachiketa was not only reconciled with his father, but learnt the secret of life and death. In this class Enzo provided these bare outlines, and did not tell us what Yama said, but definitely the story caught my attention, and I was intrigued.

After the class I went straight to the library and found a copy of the text. It contained the Sanskrit, a word-by-word translation, and then a full translation in English. First, I was filled with wonder at the beauty of the words. I had lived for years with Gita, a Sanskrit expert, and had always felt superior, and never bothered to read or look at a Sanskrit text. I wanted to rush ahead and find out what Yama had said, but then I decided to savour the words, and read slowly. What a magnificent language this was! The commentary began by explaining the difficulties in translation, and I learnt that a single word 'padam' for instance, could have more than twenty different meanings, for instance, taking a step, a foot, a word, or even a square or division on a board game.

I read only thirteen verses that morning. And I was transported to a different world. How could one fear death when Yama himself apologized for making a visitor wait three days? Of course, I knew this was just a story, but it was a story meant to convey certain truths.

From the library, I moved into the dining room for lunch. Lunch consisted of more of that bread, but this time it was toasted. There were boiled vegetables, mainly potatoes and something green that I couldn't identify, with a little salt, and boiled dal, without a tarka. Didn't anyone even know how to make dal? How could I eat this tasteless food? Peter and Alicia were the cooks that day, and they even said that they had made an Indian meal specially for me! I smiled politely, but I felt that soon I would be teaching them not just the correct pronunciation of Sanskrit words, but also how to cook Indian food.

The rest of the day passed in a sort of a blur. I was tired out and distracted. I found the afternoon work period tedious and exhausting. After all I had gone through, life in the ashram felt unreal.

Within a week, though, I had got used to the routine and the new way of life. In the morning classes I began teaching the correct pronunciation of any chants or Sanskrit words used, and adding a few comments from my extra reading, as classes continued on the *Katha Upanishad*. Enzo was proceeding very slowly, while in my own reading I had almost reached the end of the text. What I read was quite strange to me, the ideas were relatively new. I pondered over some of the phrases. The text said there was 'a fire seated in the cave' (nihitam guhayam), and translators said this was 'the cave of the heart.' What did this mean? When I asked Enzo, he said he would begin an explanation of the chakras, the energy centres within the body, after completing the *Katha Upanishad*, and I should wait till then. The Nachiketa-fire described in succeeding verses was even more difficult to understand. Then there is that crucial twentieth verse, where Nachiketa asks the main question of the text. 'When a man is dead, some say he is, some say he is not, this I would like to know.' But there are many more verses before Yama begins to impart the secret of the Self. Briefly, what he says is that there is an eternal Self hidden in the cave of the heart. This Self is ultimately the same as Brahman, which is the essence of the world, from which everything originates.

As I thought over these concepts, I felt that perhaps they appealed to me because they resonated with the words of Shakespeare, they were bringing me back to the wonder of his thoughts again. Hadn't he, in his twenty-fourth sonnet, said 'Thy beauty's form in table of my heart. My body is the frame wherein 'tis held'? Later, the more Sanskrit texts

I read, the more parallels I discovered in Shakespeare. Yet the Upanishads went straight to the point, explained things more directly. Reading them at that time I believed that I had discovered a great secret. I felt that soon I'd be able to look into that hidden cave, and find this eternal Self. Enzo gave me a mantra which he told me never to reveal, and guided me in some meditation practices. I tried, I sincerely tried. In all my free time I sat in meditation and tried to find that fire or light in the 'cave of the heart,' but I found nothing.

More than a month passed, and Enzo looked briefly at some of the other Upanishads. I learnt that there were numerous Upanishads of different types, but the earliest and main Upanishads had certain key sentences, known as 'mahavakyas' or 'great statements'. These statements, in different ways, said the same thing, that the Atman, the individual soul or Self was the same as Brahman. Later I realized that there was a lot more to be studied in the Upanishads and in Vedanta as a whole, but Enzo did not dwell on this vast theme, and instead began classes on the chakras. I already had some vague idea that chakras were inner energy centres, which could be activated, but now I learnt about them in detail. Enzo used John Woodroffe's *Serpent Power*, and I was soon studying it further in the library. I read all about the seven chakras and some additional ones, and the powers that could be achieved by activating each of them. How wonderful it would be if I could activate them all, and rouse that strange serpent power, the kundalini, said to lie dormant at the base of the spine. There were diagrams in the book and I focused on them, meditated, concentrated, read whatever else I could find about them. Woodroffe's diagrams became imprinted on my inner mind, but despite all my efforts, nothing was achieved, nothing changed. As I read and meditated on these, there was a shift in my focus. I had wanted to know the truth about life and death, and Yama's response to Nachiketa was about the ultimate aim of achieving identity with Brahman. I had tried to discover that cave within the heart, but it seemed too unattainable. And I began to think, what was the point of it? Was I ready to totally detach myself from life, and seek identity with Brahman? Maybe I could do that later in life. Awakening the chakras, particularly the seventh, the sahasrara or thousand-petalled chakra on the top of the head, would also lead to Brahman. And along the way I could also attain all those promised powers. Gita had not reached Brahman, I was sure. So where was she? I had read of the lokas, the many worlds where people went after death, depending on their deeds. Which one was Gita in? If I could activate the chakras I could perhaps gain the power to visit her, to see if she really was leading a happy life with Varun. Maybe I would find my little son too, would he be living with them? I knew these were fanciful thoughts, created by my realization that however depressed I had been, I did not want to give up on life, lose my identity, and merge with Brahman. Woodroffe's book told me that when the chakras were aroused I could even create and destroy the worlds. I would gain the knowledge of everything: past, present and future. The thought of the power I could get, somehow infused new energy into me.

***

Three months passed, and I became increasingly frustrated at my inability to see anything within me, no lights, no colours, no fire, and though instead of the space within the heart I now meditated on the chakras, I did not see them either. Nor did any one of those promised siddhis or powers arise in me. In the classes, we had returned to the Upanishads and begun on that lengthy text, the *Brihadaranyaka Upanishad*. I still helped in the class, through my reading and study I now knew quite a bit of Sanskrit. But I had almost lost interest in it all—it had seemed such a revelation to me, but now I wondered, was there any truth in anything I had read and studied? I had read that a guru could convey power or understanding to the student through a touch or a mantra. I knew Enzo wasn't that kind of a guru, he had given me a mantra that was totally ineffective, but hadn't Mr Gosain spoken of some yogi living in a cave nearby? Maybe he would give me a different mantra, through which I could activate at least one of the chakras.

Yes, Enzo said, when I asked him. The yogi was now old, he did not like to meet anyone. But as I had read, studied, and made so many efforts to meditate, he was sure the guru would meet me. He told me the guru did not need to eat in order to live, he could live on air. But, he said, one must always offer something.

Enzo accompanied me the next morning before dawn to meet this guru. He took me to the entrance of the cave and left me there. He told me I should wait there till the guru came out, that he would know I was there, through his inner powers. Then he returned to the ashram. I sat on a rock and waited. I had with me a basket with a few apples and some green leafy vegetables that grew on our grounds to present to him. It was quiet and peaceful, but cold, and I wrapped my shawl tighter. As dawn broke, I once again gained hope that today I would receive a great revelation. I even remembered the story of my birth, and wondered if the yogi in the cave could be the same as the one who had named me, and that now he had called me to him. It was not very long before the guru appeared at the entrance of the cave. He wore what seemed to be a thin white cloth, covering him from his neck to his toes. His face was beautiful and serene. Enzo had told me the guru spoke many languages, including Sanskrit, Hindi, English, Garhwali and Kumaoni.

I rose and touched his feet, and he blessed me. I was about to speak, but he stopped me.

'I know your story and your question,' he said to me, speaking in Garhwali. 'You have meditated for three months, read many texts, and found nothing. Three months is nothing. In the past, sages meditated for a thousand years or even ten thousand years to realize these truths, and you expect to do it in three months! But I will tell you something very important. Unless your heart is pure, you cannot and should not proceed any further. You will not see the true Self without a pure heart. You do not have that quality yet. And if you keep trying without that quality, you will be overtaken by disease and madness. I know, recently you have started trying to activate the chakras. That just shows that your intentions are wrong. Get back on to the right path. Seek purity within. Stop meditating. Remove all anger and all desire first. Work for others. Forget yourself. If you can do this return to me after a year.'

One year! The anger that was dormant in me after Gita's death, began to rise. I turned away, and the guru returned to his cave without blessing me again. I left the basket there at the entrance and went back to the ashram. I had thought I had found something, was on the verge of finding something, but there was nothing to be found!

Enzo was waiting for me, but I brushed past him and went into my room. I bolted the door from inside. Anger continued to rise. Once again, I thought my anger was so fierce, it was like a fire that could burn everything near me. Someone knocked on the door, but I did not open it. It was an hour or more before I began to calm down. I saw that the guru had said nothing wrong—what a fool I had been to think I could gain the true Self, or an experience of it, or activate the chakras, in just three months. Mr Gosain had benefitted from the guru—he had learnt to control his own thoughts, he had told me. But I didn't want control of thoughts. I wanted the awakened chakras, I wanted the power to create and destroy, the power of the kundalini. I wanted Shiva's power to burn people to ashes. As my thoughts wandered like this, I finally knew that to understand life and death was beyond me, and was no longer my aim. I didn't want the true Self, whatever that was. I wanted power. I never wanted to feel that sense of helplessness again, that I had felt when I saw Gita and my son dead. As the guru had not guided me towards that, I would have to find it myself.

I unbolted the door. Quite a long time had passed, I had missed breakfast, and the morning class, it was time for lunch. I went straight to the dining room.

To digress a bit: there were only twelve of us in the ashram, including Enzo. As we each performed the tasks in turn, sometimes in groups of two or three, I had had several rounds in the kitchen, and had taught a few others how to make good dal and vegetables, and even rotis. But most of them preferred their tasteless boiled or baked vegetables, and that is what we had today.

As I sat down and served myself I noticed people

glancing at me and then looking away. After a few minutes, Peter said, 'So how was your meeting with the guru?'

'It was a good meeting,' I replied, 'but he said it may take me a thousand or ten thousand years to reach the True Self. I found that depressing. I wish there was a shortcut.' I didn't reveal that I no longer wanted to reach that Self, if at all it existed, but rather the power of the chakras.

It was Enzo who replied: 'There are different paths to the transcendent. For this Kali Yuga, the path of the tantric method is considered the best'. Everyone else seemed busy eating and did not look up. Yet I sensed some kind of an undercurrent.

'Tantric path?' I queried. 'You haven't mentioned that before.'

'Well,' Enzo said, 'some of us have tried it. We thought you wouldn't be open to it. Of course it is an Indian path, but most middle-class Indians look down on it and condemn it. And that is mainly because of a lack of understanding. I will begin soon with some classes on bhakti, which is a more acceptable way to reach the divine, and later introduce tantrism in the classes next month.'

I said I looked forward to the classes on these new topics, but in fact I didn't have much hope. I believed now that I would have to find my own way towards the power I sought.

***

Enzo soon introduced bhakti. I wasn't interested in it for my own development, but I listened intently. The germ of an idea of how I could make myself powerful, so that I never had to feel helpless again, was already in me, and I was no longer looking for supernatural ways to attain this.

Enzo took a long time explaining bhakti, I think it was over a month. He seemed to have a good knowledge of it, more than of anything else he had taught so far. It was one of the three main paths to the divine, the other two being jnana and karma, the paths of knowledge and of action. Very briefly, bhakti was a type of worship that was based on love, the love of any god, in any form. One could have a motherly love for god as a child; or a pure, childish love for god as a mother or a father. God could be loved as a friend; or as a stern lord, to whom one had to surrender and offer service. I can't go into all that I learnt here, some of which I later taught myself, but at first I couldn't develop more than an intellectual interest in it. God, in any shape or form, seemed a very distant being to me, someone I could not connect with, or feel any emotion for. As for the gods of my childhood, I believed that they only existed in our villages, and I had never given them much thought.

From the time the classes began, I had a question in my mind, but I did not ask it, expecting Enzo to reach it on his own. After a couple of weeks, when he had not yet mentioned it, I posed the question. If bhakti could involve any type of love, what about romantic love? What about the love between a man and a woman? Of course, Enzo said, that was a major part of bhakti. God could be a lover, either as a handsome man or in the form of a beautiful woman, and the best way to reach god was through love for a woman outside marriage, a concept known as parakiya rasa.

This was a new idea for me, and once again, I sat for hours in the well-stocked library, and read whatever I could. Bhakti had a complex philosophy explained in the Bhagavad Gita, epics and Puranas, and through the lives of numerous later saints and philosophers, but for those who were not learned, it was also a simple approach to god. A personal relationship with god could be established by anyone, of any caste. Bhakti had led to wonderful art, and some of the most divine and beautiful poetry, and as I read, the verses resounded in my head, as had Shakespeare's, in what now seemed like a different age to me. 'Sandal and garment of yellow and lotus garlands upon his body of blue...' this was from the *Gita Govinda*, about Krishna, the god usually chosen as a lover. Krishna was married to Rukmini, but his greatest love was Radha, a woman older than him. All over north India, there were temples to Radha and Krishna, and I had visited some of them, without giving it much thought. Enzo explained that even the elaborate forms of worship of deities in temples was a part of bhakti. I stored all this knowledge for later use.

The bhakti classes came to an end, and in the last class Enzo described the life of the fifteenth-century bhakti saint, Chandidas, and how he had reached god through parakiya rasa, through his love for a washerwoman named Rami. In the evening, I sat in the garden thinking over what I had heard and studied. I knew that human beings had invented some of these concepts, but still, I could understand that love, that grand emotion, could lead to the divine. I remembered how I had felt in the early years of my love for Gita, and even when I loved something like the words of Shakespeare. But why did it have to be love outside marriage? Was it a matter of sex, and not love? Was reaching god all about sex? Or was there a purity in love that was not confined within accepted social norms?

Thinking these thoughts, at night I had a strange dream of a wonderful, beautiful woman. She was draped in a white sari worn over a white petticoat and a blue, long-sleeved blouse. The sari was transparent and sheer, though the blouse and petticoat covered her adequately. Her light brown complexion was luminous, her deep brown eyes, focused on me with an expression I could not fathom—was it love or desire? As I gazed into them I feared it was neither—they seemed to look on me with pity. Yes pity, not that grander emotion of compassion. I shifted my gaze and saw her black shining hair, straight and smooth, down to her waist. And then she turned and I couldn't breathe any more. Her smooth brown back was visible, the blouse just fastened by two sets of strings at the back, the pallu of her sari, draped over her left shoulder, tantalizingly leaving half her back visible, and the other half barely concealed. If she was god, I believed I could develop a love for her.

That was what I thought in my dream, but then I woke, and tried to analyze what I had seen. I told myself it was just a dream, generated by my thoughts of the previous day, and by what I had studied and learned over the past month. And what did I mean by love? It was desire that arose in me, and surely desire was different from love?

I had to shake off my thoughts and get ready, and soon I had more to think about as that day Enzo began his series of classes on tantrism. All I knew about tantra was that it was somehow related to sex. I mentioned this, but Enzo explained that there were two broad divisions of tantra, known as 'right-hand' and 'left-hand' sects. The right-hand sects were acceptable, and could hardly be distinguished from conventional practices. They used mantras or sacred chants, yantras or cosmic diagrams, and other meditative and breathing practices. The left-hand group negated and overturned all normal practices. The two groups were not mutually exclusive, and there was some overlap between them. Worship of a deity too could be part of tantra. Shiva could be considered the presiding god of tantra, he said, and Shakti, the goddess. Shakti means 'power' and there were several goddesses who could represent Shakti, such as Kali, Devi, Bagala, or one of a number of others. Rather hesitantly Enzo said that a young virgin girl could also be worshipped. This was known as Kumari-Puja. There is no uniformity in the methods used, he said.

He went into the origin of tantra and explained that it was not confined to Hinduism, but was also a part of later Buddhism. Tantra was not liked by mainstream religious sects, said Enzo. Therefore, several tantric texts in both Sanskrit and regional languages remain untranslated, and many were destroyed. But at the same time there are new and modern explorations of tantra. Enzo then described some more aspects of tantra, and what an ideal text on tantra should contain.

This introductory class was so packed with information that I could not take everything in. I pondered over my notes at night. Was tantra an easy way of uniting with god? Or was it an easy way of gaining the power that I deeply desired?

I put my question to Enzo the next day. 'To my mind,' he replied, 'it is a path to the divine for the present day. It can also be used to gain control over all the forces of nature, and to obtain the power to accomplish any task. But I should add that some consider it a very dangerous path and believe that a guru who constantly guides the student is essential.'

'On the day I visited the guru,' I reminded him, 'you said that some of you had tried it. What did you mean? And what are the dangers?'

'Perhaps, I gave you the wrong impression,' he said. 'But we did dabble in the five Ms. And achieved some peace, as well as some pleasure.'

'The five Ms? What are those?'

'I'll explain in my class today,' he said.

I was eager to know about these mysterious Ms. After breakfast and the morning chores, I rushed to class and waited for Enzo. Peter and Katy were my only fellow students that day.

Enzo began the class by talking about seven tantric paths accepted in Hinduism. He then said that all tantric sects seek to raise the Kundalini, the hidden energy centre at the base of the spine, through the lower chakras, to the Sahasrara Chakra at the top of the head, arousing these centres along the way. He added that while it could be used for union with the divine, at its lowest level, the powers generated could be used to harm others. I hadn't realized till now, that the chakras whose powers I wanted to arouse were related to and a major part of tantra. He had already described them, I had read intensively and meditated on them, and it had got me nowhere. I was looking for something new, and he seemed to be repeating himself. I was getting impatient. 'You said you would talk about the five Ms,' I reminded him. 'I am keen to know what they are and how you experimented with them.'

'Yes,' he said, 'I was getting to it.'

Left-hand sects, he said, particularly use the pancha-makara or pancha-tattvas, commonly known as the five Ms. These, he explained, are Madya or wine, Matsya or fish, Mamsa, meat or flesh, Mudra or parched grain and Mithuna, sexual union. I was amazed. And I should say, quite shocked. How could these be a part of religion? But perhaps it was no stranger than parakiya rasa and Kumari-Puja. Anyway, I tried to conceal my feelings, and asked him how they experimented with these, and in what way they had benefitted.

He did not explain properly. These things were meant for enjoyment, he said. And enjoyment led one close to the divine. One had a good meal with meat, fish, liquor and grain. And then one had sex, a union with no strings attached, without love, just for pure pleasure. One could have as much sex as one liked, with several partners. 'I assure you,' said Enzo, 'that after all that there are just no thoughts in one's head. The body and mind are totally relaxed and free. In that state if one focuses on the divine—an image, a symbol, or a concept—the image becomes imprinted in the mind and heart. It is a great and easy process. We still have Five M get-togethers, if you would like to join us and experiment. We start late at night so that we don't disturb anyone who does not participate, and we end in the early hours of the morning—the time before dawn is brahma muhurta, the time for god, when it is easiest to come in contact with god.'

I think my face was turning red. I couldn't believe what I'd heard. And he was inviting me to participate! My inner self shuddered with aversion. It was one thing to read about it in theory, I couldn't believe they actually practised this. Anger rose in me, despite my attempt to control myself.

'You foreigners!' I blurted out. 'You have no morality! And you talk about reaching god!'

'It's an Indian system,' said Enzo quietly, a faint smile on his face. 'Don't forget that.'

I rushed out of the room before I could say anything that was more insulting. My heart was hammering; I was furious. Had I come here to be deceived like this? No wonder I couldn't find that inner Self or achieve any powers through my meditation. They were all fakes here. I was determined to leave the ashram the very next day. I was not a vegetarian but had never eaten much meat. As I said earlier, my father too was against it. And I had never drunk alcohol. City life had influenced me, and I thought alcohol and too much meat-eating were for the lower castes. I thought they were talking nonsense, and trying to fool me. It was not yet lunchtime that day, but I began packing my bags, though I knew I couldn't leave till the next morning. It would not be possible to get off the mountains and into the plains without proper planning and a guide.

Enzo knocked on the door. I opened it in a fury, but he quickly handed me a book, and left. What is it about books? Even in the middle of my packing, and in my state of anger and disturbance, I looked at the title, and soon I had started reading. The book was called *The Basics of Tantra*. Our classes on tantra had only lasted two days, and somehow I hadn't yet followed my usual practice of going to the library and reading further.

As I read I calmed down. I was sure the tantric path was not for me, but I realized Enzo wasn't inventing the pancha-makaras. And I realized too, that I had already been thinking of the bhakti path of passion for god and pondering over Kumari-Puja, and wasn't my dream of that tantalizing woman related to sex? Was I pretending to be shocked by what Enzo suggested because I could not accept my own desires?

I felt extremely tired. I was hungry too, though I knew lunchtime was over. I thought I'd go to the kitchen and find something to eat, but I just lay down on the bed, my mind again going over all that had happened. I had hardly lain there for a few minutes, when there was another knock on the door. The blue-eyed Cynthia entered, and just like on the first visit, she brought me a bowl of warm vegetable soup. She sat at the side of my bed as I propped myself up and began to eat. There was freshly baked brown bread with it, and I dipped it in the warm soup and as I ate, I felt strangely comforted.

'I heard what happened in the class,' Cynthia said. 'Don't worry about it, Dev. There is never any compulsion on anyone to participate in something they do not want to. And we are all your friends here.'

It was a long time since anyone had called me Dev. I began to feel they were all indeed my friends. How the mind changes and jumps from one extreme to the other!

Cynthia had heard what had happened, but I wondered why she hardly ever attended any classes. I thought of asking her, but was overcome by drowsiness. 'I think I'll take a nap, Cynthia,' I said. Maybe I would ask her later. Maybe I could find a friend in her, or even something more.

'Sure, Dev,' she said as she picked up the tray with the now empty soup bowl. At the door she turned and looked at me. Yes, there was something growing between us, though I was not sure what. I got under the quilt and soon drifted into sleep, very rare for me in the middle of the day.

I woke in the early evening, still feeling somewhat tired. In a somnolent state I went into the kitchen and got myself some tea. Then I looked for Enzo, as I thought maybe I should apologize to him for my outburst. I found him in his study, where he usually sat in the evenings. He was reading and making notes in the light of his lantern. I knocked and went in, and he gave me a friendly smile. Before I could speak he said, 'I could understand your response. Now don't give it a second thought. Go for a walk, watch the setting sun...later we will have a talk if you like.'

I wrapped up warm and did as he suggested. The sun had set, and in the twilight, the cold air was refreshing. I began to plan my future. In a month, or at most two, I would leave here. And then I would begin a new life. One in which I had power and respect. I just needed a little more study and practice. But practice of what? Meditation had got me nowhere. And I definitely would not try those five Ms. I thought I would discuss this with Enzo, and returning from my walk, I again went into his study.

I had thought out what I would say. I would not disclose my desire for power, but would ask a more general question. After he had invited me to sit, given me a cup of hot herbal tea from a boiler that was set on burning coals in a corner of his room, and we had exchanged some preliminary comments on the weather, I got to the point. 'Enzo,' I said, 'I have learnt a lot here. I have picked up Sanskrit, learnt about the Upanishads, the chakras, bhakti, tantra, and so much more. But you know that despite spending hours in meditation, I have not seen any divine light or got any sense of god, or even of those energy centres within. I hear some of the others talking here—saying they have seen some brilliant lights, or some divine being, or that one of their chakras had started whirling. But I have not had any such experience. I don't want to try those pancha-makaras, but isn't there another way? Isn't there some way I could get at least some sense of the divine?'

'You have perhaps read and studied enough,' said Enzo. 'But some practices bring results for certain people, and different practices for others. In fact, I have invited a very good yoga teacher here—he should reach in about two weeks. Somehow, I have a feeling that yoga will suit you. And I will just add—very often people invent or imagine visions of god or divine lights. Don't let it bother you.'

'You have invited a yoga teacher? But Mr Gosain said the yogi who lives in the cave on the hill, and whom you took me to meet, used to teach here.'

'He used to at one time, but that was long ago. Now he is at a different stage in his life, he lives in seclusion and meditates—he is almost ready to take samadhi.' After a brief pause, he added, 'For a couple of weeks, till the yoga teacher arrives, I won't be teaching any more classes. I think those on tantra were not a success! Read what you like, and discuss with others here—it may help you.'

I was at peace that day. I slept well and the next day began a somewhat eclectic course of study on my own.

I felt that bhakti and tantra were related. I found three or four more books on tantra in the library. There were some original texts too, but the Sanskrit was difficult to understand. As I began to read on tantrism, it seemed to me that these texts were only an overt expression of what existed in all parts of religion, that is, sex. I, who had never been plagued by sexual desires, now saw sex everywhere. Wasn't the Samudra Manthana story, the churning of the ocean of milk to gain divine Amrita, merely a metaphor for sex? Was sex then the elixir of life? And wasn't the whole bhakti movement, which was so respectable because love was focused on god, just sex subsumed? And sometimes, as in parakiya rasa, it crossed the finely marked boundary and became overt. Of course, the left-hand tantras formalized sex, raising desire to a height with ritual.

I had not studied or thought about any religion deeply

until I came to Enzo's ashram. Our Jad religion had been gradually absorbed into Hinduism, and, I knew something about Hinduism, though not very much. I was aware that in contrast to tantra, there was the ascetic path in which sex was forbidden, and a similar path in Jainism and Buddhism. I looked up an encyclopaedia and tried to discover what each religion said about love. I found the ideas of the Sufi saints of Islam similar to bhakti. It seems as if they kept love and sex separate, but some Sufi sects weren't against sex, it wasn't forbidden to them. As for Christianity, I liked the Bible, and the beauty of the psalms. I had read all that earlier as it provided insights and the background to much of English literature, and I had not looked on it as religion. I knew that Gandhiji liked the Sermon on the Mount in the New Testament and that his favourite hymns were 'Onward, Christian Soldiers', and 'Abide with Me'. Now I tried to learn more. I had believed that Christianity was somewhat monolithic, and as I read I discovered how ignorant I was. The history of the religion and the enormous variety of Christian sects were both fascinating and bewildering. The Catholics had this immense concept of original sin, which I could not quite understand. Apart from the numerous Protestant groups there were early breakaway Christian sects such as the Cathars, which seemed to have some different views. Somehow, I chanced upon the Jewish Zohar, which saw the Sabbath as the bride of god. The more I read, the more confused I became at the variety of ways of looking at religion, and of the role of sex in religion. Of course, all this was just superficial knowledge, I hardly knew the depths of any religion or sect. On the whole, it seemed as if each religion had an ascetic path where sex was out of bounds, while for the ordinary person, religions made attempts to control and confine sex within reasonable limits. And then there were those sects which actually prescribed sex.

Years later, when I gained more knowledge by reading the untranslated tantric texts, I realized how ignorant both I, and Enzo and his co-revellers were at that time, even about tantra. The tantric method is extremely complex, and many texts are mysterious, the true practices are not revealed in them, and a guru is essential. I did not pursue that path and never understood its secrets, though, of course, I too began to misuse sex in the name of spirituality.

Discuss with others, Enzo had said, so I decided maybe I should do that to gain some clarity. At first I hadn't bothered much about my fellow students. I was absorbed in my own reading and my own thoughts. The morning classes had stopped and had never been compulsory. Apart from me, Cynthia, Ono and Jeremy were usually there, but not always. Sometimes Peter and Katy came, but often it was just us four. I couldn't figure out why Laurence, Edward, Petra and a few of the others were in the ashram. Some of them not only did not attend classes and meditation, but did not even come for the evening discussions. I saw everyone in the dining room, and I think they all did the work assigned to them. But why were they there? Apart from Ono, surely they were all Christians? And whether they were Catholics or Protestants or some other sect, didn't they find enough in Christianity to live by? I thought I would begin by asking Enzo what he believed in. He had a lot of knowledge, but why had he come here?

When I enquired, Enzo said he was born a Roman Catholic, but had lost all interest in Christianity. He had come across a book by Schopenhauer, who had praised the Upanishads so highly, and then decided to come to

India. After some time in Rishikesh, this ashram had been recommended to him. It was then run by an Englishman, a theosophist named Charles Duncan. He was an extremely learned man, but he died within a year of Enzo's arrival, probably of cancer. Before his death he asked Enzo to take over the ashram. 'Everything I teach is based on his notes,' Enzo said. 'I would never have been able to read so much, and to distill its essence.' Theosophist? There was another new term for me. I asked Enzo. He was taken aback. Surely, he asked, I had heard of Annie Besant and Madame Blavatsky? And J. Krishnamurti, the great philosopher? No, I said, I hadn't heard of any of them. 'Any student of Indian history knows Annie Besant,' he said.

'I don't remember hearing about her in school,' I replied.

'I am not going to hold classes on them,' said Enzo. 'But you will definitely find some books on them in the library.'

That day when I went to the library I found a book on Annie Besant, and also a three-volume work of Madame Blavatsky called *The Secret Doctrine*, but could not find anything on J. Krishnamurti. The work on Annie Besant was a biography, and was mainly on her association with the freedom movement. However, in this book there was one chapter on theosophy, and I learned that the Theosophical Society was founded in New York in 1875, and later established in India. I liked its three main principles, which were about universal brotherhood, studying comparative religion, and, most important for me, investigating 'unexplained laws of nature and the powers latent in man.' I also learned that they had a hierarchy of hidden masters, and that Master Kuthumi and Master Morya, who among many others, occupied the fourth level in the hierarchy, were the two in charge of India, though they only existed in another dimension. It seemed strange to me, and when I asked Enzo, he said that as far as he knew if one joined the Society one could get to know more about all this.

Next, I had a look at *The Secret Doctrine*, but found it confusing, though I was intrigued by whatever I read. Madame Blavatsky had some mysterious powers, could I gain them too? More than anything else, I would like to be Sanat Kumar, head of the whole universe, according to the theosophical hierarchy. How did he get there, what was his origin? I asked Enzo about J. Krishnamurti, and he told me he had been adopted by the theosophists when he was a teenaged boy, and considered a messiah, until he rejected that role himself, and turned into an independent philosopher. I wondered if I could get Enzo to promote me as a messiah? I'd never reject the role. My thoughts were flying in all directions. I took a deep breath and tried to calm down. As I walked out of the library I met Enzo again.

'I forgot to tell you,' he said, 'tomorrow evening we have a new resident joining us—he is the yoga teacher I told you about. He will be teaching hatha yoga, but before that will look at the ideas in the *Yoga Sutra*. What I have noticed, and am sure you have too, is that most of the residents just don't attend my classes. I do find it a bit disheartening. I am sure you will benefit from yoga, and I'm hoping that yoga may generate an interest in them too.'

I looked forward to the new sessions on yoga. Meanwhile it was time for my afternoon work period. As I went into the garden, for it was once again my duty there, I saw that Peter was already busy raking leaves. He waved and smiled at me. I started on the other side, clearing the leaves with a broom. After about forty-five minutes Peter took a break and sat on one of the benches. I thought it was a good time to ask him what he believed in, and went and sat beside him. 'Peter,' I said, 'I hope you don't mind me asking, but are you a Christian? I mean, you must have been born one, but are you a practising Christian? Or do you follow one of the systems Enzo talks about?'

Peter did not seem to mind my question. He replied, 'I? No. I follow the Emerald Tablets of Thoth. They resonate with something deep in my spirit and I believe they are the truest texts ever revealed.'

Emerald Tablets? I did not know what to say as I had never heard of them. History had been a subsidiary subject in my college days, and early Egypt had roused my interest at that time. Thoth as far as I knew, was an Ibis-headed deity of ancient Egypt. I said as much, but Peter explained, 'I like you,' he said, 'so I'll let you into a deep mystery, a great secret. Thoth may be a god of Egypt, but he is also something much more. He was a priest-king of Atlantis. And when Atlantis was submerged, Thoth ruled over Egypt from 52000-34000 BCE. He was later reincarnated as Hermes. And as Hermes, he wrote the wonderful Emerald Tablets.'

'Can I read these tablets, Peter?' I asked, realizing as I spoke, that he was talking about some spiritual theories that had nothing to do with traditional history.

'The tablets are secret,' he said. 'They are only for the followers of Thoth. Maybe you will read them one day if you are worthy of them, but I cannot give them to you. But since you are interested I'll tell you something more about them. In around 1300 BCE, Egypt, then known as Khem, was in turmoil. The Emerald Tablets were in the possession of a group of higher priests. Taking these with them, they and a few others migrated to South America, where they founded the Maya civilization. When the

Spanish invaded the region, the Tablets were returned to the Great Pyramid of Egypt. A copy was made known in 1925 through a member of the Great White Lodge.'

At first this seemed like a lot of nonsense to me. It was only some months later, in a different phase of my life, that I read some related books and realized there was a whole occult world of which I knew almost nothing. After talking to Enzo and Peter about their beliefs, I felt I could not take in any more and posed no more questions. I thought I would just carry on with my own reading until the yoga teacher arrived. I had heard that with yoga one could gain control of oneself and of the environment, in a simpler and less dangerous way than through the practise of tantra. I asked Enzo if it was true. 'You are thinking of hatha yoga,' he said, 'and that will be the focus of the yoga teacher. But yoga means "union" and is a method of uniting with the divine.'

Why was everyone so keen on uniting with the divine? I couldn't figure it out. I hardly knew what it meant. Despite all I had read about the world being unreal, and about divine union and bliss, the world seemed real to me. I wanted happiness in the world, and I believed that power would give me happiness. Now I wasn't so sure I wanted to know about yoga.

The teacher, who told us to call him Sundararaman-garu, arrived that evening. His accent was odd, and I learnt he was from the south. In those days, our region was a bit backward. Of course, there were people from south India, even the rawal of Badrinath came from the south of India. But on the whole, we looked down on people from the south, and called them 'madrasis' after Madras. I presumed Sundararaman was mispronouncing guru as 'garu'. When

I addressed him as Sundararaman guru, he immediately corrected me with a smile.

'Young friend,' he said, 'knowledge of all kinds is important. I am from Andhra Pradesh. There we do not use the term "ji" at the end of names, but its equivalent, which is "garu".' I realized I had a lot to learn. After that I respectfully called him 'Sundararaman-garu', but as we became friends, he asked me to call him Sundara.

At first, I was disappointed with what he taught. He said he would start with the *Yoga Sutras of Patanjali*, and claimed it was one of the greatest texts ever written. He spent more than an hour on just the second line 'Yoga-chitta-vritti-nirodhah'. To put it briefly, all this means is that yoga is stillness of the mind. But Sundararaman explained this at great length, dwelling on the numerous possible different meanings of each word. I wanted him to proceed further, I wanted him to tell me something about power. As the classes proceeded, I learned there were eight steps in yoga. The first two were basic ethics grouped together as yama and niyama, and the last four went rather deep. It was the second two I became deeply interested in, asana and pranayama, and to some extent, the next two, pratyahara and dharana.

After explaining these basics, Sundararaman did not spend much time on the *Yoga Sutras*, but plunged into practical lessons. And, as I closely followed and practised what he taught, I found something of what I was looking for. No, I did not find that supreme inner Self, that I had almost given up wanting. Nor did I see any brilliant lights or divine beings or whirling chakras. But as I practised the asanas (physical postures) and pranayama (breathing techniques), I gained poise and confidence. I had always been physically fit and strong, but I sensed that I was gaining a different kind of strength, a strength that led to endurance. Pranayama led me to reduce my food, and to eat differently. I hardly wanted tea any more, and did not crave spices and chillies as much I used to. I felt this strengthening of my inner and outer self could be the first step towards attaining the power I craved, both over myself and the world.

Gradually, I went on to learn and practise the bandhs or locks, through which I gained more control over my body. Sundara told me of Sufi saints who only needed to take one breath in twelve hours. I couldn't reach that level, but I could slow my breathing considerably. I was progressing fast, while most of the others who came for the class were treating it as a kind of entertainment. Ono was serious to some extent, but even he was way behind me.

This was taking longer than I expected, and two months passed. Sundara said he would remain one more month, and asked me to begin some higher practices. He said he had never had a student like me.

In this last month I began initial practices in pratyahara and dharana. I was not so successful in these. Pratyahara was essentially a question of withdrawing all one's senses from the outer world, and dharana was a term for concentration and focus. They were the preliminary steps for dhyana, contemplation, and samadhi, merging with the divine.

I had come to the ashram with a desire to understand life and death, but as I came to know something about the ancient texts, the concept of merging with Brahman did not appeal to me. Perhaps those initial ideas also faded away as I began to feel better in the ashram, with regular meals, a work schedule, and new thoughts. When Gita receded from my mind, certain aspects of my personality, that I had almost been unaware of, began to surface. Had the desire for power always been dormant in me? As I analyzed it, it must have been so. In the controlled and responsible life I had lived until Gita's death, there had been no space for such desires. Her death had sent me into a downward spiral of grief and turmoil, and had led me to think about life and death, and look desperately for reasons and causes. The ashram had to some extent healed me. Also, it was liberating. No one knew my past, and I was free of my life of responsibility, conditioned by tradition. Though I could not feel totally free, or 'enjoy myself' as Enzo had suggested soon after I arrived, I think that I was becoming more myself, a different nature was being revealed.

Though I had not revealed my thoughts to anyone, for some time now, I had been thinking of becoming a guru myself. I thought it would be an easy way to gain both power and wealth, and to fulfil my occasional desire for women—desires without love, without giving them any hold over me. I couldn't reach the point of joining Enzo and his friends in sexual orgies, but desires were there, and somehow they had been growing.

Yet, practising pratyahara and dharana, even this desire for power subsided. In the first stage of pratyahara or withdrawal from the world, Sundara had taught me a technique—I had to sit still in padmasana, shutting my ears with my thumbs, and my eyes with my fingers. Then, I was to withdraw my mind from the events of the world, from my past and future, and think only of the impermanence of everything. Then I practised dharana, concentration, focusing on the flame of a candle, or on the symbol of Om. Sundara taught other complicated techniques and mantras that I cannot describe here. As I said, I did not feel close to god or see divine visions, but I had a few moments of indescribable peace, of a stillness and silence beyond words. At the end of that month of intense practice, my desire for power had faded. Yet I felt inadequate, unable to master some of the complex practices. 'That doesn't matter,' said Sundara. 'I am teaching you far more than you could possibly take in in one month. But you have made your notes and you have an excellent memory. You can practice these anytime, anywhere.'

Finally, it was time for Sundara to leave. On the last day, I hesitantly approached him with the question that had been in my mind all these months, and that all my reading on religion had not resolved. I put it bluntly: 'Does sex have a role to play in reaching the divine?' I asked, even though I had guessed from his personality and nature, that Sundararaman was on an ascetic path.

He frowned. 'Do not listen to anyone who tells you that. The most basic steps are the yamas and niyamas that I have already taught you right at the beginning. Never forget them, or you will slide downwards. Brahmacharya is the fifth yama. Brahmacharya is often taken to mean celibacy, but it is far more than that. It means, as you know, to live as god lives. God has no desire, and in fact has no shape or form. Where then, does sex come in?'

'I have read of the many gods,' I said. 'The gods have consorts. Shiva has Parvati. Vishnu has Lakshmi. Rama has Sita.'

'The gods are a great mystery,' he replied. 'Their outer forms are for the ordinary person. Their true meaning is for the one on a spiritual path. One day you will understand that the gods do not in fact have any form, and that they are all one. I will give you one last teaching from the Upanishads. In fact, I know that you have already studied the *Brihadaranyaka Upanishad*. Let me remind you of its explanation of how the innumerable gods represent only one. In this text, as you know, the great rishi Yajnavalkya explains that there are basically thirty-three gods, the others being their manifestations. The thirty-three can be reduced to six, which represent fire, earth, air, sky, the sun and heaven. Further, they are reduced to three, representing the three worlds and all they contain. Then they can be reduced to two, matter and the life-force, then to one and a half, and lastly to one, the cosmic prana, that is the same as Brahman, the essence of all that is, the ultimate source.'

Yes, I did remember, I said. But, I added, the *Brihadaranyaka* was describing Vedic gods which were largely elements of nature. What of the later gods and goddesses? 'All divine beings,' said Sundara, 'are aspects of the One. And in fact, so is all of creation. Remember the mahavakyas? There is no second, there is only One.' I knew those words by then, but there was just so much, so many different theories. What was true, what was not? Sundara was a great yoga teacher, and in philosophy, he followed Advaita Vedanta. What did I believe in? I had no beliefs, only some thoughts and ideas.

Then Sundara added, 'I will tell you one more mystery, Dev. Maybe you will not understand it today. A male god and his female counterpart only represent the male and female aspects within each person. When they marry or unite, the true meaning of the word "individual" is revealed. It means "undivided", or "whole". Shiva and Parvati, Vishnu and Lakshmi—they are just symbols of one's inner self. In fact, there are some texts which teach you to visualize the marriage of a male and female god within the heart chakra. And the entire yearning of the gopis for Krishna, and so much that is similar in bhakti, it is only the yearning of a divided self to become whole.'

I listened, but could not take in everything. Anyway, I touched Sundara's feet, and presented him with a gift, a scarf I had knitted myself. I had learned to knit before my marriage to Gita, and I could still knit adequately. In the hill regions, many men knit, at least they did in those days. The scarf was in two colours, orange and yellow. Sundara thanked me, and wrapped it around his neck. 'I will treasure this,' he said. 'Made by the hands of the best student I have ever had.' Then he added: 'One word of advice before I leave. I am not an astrologer or a prophet, but we have spent three months together, and I sense certain things in you. You could become a great teacher, a yogi, and advance further in a spiritual direction. But there is also a negativity in you. I can sense some dark thoughts. Please, never think that the yamas and niyamas are not important. They, and not the asanas and higher techniques, are the most important part of yoga. Follow them to the letter, always remain celibate, and you are safe. The divine path has been compared to walking on a razor's edge. If you surrender the basic ethics essential on this path, you will be on a downward spiral, and it will take you many lives to return to where you are now. And, remember, if you want to study more you can find me in my ashram in Anantapur.' I said I would always remember his advice. Then he presented me with a copy of the *Yoga Sutras*. It had the text, along with a commentary that he had written himself. 'When I came here,' he said, 'Enzo wanted me to focus on, and teach practical aspects of yoga. There is a lot more in this book that we could not study together. Please follow everything in this book, and do not get diverted from the true path.' Sundara, from whom I had learnt so much, left soon after.

***

I was quite influenced by his final words. As I said, I had never bothered about the yamas and niyamas, but now I went over them in my mind. Ahimsa-satya-asteya-brahmacharya and aparigraha were the five yamas, that is, non-violence, truthfulness, non-stealing, celibacy, and non-greed. Shaucha, santosha, tapah, svadhyaya, and Ishvara-pranidhana were the five niyamas. These can be translated as cleanliness, contentment, spiritual practices, spiritual study, and surrender to god. To understand these fully, and make them a part of my life, was a huge task in itself. And those higher practices—even a lifetime was not enough to perfect them.

I realized these three months had transformed me. Yes, the earlier time I had spent in the ashram had given me considerable knowledge, but it was Sundara who had provided me with a new direction in life. Now I felt, I would go and study further with him. Before that though, I would try to teach what I had learnt, instead of teaching Shakespeare. It was true, there were some similarities between parts of Shakespeare and Vedanta, but it was not philosophy I wanted to teach, but the practical steps of yoga. I had been in the ashram for six months, and my savings were almost gone. I had paid six months' rent in advance on my house in Dehradun, and I had given Mr Gosain access to my account for miscellaneous expenses. In addition, Enzo's ashram, unlike most places of its kind, was not free. A small amount had to be paid every month for food. It was time for me to return to Dehradun, sort out things there, and see if I could put my new plans into practice.

I stayed in the ashram another week and then I set off homewards. I had come to the ashram in February, and now it was the end of August. The monsoon had begun two months ago, and though the rains had slowed, I could still be caught in a downpour. I had to walk down to Almora, and there could already be problems with flooded rivers and landslides. I decided not to wait any longer, and asked if I could get Bholu again as my guide.

Meanwhile, there was a farewell party for me. Petra had left a month ago, and Jacob, a backpacker from Israel, Tom from England, and Corvin from Canada had arrived. Cynthia baked a lemon cake, and Peter made some special rolls. There was hot coffee in which just a spoonful of rum had been mixed. It was my very first taste of alcohol, and it was surprising that I liked it.

Enzo said I was always welcome to return, I had been a real asset to the ashram and had contributed so much—had even taught them to make Indian food! I said I too had learned so much here. Everyone wished me so warmly that I was touched.

***

Nityananda

I read the second part of Dev's story with interest. It may sound odd today, but I and many of my friends were celibate before we married. Of course, Dev was older than me and married later than I did, I was only twenty-two when my marriage to Kusum took place, but it wasn't unusual in those days to refrain from sex outside marriage. But then there were others too, like Gita and Ajit.

I'll confess, that though my wife Kusum died two and a half years after our marriage, I never had sex again.

Enzo's ashram did not seem to have been the right choice for him. I could not make out what Enzo was doing there, but from the description, he was not a true guru. He conveyed a hodgepodge of knowledge, and not in an organized way. It wasn't even his own knowledge, he was just using his predecessor's work. I was shocked when I read about the tantric experiments. How innocent Dev was at the time! Fortunately, Sundararaman had provided better and true guidance.

I mulled over what I had read about the people in the ashram. Apart from Enzo, I couldn't understand what the other students were doing there. They did not seem interested in spirituality. But I could see that Dev had imbibed certain things from the organization of Enzo's ashram, and incorporated them in his own. Like Enzo's ashram, Dev's was purely vegetarian, and all the work was done in rotation by the students. But, of course, Enzo's tantric experiments used alcohol and meat, which Dev had strictly forbidden. I wondered if Enzo's ashram still existed. I knew of another ashram in the region, Mirtola, run by Krishnaprem, who was also a foreigner, and had once been Ronald Nixon. But that was run according to Vaishnava rules and rituals, it wasn't a relaxed place where one could do as one liked.

Dev seemed to have a fine mind and a good memory. He never forgot the Shakespeare that had once enchanted him, and he picked up and learned Sanskrit so easily. By now he was quite good at the language, though not an expert as I was. I too had read and studied the *Katha Upanishad*, and perhaps a thousand other texts. The Nachiketa fire was difficult to understand, but Shankara had explained it in his commentary, surely Dev had read that? It would seem that this Upanishad was also providing instructions on fire rituals, which, when practised along with meditation, led to heaven. As for 'nihitam guhayam' I knew that cave; I had seen the white light there. Of course, the mahavakyas were the key statements of the Upanishads. Aham Brahmasmi, I am Brahman; Tat tvam asi, You are That, etc., statements every scholar would know.

Woodroffe's *Serpent Power* was a good introduction to the chakras, but there were a number of other books. There was Charles Leadbeater's version, and then there were mystical texts in regional languages, some of which referred to the chakras as mandalas. Today incorrect information is being spread about the chakras by New Age and Western literature. Chakras do not follow the colours of the rainbow, as they describe. Strange claims are also made about 'opening the chakras,' or 'clearing the chakras,' by people who have absolutely no knowledge or experience. I know from my own experience, if even for a few seconds you can 'see' a chakra, there is total transformation. And it is only in a state of utmost inner purity that such a vision is possible.

I was amused by his meeting with the old guru in the mountain cave, obviously one of those few genuinely spiritually advanced people.

Enzo seemed to have a fairly good understanding of bhakti, though he had not practised it. And certainly, there were schools of bhakti that merged with tantrism. To me, parakiya rasa was just an excuse for indulgence, and Dev's dream of a woman in white seemed to be his hidden desires coming to the fore.

Dev had wondered whether reaching god had more to do with sex than love. In one way or the other, sex plays a role in all spirituality. Either it is rejected and shunned, celibacy being promoted, or it is encouraged as a path to the divine. My own view was that celibacy was essential for spiritual progress, I agreed with Sundararaman on that.

There were also different views on the kundalini, which Dev did not seem to know. While most tried to raise it from below, from the base of the spine, others stated that it descended from the top of the head.

Though Dev looked at the basics, there was a lot on theosophy, J. Krishnamurti, other Indian philosophers, and even the Western occult, that he hadn't explored yet. He hinted that he read more about this a few months later, but even when I knew him, his knowledge of both Eastern and Western philosophy and of occult practices, was limited. He had never mentioned the Emerald Tablets to me, and until I read this, I had not heard of them. I had read quite a bit about the mysterious city of Atlantis, believed to be a very ancient centre of a great civilization, before it was swallowed by the sea. I was interested in buried cities, but that was from the point of view of archaeology. I could not understand this belief in Thoth or the Mayas. The Mayas were involved in strange rites and gory human sacrifices, why consider them superior? But as a historian it was interesting to see so many in the West attempting to return to earlier beliefs, beliefs in ancient gods and practices. Would the superimposed monotheistic religions die out some day?

I was intrigued by the changes in Dev's thought processes in the ashram. He went from wanting to know the truth about life and death, to desiring power, to aiming to be a simple and peaceful yoga teacher. As I looked back at my years with him, I felt these aims and desires were not mutually exclusive, perhaps all three trends were with him throughout his life. When I went to visit Dev, I said that his studies in Enzo's ashram seemed disjointed and incomplete, and even in yoga the emphasis had been on physical aspects, except for that last month which had brought about a change in his thinking. Dev agreed but said he had studied more later, Enzo's ashram had only been the beginning. He remembered everything about it, because it was where a glimpse of the world of religion was first revealed to him.

I had listened to just a few of Dev's talks, and of course, it was true that they were coherent and well thought out. His main theme was always Raja Yoga, that he had first studied with Sundararaman, and had explored further later. Though he explained all the eight steps in his talks, at a personal level, he ignored their most basic principles that Sundararaman had emphasized, the ethical precepts of the yamas and niyamas, and I think no longer tried to practice the four higher aspects. He seemed to have a natural inclination for the practice of asanas and pranayama, with both practical ability and an indepth theoretical knowledge of them. As he had with me, Dev also usually spoke on karma, that mysterious process by which all that happened could be justified. And sometimes, he brought in parallels with Shakespeare, the love of his youth, and this gave his talks a unique flavour. But I think it was not because of what he said, that people followed him. It is not so simple to be a guru. I too was a swami. I was at least equally learned, better at Sanskrit, and more honest. Yet, though people respected me as a teacher, I did not have a large following as a guru. To be honest, there were not more than ten or twenty people who had approached me for spiritual guidance. Dev had thousands of followers, perhaps lakhs. In India, these were largely the ordinary people who lived near our ashram, or villagers from nearby districts who had heard about him. His Western disciples were those looking for answers in the mysterious religions of the East. Why did people follow him? Not everyone could gain a following like that. He wasn't exactly a good person, so what was his charisma? Was it the power he emanated? Was it the money he distributed? I asked myself again why I had followed him. At first, I came to the odd conclusion that it had little to do with Dev. It was a combination of my own lack of direction after Kusum's death, and of the traditions that surrounded us. I and my friends had grown up imbibing the idea that following a guru was right and acceptable, and was a way to overcome or come to terms with personal problems and difficulties. All through life we heard the statement, "when the time is right, the guru will appear", and I felt, it was this background of conditioning that led me to follow him. Perhaps, I thought, it was the same with most of the others too, but this line of thinking did not explain why so few people had followed me. No, there was something else, some mystery, about how and why a guru gained followers. Even now, when I had begun to doubt so much about him, I could not turn away or totally reject him. Thinking further I felt it must be his compassionate and charismatic gaze that had worked its magic on me too, that compelled people to follow him. But then, wasn't the way he looked at people, held their eyes, emanating from something deep within him? Whatever it was that drew people to Dev, must be what all gurus had in common. I had read of many gurus accused of far worse crimes, who had even more followers than Dev. It was difficult to understand, what was the secret, what had made people respect and worship him and so many other gurus like him?

As I was thinking over all this, he handed me some more pages that he had written.

7. The Return Home

Dev's Story

When Nitya told me about Gita's affair, and the probable cause of her death, I heard the story with pain. Yes, somewhere in my heart, I had always known of Gita's unfaithfulness to me. Perhaps I had only pretended to believe in her visions as I could not bear the thought of her treachery, but I did not have a hand in her death. And, truly, I had no knowledge of Madhav Kumar, land takeovers, or fake financial deals. Had they actually happened, or were they just rumours being spread by my enemies? I hope Nitya can discover more.

***

Let me continue my story as I do not have much time left.

Bholu arrived that same night, and we set off early the next morning at 4 a.m., while it was still dark. We had got up even earlier and had some bread and coffee, so that we would not need too many stops along the way, and packed some buns in our bags for the journey. I looked back as I left a place I had almost come to love, the low, white simple buildings and the vast land around it, the trees whose leaves I had swept and gathered…I remembered the day I'd reached here, so weak and tired, my mood so despondent. And now I had forgotten my past, I would teach what I had learnt, help others…

Bholu was already on his way, plodding along at a steady pace, head bent, backpack in place, and I had to cut short my thoughts and hurry to catch up. It was a clear morning and his plan was that we proceed as fast as possible and try to reach Almora today. We would stay at Girija Kumar's guesthouse again, and he had already been informed that we may reach there late at night. Now I was much fitter and stronger, and was able to match Bholu's fast pace. Going downhill is sometimes trickier than climbing up, and we both spoke little on the narrow and treacherous path, slippery and wet from the recent rains, and covered with loose boulders and stones. We made good progress with just a few brief stops to drink water from fresh springs on the mountainside. Memories of my childhood flooded back, but there was not much time to think, I had to focus on maintaining my balance and walking as fast as possible, without falling.

The weather held and by noon we were almost halfway—the steepest parts had been transcended, and now the going would be easier. We stopped to eat our buns, I was hungry, and quickly swallowed three. Bholu said two were enough for the present, more would slow him down. Just as we started again after the half-hour break, it began to rain and we had to look for shelter. We had passed two large trees a little while ago, and we went back quickly to reach them, hoping the rain would stop soon. But the rain increased just as we returned to the trees, and a fierce wind rose. We took our raincoats out of our backpacks, and crouched behind the trees, avoiding the direct blast of the ferocious wind spraying us with icy, stinging rain. We had to bury our heads in our knees, and to add to the rain, from some distant field, hay from several haystacks had been lifted by the wind and was blowing across with it, getting caught against trees, and against us. Rain turned into hail, and despite sheltering behind the tree, hailstones were hitting us. We moved around the tree to avoid the wind and hail, but the wind direction immediately changed. I somehow had an eerie feeling that this was a bad omen. There was no way to lift one's head or to speak and we crouched together, waiting for the storm to pass. The hail stopped after about twenty minutes, the rain continued but was not as fierce, and gradually slowed to a drizzle. Now we were able to stand, though I felt bruised and frozen. We waited for some more time, but the drizzle showed no signs of stopping.

'We have to move on,' Bholu said, 'this may not stop all day.' I agreed, and we began to walk downhill again, the path now wetter and more slippery than before. After about an hour, we walked out of the rain, the drizzle continuing behind us, with the path ahead dry. Another half an hour brought us into the sun. It was 3.30 p.m., and sun and cloud were intermixed as we proceeded. Soon the sun was setting, but there were no further mishaps though I was still feeling cold and miserable. The path was now not so steep and by 8 p.m., sooner than we had expected, we were at the guesthouse. Mrs Kumar was expecting us, and hot masala chai was quickly served. Seeing our damp clothes, she suggested we wash and change before eating, and hot buckets of water were soon ready, placed in two different bathrooms. I was appreciative of them taking this trouble for Bholu too, and treating him as an equal. It was wonderful to have a hot bath, and wearing fresh dry clothes, I felt revived. Parathas, rajma and potatoes fried with jakhiya, our local spice, formed our delicious meal, and then we were both ready for bed. Bholu was accommodated in the same room as I, and once again I marvelled at their concern for him. We were so tired out, that I had no further thoughts that night, and dropped into a deep sleep.

I woke around 6 a.m., feeling warm, drowsy and comfortable. As I took in my surroundings and thought that now I would have to proceed further by bus, and would be back in Dehradun in two or three days, I was filled with panic. Memories of all that had happened, of Gita, my son, and the terrible days before I left there, rushed through my mind. I had planned on returning, living in the same house, getting it repaired, and earning a living through teaching yoga, but now a dread overcame me; I felt I just could not return.

Bholu came in to meet me. He was ready and dressed for his return journey. I got up, and gave him an envelope with some money in it. I insisted he take it, pushed it in his pocket when he refused, and he gave in. 'I am ready to help you any time you need me,' he said, and then he was on his way. I got ready myself, fear and apprehension rising within me. What was the use of all that I had learnt, studied and practised, when I could not control these feelings? I had calmed down a bit by breakfast, enjoying the puri and aloo Mrs Kumar served, which I had not eaten for so long. As I sat in the drawing room after breakfast, drinking more hot masala tea, Mrs Kumar asked me about my future plans. I said I thought I would return to Dehradun and teach yoga instead of English, but that I was apprehensive about returning. 'You look very different,' she said. 'Your stay at the ashram has clearly transformed you. I am sure you will manage fine.'

There was not much more to say. I walked around the town, and had a haircut before returning to the guesthouse. My hair had already been long when I reached Enzo's ashram, and I hadn't cut it for all the time I was there. I wore it in a pony-tail, as I had seen Ono doing, though Cynthia cut and trimmed hair for anyone who asked her to. I couldn't go back to Dehradun with long hair—it wouldn't be acceptable there. And I had to meet my parents too—they knew I was in the ashram and were waiting for me to return. Back in the guesthouse, I enjoyed a good lunch, had another cup of tea in the evening, thanked them profusely, as they still refused to accept any payment, and left on the night bus for Delhi, as there had been new landslides on the direct route to Dehradun.

There was some rain along the way but we faced no major problems, and we reached by 6 a.m., only an hour late. I found a bus leaving for Dehradun almost immediately, and once again the journey was uneventful. It was past one o'clock when the bus pulled into the Dehradun bus stand. I found an auto which dropped me home in half an hour. Everything was so familiar, the roads, my house, but the garden was totally overgrown, creepers winding up along the walls. I unlocked the house and went inside—yes, there was the expected leakage, damp, and termites in some corners. I had a lot of cleaning up to do, yet all I wanted was some tea and a rest. There was nothing in the house to eat, and nothing to cook on either. I stirred myself and went to a dhaba for tea and parathas. Then to the local store where I bought kerosene, matches, tea, and some dal and atta. I made a mental note to apply for a gas connection, instead of cooking on an oil stove. Back home I changed the sheets on the bed, and lay down. By a miracle the electricity was still functioning. Mr Gosain must have paid the bills on time, but that was no guarantee that the wiring would not have broken or burnt through a short circuit.

For the next few days I kept Gita out of my mind. I cleaned and set the house in order, scraped off the termite trails and filled the holes with mustard oil and then cement, and got the leaking roof fixed. Then I had to sit down and take stock. I went to visit Mr Gosain to thank him for paying my bills and sending me the money I needed, and to tell him I had returned.

Mr Gosain greeted me warmly. He too said I looked transformed, and enquired about my stay in the ashram. I gave him a brief summary. He suggested I return to teach English in the school, he had kept an opening for me, as he had promised. I said I would let him know in a day or two, and asked if I could teach yoga instead. He replied that he could not have a fulltime yoga teacher. Yoga was something new in schools, but if I taught English as I used to do earlier, I could also organize some classes in yoga. After all, the students practised dance, badminton, hockey, volleyball and various sports, so a few may opt for yoga as an extra activity. He served me sweets, tea and biscuits, and I went home.

I didn't like the idea of going back to work as an English teacher. But I hardly had enough money left out of my savings to live for another month. And I had heard that my father wasn't too well—my mother wanted him to have a check-up in a Dehradun hospital. It was now time for me to support my parents and forget about my own desires.

Inadvertently, my thoughts kept veering towards Gita. Now that I knew some Sanskrit, and had begun to appreciate the language, we could have shared so much...

The next day, I met Mr Gosain and agreed to rejoin as an English teacher after a week. But what had happened to my plans and dreams? I had hoped to discover the truth about life, but in the ashram my focus had shifted and I thought I would set myself up as a powerful guru. Then after my association with Sundararaman, I had dropped the idea of pretending to be something I was not, and focused on the simpler aim of becoming a yoga teacher. His influence on me had been profound. But now I was back to square one. I told myself I would put an ad in the local paper, and start yoga classes in my free time—Sundays, evenings. I made a brief visit to my parents. My father's health was better and they had no plans for an immediate trip to Dehradun. They were happy that I was back to normal, in fact, they said, I looked fitter than ever before. My mother tentatively asked me if they should look for someone for me to marry. I said I was not ready for it, and she didn't push me. I knew, though, that she would keep looking for some other educated girl.

On the first of September I rejoined the school. Almost a year had passed since Gita's death, it was last October that those terrible events had taken place. I tried not to think about it, but I couldn't help reliving those days. I began teaching *Macbeth* to the senior classes and a summarized version of *Romeo and Juliet* to the junior classes, alongside grammar, how to write essays, and the other things that formed part of teaching English. Despite my new insights into Shakespeare, I had no enthusiasm for it now, and taught mechanically. An optional yoga class was scheduled for Saturday afternoon, but even after one month, there were no students. Two ads in the paper had also not brought me any student at home.

Frustration and anger were rising in me. I had had a good plan I thought, and Sundararaman had misled me. I gave up my daily yoga practice and brooded. Memories of Gita were back to haunt me. As the days passed and nothing changed, I began to feel almost as bad as before I had left for Enzo's ashram.

***

Nityananda

I read the pages of his return and was waiting to see what happened next. Dev had learned a lot in the ashram, he had been in the process of transforming himself, but the transformation was incomplete, and it was clear that he was not at peace when he returned. When I went to see him a few days later, there were more pages ready for me.

I don't know if Dev refers to Bholu again, but Bholu lives at our ashram in Rishikesh. Dev had told me that he arrived there soon after the ashram was founded, in the mid-1980s, bringing with him a four-horned ram. At that time, I did not know the story of how they had first met, Dev had merely said he was someone he knew from long ago. Now I guessed that Dev had kept in touch with Enzo, and Bholu had learnt about his ashram through him. Bholu not only had a way with animals, but a love for them. This ram from his village was one he was passionately fond of, but its unique four horns had led it to be chosen to lead the Nanda Devi Raj Jat, a yatra, or pilgrimage that takes place every twelve years in the Kumaon region. The pilgrimage centres around the story of the goddess Nanda Devi, also the name of a mountain. Every year the goddess is said to pay a brief visit to her parents, before returning home, and there is an annual pilgrimage, apart from the more major twelve-yearly one, in which the procession is led by a four-horned ram. Accompanying the goddess on her return journey could be considered a privilege for the ram, but Bholu was sure that it would not survive, as when the villagers turn back, the ram is left to proceed on its own. Wrapping its ears and head in a shawl to hide its horns, Bholu somehow walked with it from his village, located the ashram that he had only heard about, and was lucky to find Dev there at the time. He asked Dev for sanctuary for himself and his ram, which of course was granted. Dev named the ram Heryshaf, after the Egyptian god, but Bholu turned this into Hari. Hari was less than a year old when he arrived, and has grown old in our ashram, living much longer than most sheep, and leading a happy life.

Bholu was away at present, visiting his village. Hari was being cared for by the ashram cook, a middle-aged man named Bhagat. In all of Dev's ashrams across the world the student residents along with teachers and administrators took care of the daily work in turns, just as they had in Enzo's ashram. In Rishikesh, though, we followed the Indian way, with paid staff, a cook, gardener, sweeper, and administrator, that last being Bholu.

Now I realized that Bholu would be a good person to ask about who had stayed in the ashram over the last year, to try and figure out the people responsible for the land grab and financial deals. I would ask him as soon as he returned.

8. Cynthia Arrives

Dev's Story

Now, to continue with my story, I had been teaching for a month and a half. I still had no yoga students, either at school, or at home. I returned every day in the late afternoon, cooked my simple meal, tidied the house a bit and listened to the radio. That was all I was able to do. I was almost reconciled to living like this forever. The inner spark and potential for joy that had once been within me, was dead.

One day, as I returned home, I saw from the distance that there was someone or something sitting outside my gate. At first, I thought it was a dog, I had taken to feeding some stray dogs with my leftover food, I felt a kinship with them, as lost and forlorn as I. But I only fed the dogs at night, they did not usually sit near my gate. As I walked closer, I saw it was a person, wearing a hooded shirt, sitting on the ground, and leaning against the gate. As I drew nearer, I realized who it was. Cynthia! And that marked the beginning of the changes in my life.

She seemed to be asleep. I stood in front of her, not knowing what to do. I whispered her name, but she did not move. After a few minutes, I moved past her, and began unlocking the gate. As I opened it, she woke and got to her feet. With a huge smile, she flung her arms around me in a tight hug. I was taken aback, and stood there stiffly. Had she mistaken me for someone else? Stepping back a bit she spoke, 'Dev,' she said. 'I had to come to you. I've left Enzo.'

I remembered how she had called me Dev before. 'You've left the ashram?' I asked.

'Not just the ashram. I have left Enzo.'

I was puzzled. 'What do you mean?' I asked.

'Don't you know I was in a relationship with him?'

A relationship? It may sound odd, but I hadn't heard the word used in that context, though after a few moments I thought I understood what she meant.

'I didn't know,' I said, 'but why did you leave him?'

'I am in love with you.'

The house and gate keys were still in my hand, the gate half open. I stood still, and did not know what to say. In the benumbed state I was in, it did not mean anything to me. In fact, it was just an irritant. I saw that she had a small travelling bag at her feet.

'You can't stay here!' I exclaimed.

'But why not?' she said, picking up the bag and moving inside the gate.

'I live alone. There is no one else in the house.'

'That's ideal then.'

'You don't understand. It's not acceptable. This is India. This is a small town. People will be against it. My landlord may ask me to leave.'

'Do you mind? Does all that matter to you?'

I was silent for a few moments. Did it matter? No, nothing much mattered. But I still felt I did not want Cynthia in my house. I looked at her. The woebegone look on her face made me feel bad that I had been so unwelcoming. I moved forward and unlocked the door, and when I went in she followed me. 'Do sit,' I said. 'I'll make tea.' I escaped to the kitchen. As I boiled the water and got the tea ready, I felt my deadness lift. At least something different was happening today, something less dreary and routine. Still, I was worried. She couldn't stay in this house. There was just one bedroom—again I remembered Gita and how cosy and comfortable we had been together. It was mid-October now, winter just setting in, and at this time of the year Gita would be putting the razais in the sun, airing the warm clothes. I would go to the market and buy a quintal of wood, we had a fireplace, and we would light the wood fire in the evenings. We used to get chestnuts sometimes, and roast them in the fire, cracking the soft shells, eating them while they were still warm. Remembering all this, my eyes filled with tears, for it was almost exactly a year ago that she had died.

I brought the tea out on a tray, with a bowl of salty snacks. Gita used to make these herself, but now I had to buy them. Cynthia sat in one of the chairs, looking tired and sleepy, her travel bag on the floor near her. When I put the tray down, she asked if she could use the bathroom. Of course, I said. I wanted to refuse, but how could I? The only bathroom in the house led off from the bedroom. And in the bedroom were all my memories of Gita. I didn't want Cynthia to enter that sacred space. In later years, I learned that in the Western world people are tough. They say what they feel and do not let anyone do anything they do not like. Here in India we are brought up on a tradition of politeness, at least we were in those days. I couldn't say no, and led Cynthia to the bathroom.

She was out in a few minutes. We sat opposite each other and drank our tea. Cynthia still seemed tired, and did not speak. Nor did I, as I could not think of anything to say. Then she broke the silence by saying, 'I've been travelling for the last three days, Dev. It took me two days to walk down to Almora. From there I took a bus to reach here. The roads were terrible, and the bus was so rickety and old, I was jolted around all the way and couldn't sleep a wink. Could I take a nap?'

One part of me, traditional, conventional, wanted to insist that she leave. The other part of me was experiencing something else. She was attractive. She had always been kind, concerned, motherly almost. A desire arose in me, which wasn't just sexual. I wanted to bury myself in her, to forget, to get some peace. I suggested she could nap on the sofa in the living room—I gave her a couple of sheets and a pillow, and she lay down there. She covered herself with the sheet, closed her eyes, and was soon asleep.

I wandered outside in the garden and watered the few plants—after my return, I had cleared the weeds and planted petunia and pansy seeds, and some small shoots had begun to grow. I tried to think about what I should do, but my mind was blank. Back in the house I went into the kitchen and made aloo parathas, dal and raita for dinner. Next, a visit to the market, where I bought some tomatoes and cucumber for salad and some gulab jamuns from the sweet shop for dessert. I hoped that Cynthia would like the dinner I had made.

I waited for Cynthia to wake, but she continued to sleep deeply. Around 8 p.m., I sat down near her and put on the radio. I listened first to the news, and then to Hindi songs. I had put it on softly, but gradually the sounds penetrated into Cynthia's sleep, she began to stir then came awake and sat up.

We had dinner. She complimented me on the food. 'It's delicious,' she said. 'The best I have ever eaten.' She had never eaten gulab jamuns before, and loved them.

We talked a bit, but I did not try to find out more about why she had left the ashram and why she had come to stay with me. After a while I said she must be tired and it was time to sleep. She could sleep on the sofa I said, and gave her a blanket in case she felt cold. She said she would be fine there, and after a wash, settled herself on it and snuggled under the blanket. I switched off the light and went into the bedroom. I had mixed feelings. I wanted her, and yet I was afraid. I felt I could never again trust or love anyone completely.

I had some corrections to finish for two tests I had given in school. I sat at the desk in my bedroom working on them and was up till midnight. Focusing on this had stopped me from thinking, and I went to bed and fell asleep despite all my worries.

I was in a deep sleep when I felt someone's hand on my face, and I woke to find Cynthia in bed near me, gently caressing me. I did not stop to think, I responded and we made love. After more than a year of abstinence, it was a wonderful experience. But soon after I felt an uncontrollable grief rising up in me, I began to weep, it was the first time I had wept since Gita's death. Between my tears I blurted out my tragic story. I am not sure what Cynthia understood of it, but she comforted me, and after a while we made love again. And then, at peace, I slept. When I woke the sun was on my face. I was bewildered and looked at the clock—9 a.m.! School would have started an hour ago. I jumped up and saw the rumpled sheets on the bed. Then I remembered what had happened at night. Panic and regret filled me. What was the point of this?

Cynthia was not in the room. I hoped she had realized the folly of coming here, and had already left. I peeked into the front room, but she was there—sitting and reading a book. I went back into the bedroom, had a bath, got dressed. Then I went out to meet her. She hadn't changed her clothes and didn't seem to have had a bath. The first thing Gita and I would do every day would be to bathe and wear clean clothes, and her sloppiness was off-putting. She greeted me warmly, but I could hardly respond, flooded with regrets of the previous night. Cynthia didn't seem to notice my coldness. She got up, put her arms around my neck, and kissed me on the cheek, as I averted my face. 'You've been through a lot, Dev,' she said. 'Now there is no need to worry. I will take care of you. I am just making our breakfast.'

She moved away from me into the kitchen. I had to admit, that I was attracted to her once again. She was back in about ten minutes, with a plate of steaming hot pancakes. I'd eaten her eggless and spiced pancakes in the ashram, and knew they were delicious. She must have mixed the batter earlier, and kept it ready. We sat down to eat at the dining table together. 'I didn't know that you would find all the ingredients for these in the kitchen,' I said.

'No, Dev,' she said. 'I went out and bought what I needed.' I froze. She had been out to the nearby market? Now everyone would know she was living in my house. No one would accept it. And then I hadn't even been to school. I could lose my job. If Mr Gosain came to know he would say I was a bad moral influence. Times have changed, it would not be like that today, but in those days, and in the somewhat lower middle-class neighbourhood in which I lived, I could predict what would happen.

The pancakes were good though, I enjoyed them. I tried to think and plan, but my thoughts wandered. If I had to leave here I could return to Enzo's ashram, life had been better for me there. But I couldn't stay there free of charge, and I still had to make some money. And then, I thought, Cynthia would not come with me. Or if she did, she'd get back with Enzo. I wasn't sure how I would feel about that.

After we had eaten the pancakes, Cynthia went to make tea. It was nice having someone to do all this after so long. Maybe we could live together, I'd make dinner, she'd cook lunch. If we got married, society would accept her. Sipping tea, I began to dream.

And the next few days were dreamlike. We behaved like a married couple. I resumed going to school, Cynthia shopped and cooked and took care of the house. One of the neighbours did ask who she was, and I replied truthfully that she was a good friend. No one said anything more, and I began to think my fears were unfounded. The nights were filled with pleasure, and the comfort of having a loving companion. Yes, I almost began to love Cynthia. It was perhaps too soon to propose marriage, but I thought it would happen. Now I believed I could one day forget Gita.

Perhaps ten days passed like this, and then there was a bombshell. Mr Gosain came over one evening while Cynthia and I were together in the sitting room, drinking tea. I introduced Cynthia to him. She offered him a cup of tea, and he accepted. When she went into the kitchen to get it for him, he said, 'Look, Dev, this won't do. I heard about this woman living with you. You know that teachers at our school must maintain certain standards.'

I was curious about how he had heard and asked him. 'Many of the teachers know about it,' he said. 'I don't know how.' Cynthia returned with his tea, and I asked her if she could leave us alone for a while.

When she had left, Mr Gosain said, 'I understand the attraction of a beautiful woman like that. And, in fact, I am happy if you have got over that terrible tragedy. But you know that this is not permissible in our society, particularly when you are a schoolteacher.'

I remained silent.

'I can give you a little time,' he continued. 'If you decide to marry her it would be acceptable. Otherwise you have to ask her to leave. And soon.'

'Okay,' I said. 'I'll see what I can do.'

He finished his tea and got up to leave. After he left, Cynthia asked me what he had said, and I told her. In fact, I was rather happy with his visit. I liked the thought of marrying Cynthia, and I felt now she would suggest it herself. But all Cynthia said was, 'I didn't realize you people lived in the nineteenth century. Or is it the eighteenth?'

I felt a flash of anger. The 'you people' made me want to spring to the defence of my city, my country. But all I said was, 'Things change gradually here, Cynthia. Why don't we get married? You said you loved me, and I have become fond of you too. So why don't we take that step?'

I hadn't expected Cynthia to laugh, but that is what she did. 'You are funny, Dev,' she said. 'I have been here less than two weeks. Are you crazy that you expect me to marry you?'

'I married Gita after just meeting her twice. So I don't see what the problem is.'

'The problem is the difference between East and West. I can't get married like that. And besides there are so many things to think about. I can't see myself living here all my life. Or maybe I could, but it is far too early to decide. You know, at first I thought I had found the perfect partner in

Enzo. It was only after I had been with him a few months that I realized he may not be right for me. Then, by the end of a year, I knew he was definitely wrong for me. And I met you, so bewildered and innocent, so different from him. And you are a genuine scholar too. Let's live together for a year or so. Then we can decide.'

I began to feel that Cynthia was too independent for me.

'I agree with you in theory, Cynthia,' I said. 'But the problem is I can't retain my job here if you remain here and we don't marry. You would have to leave.'

'Well, Dev,' she said. 'Why don't we both leave?'

'But where will we go? What will we do?'

'We will go to Delhi,' she said. 'Before going to Enzo's ashram I had stayed three months in Delhi. I know it is hardly 250 kilometres away, but it is very different. It is more liberal. People manage to live together without being married. Neighbours are less nosy and inquisitive.'

'But what will I do there? I could apply to schools there, but it won't be easy to get a job. I don't have any savings.'

'Oh, don't worry, Dev,' Cynthia said. 'I have money to tide us over for a few months. And I think you could do better there than becoming a schoolteacher. I can see that you don't like your job at all. I had already been thinking of a different option for you. Mr Gosain's visit just means that we need to consider this sooner than I had thought necessary.'

With a start, I realized that I knew nothing about Cynthia. I had blurted out my entire life story and wept on her shoulder, but I had asked her nothing about her life. I knew she was originally from San Francisco in the US. But I hadn't bothered to find out about her family, her life in the US, or why she came to India. She wasn't that young.

She must be my age at least, and probably older, maybe she had had a job, maybe she had been married. I felt a bit ashamed. Perhaps I was still an unbalanced person, I had not recovered from the loss of Gita and my son. In the relationship with Cynthia I had thought only of myself.

'Cynthia,' I said, 'I know in suggesting we get married straight away, I was not thinking clearly. Though I think it could work out, you are probably right, we do need to know each other better. Regarding going to Delhi...let's think it over. Mr Gosain has given me some time. Let's talk and decide in a week or so.'

'That's fine with me,' said Cynthia. 'We won't rush into anything. Now you go ahead and finish your corrections. I've seen the pile of books you brought home. I'll make dinner.'

'Thanks,' I said, and went to my desk. Correcting the essays on *Macbeth* was almost a mechanical task, but I had fifty to glance through. While I worked I was aware of a rising excitement at the thought of leaving this job and going to Delhi. Yes, we would discuss it further, but first I decided I would find out more about Cynthia.

We had dinner around 8 p.m. though I had not quite finished my corrections. Cynthia had made a vegetable stew and potato cutlets, along with a dessert of bananas cooked with jam. It all tasted good. Across the table I looked into her deep blue eyes, I followed the way her dark hair curved on her cheek. I didn't want to let her go, not yet, perhaps never.

I got back to my work after dinner. By the time I finished, Cynthia was sitting up in bed, reading. Cynthia spent a lot of time reading. Gita never read in bed. But then perhaps she had more to do, what with her own classes, then coming home and making snacks for tea, then dinner, then corrections. We both used to get up early too, to set off for school. Cynthia did wake when I left, but I think she usually went back to sleep.

I nuzzled close to her. 'Cynthia,' I said. 'I know I have been selfish, thinking about myself. I want to know something about you now. Tell me about your life from the time you were born.'

'That's a bit much—I can't tell you everything at one time.' But still she told me this story.

'I lived with my grandparents in San Francisco as my mother died when I was three. They were good to me but somewhat distant. I used to dream about living with my father, but he did not want me. Then, when I was about thirteen I fell in love with a wonderful boy. We stayed friends all through school and even through university. He seemed to fill all the gaps in my life.'

'Isn't thirteen a bit young?' I interrupted.

'Thirteen is not young at all. After getting our undergraduate degrees we married,' she continued. 'We were both twenty-two. Both of us wanted to study further, and my father decided to make up for his years of neglect and support us. I did my masters in anthropology, he became an accountant, and soon got a job.

'We were happy together, but Carl, my husband, did not like taking money from my father, now that he had a job and his own income. Carl said my father had done enough. I agreed, but I felt it would ruin my newfound relationship with my Dad, that it would be a rejection of him. Anyway, I met Dad and told him what Carl felt. My father suggested that I go on taking the money and keep it in a separate account for emergencies. He said there was absolutely no reason why he shouldn't share his wealth with his own daughter, and if Carl didn't like it, he must be old-fashioned and out of date. "I'd like to know I've given you something and helped you in some way, even though late in life," he said. I saw his point and agreed to take the money. I did not tell Carl and thought there was no harm in it.

'I found it difficult to get a job, but managed to get one in a research organization, doing various kinds of surveys. Carl himself suggested that I keep my money in a separate account and use it for something special, as he was earning enough to provide for both of us. I added the small amount I earned to the large sums my father sent me from time to time. Things went smoothly for the next four years. We both agreed to postpone having children for a while. Carl wanted to reach a higher position in the finance company in which he worked before we had a child, so that we could provide for it better. Of course, I knew there was no need, but I could not tell him that. We remained close and loving, but the fact that I had a secret was becoming a burden on me. I spent some of the money on elegant clothes, a handbag, hairstyling and fashion accessories, and even on some beautiful art objects for our home. Carl never realized how much all this cost, and thought it came out of my small income. Money in my private account kept growing. My father got into the property business, and was making huge profits that he shared with me.

'Gradually, I began to notice that Carl's behaviour was not the same. He was irritable, often came home late, and when I questioned him, he said he had a new boss and had to work extra hard. I accepted his explanation, but it was when I accompanied him to an official party, that things began to fall apart. I wore a Dior dress and a necklace and bracelet of blue sapphires set in gold. Carl commented on them, he said they were beautiful and must have cost the earth, but I said not that much, it was just glass beads and the base was silver with a gold wash. I knew Carl would not know a sapphire from glass.

'At the party, I received many compliments for my looks, my flowing floor-length dress, and my jewellery. As we drove home Carl said to me, "I am so proud of you. You were the most beautiful woman in that room." That night we made love after quite some time.

'I woke next morning confident and happy, and made pancakes and coffee for Carl before he set off for work. He too looked happy, and gave me a hug and a kiss when he left, something he had failed to do recently.

'But then everything went wrong. Carl's boss was not as simple and ignorant as him, and his wife came from a wealthy family. During the course of the day, Alfred, the boss, asked Carl how he could afford to get me a designer dress and a gold necklace studded with sapphires. Carl insisted it was just an ordinary dress and glass beads that I bought for myself from the amount I earned doing anthropological surveys. Alfred, it seems, laughed, and told him he was a fool. "Get it checked by a jeweller," he told Carl, "and then you will know the truth." Carl's suspicions were aroused. He was distant to me that day, though I did not know why. Two days later he got the opportunity to take the necklace out of the house without my knowledge. He took it to a jeweller and there he learned the truth.

'He came home straight away. He did not pretend that he did not know. I still remember that day when he returned unexpectedly at three in the afternoon. As he came in he took the necklace out of his bag and held it out to me. "Explain this to me," he said, and I knew that he knew.

'I did not make things worse with more lies. I told him about my father's continuing contributions, though I did not tell him how much money I now had. I am sure he believed what I said, but he was angry. He said he did not think I was telling the truth even now and it must be the gift of a rich lover. Then we both began shouting at each other and said terrible things. It was the first fight we had ever had, and also, the last. To cut things short, Carl said he could not live in a marriage based on deception. He wanted a divorce. I tried to explain, to apologize, to tell him how much I loved him, but he was adamant.

'It took a few months but the divorce went through, and I felt broken and shaken. It was my fault, but why couldn't he be reasonable? We had known each other, liked and loved each other from the age of thirteen. We had been in harmony with each other for seventeen years. How had this happened? What a fool I had been. Carl was far more important to me than my father. I blamed myself, and I missed Carl terribly. I'd never been someone who had many friends. I was alone and drowning in grief.

'It was about a month after the divorce that Alfred's wife, Leslie, visited me. I would have liked to send her away from the door. She and Alfred were the cause of my problems. I stood at the door trying to summon the will to shut it in her face, but she pushed passed me. I didn't ask her to sit down, and we both remained standing.

'"Look Cynthia," she said, "there is something I want to tell you. I am sorry your marriage ended, and perhaps the spark was set off by me and Alfred. Originally, I thought you too must have a lover and that he was giving you those expensive gifts, but then I heard you were very depressed, almost having a breakdown, and thought perhaps it wasn't so."'

'"It was my father's money,"' I mumbled, wondering why she had said, "you too must have a lover."

'"And you told Carl that?"

'"Of course."'

'"Then don't blame yourself. And don't blame us either. Carl was looking for an excuse to break the marriage. He was already in love with Alison, his secretary. And he is marrying her next week.'

'I gazed at her in shock. That couldn't be correct. Carl getting married? Carl in love even while we were married? "But we are soulmates," I blurted out. "It can't be true. We'll marry again when he gets over his anger..."

'She looked at me in pity. "Ask him yourself, Cynthia," she said, as she went out of the door.

'Was it true? I didn't think I could confront Carl. I sat there shaking. Then I thought I would speak to Alison instead.

'I phoned Carl's office and she answered, I recognized her voice. I had heard it hundreds of times when I was trying to reach Carl. "Lyman Accountancy, how can I help you?"

'"Alison," I said, "I just want to congratulate you on your marriage to Carl."'

'She recognized my voice too. "Thank you, Cynthia," she said, after a brief hesitation. "I hope you don't mind. In fact I wanted to send you an invitation, I would like us to be friends, but..." I put down the phone while she was still talking.

'So, it was true. I couldn't do anything more that day.

While the divorce was taking place I had gone to a doctor and got a prescription for sleeping pills. I hadn't taken them too often, but that afternoon I took two and curled up in bed. I slept a deep and heavy sleep. It was midnight when I woke. I made myself some coffee, ate a toast and then went back to sleep.

'I felt better in the morning. After my fight with Carl and the initiation of divorce proceedings, I had told my father what had happened. I wasn't irrational enough to blame him, after all, he had only sent me money, he hadn't urged me to buy expensive things and flaunt them. Looking back, I saw that I had got a lot of pleasure, even happiness, from the small luxurious items with which I had surrounded myself. Now I phoned and told him that money hadn't been the cause of our break-up. My Dad was relieved because, I guess, in some way he did feel responsible for what had happened. He urged me to travel and forget the past, and I decided to do just that. I went to Europe first—to London, Paris and Rome. It had been great to see the museums, the art and architecture of Paris and Rome, but it was London I liked best. I had visited it first and later returned there, renting a room from an Indian couple. I was with them about two months, and I got to know something about India, and thought it would be a good place to visit, somewhere entirely different and new. I was in Delhi for a few months, and then I heard about Enzo's ashram and went there. And now here I am.'

'Well, Cynthia,' I said, 'I'm glad you are here. And you too have suffered sorrows and disappointments like I have. Thanks for sharing your story. Maybe we do have a life together.'

'Look, Dev,' she said, 'let me tell you my idea of what

you could do in Delhi. You could run yoga classes. You would be a big hit.'

'I don't think it will work. I tried here but did not get any students.'

'I guarantee you it will be different in Delhi. I assure you. And later we could even go to the US, and you could teach yoga there.'

Right at that moment I decided that I would take the plunge and give up my job. I was desperate for something new. I did not say anything then, though I had made up my mind.

The next day Cynthia said, 'I have another idea too, if you don't like the one about going to Delhi.'

'What?' I asked.

'We could set up a yoga resort cum guesthouse, in your own area, somewhere near your village on the banks of the Ganga. Foreigners could come there, just as they do to Enzo's ashram.'

I said I would think it over, though I did not like the idea at all. After a few days, I told Cynthia what I had decided—we would go to Delhi. I said that though I liked the idea of setting up a resort near my village, it would be impossible for us to live together there.

Now it was time for me to resign from my job. I felt bad doing this as Mr Gosain had done his best for me. It was he who had suggested Enzo's ashram and kept my job for me for a year, re-employed me mid-term, and even not gone overboard over Cynthia staying with me. I knew he could not have done more. Anyway, I went and met him and told him what I had decided. 'You have made the right decision,' he said, to my relief. 'It is mid-term but then we already have an extra English teacher. I accommodated you because I had promised to keep your job for you, and of course also because you were the best this school has ever had. But I can see that your heart is no longer in teaching or in Shakespeare. You still teach very well, but the passion you had earlier is missing. Now I can't keep your job for you any longer. But if you are sure about this, go ahead. Write and let me know how you get on.'

I thanked him profusely. I had not expected such a positive response.

I decided I would not keep the house on. It was time to make a clean break. I liked the idea of leaving everything behind and moving forward with just a couple of suitcases. I had to meet the landlord, tell him I was leaving, sell the furniture, give away a lot of other items. I gave all the pots, pans, and other stuff from my kitchen to the Cheshire Home. A lot of clothes, blankets, sheets, curtains, and some furniture which hadn't sold was given there too. Then there were Gita's clothes and personal items. I hadn't opened her cupboard since she died, though I had thrown away anything that belonged to her that had been on the table or in the bathroom. Her jewellery had been put in the bank locker earlier. Now I asked Cynthia to pack up all Gita's things and when that was done I gave them to the Home as well.

Finally, everything was done. I was impressed by Cynthia, who had been in India more than a year, and had only a backpack with her. Taking a cue from her, I reduced my possessions to just one medium-sized suitcase.

9. Life in Delhi

Dev's Story

We had booked our train tickets and on the night of 15th November, 1975 we left by the Mussoorie Express for Delhi. The train was slightly late, but as it crossed the Yamuna Bridge around eight the next morning and drew into Old Delhi station, I felt a thrill. My new life was about to begin. When we alighted, the crowded platform and the difficulty in getting transport left little time to think. Cynthia said she had reserved a room for us at the India International Centre, the IIC as it was popularly known. She had become a member there, she said, when she had stayed in Delhi. I hadn't seen the place but had heard about it. Someone had told me that getting membership there was very difficult. 'It's easier for foreigners,' Cynthia had said, and that had made me angry, though I had kept quiet, focusing on my original plan. Sundararaman had diverted me from it, but in fact had provided more knowledge which could help me to reach my goal. I kept my plan a secret from Cynthia, but now it was firm in my heart. I was going to be a guru. I was absolutely sure this would take place soon.

We got a scooter, as people in Delhi used to call them then, a three-wheeled auto-rickshaw for hire. Seeing Cynthia of course the driver refused to use the meter and charged about five times the amount. I tried to argue, but Cynthia said it didn't matter. This would be the norm whenever I travelled with her. Most drivers felt foreigners were super-rich and would not mind paying more, and they were often right.

We reached the IIC where we had a double room. Though the room was quite simple, I could not get over its pristine cleanliness, and what seemed to be an absolutely luxurious bathroom. The white towels, changed every day, running hot water, shower, and long tub were things I had never known before. And both room and bathroom were heated! Not with a fireplace and a wood or coal fire as we had, not even with an electric heater, but from some vents in the ceiling. 'Central heating,' said Cynthia knowledgeably. 'We have it even in our houses in the US.'

In later years, I lived in far more luxurious places across the world, but the IIC was always a special place for me. I became a member a few years later, and whenever I visited Delhi, I would stay there.

Cynthia had not spent a lot of time in Delhi, but she seemed to have a number of contacts. Perhaps it was through them, and not just because she was a foreigner, that she had become a member at the IIC so easily. The very next day she located a Buddhist centre in the posh colony of Safdarjung Enclave. They would permit me to teach yoga there, on a profit-sharing basis. That is, one-third of the fees would go to them. Cynthia booked the hall for two hours every morning, beginning from 1st January. That was almost a month and a half away, and I wanted to start sooner, but Cynthia said it was important to advertise first in order to get sufficient people. She said I would find plenty to do in Delhi.

I started wandering around Delhi, appreciating its roads, greenery and gardens. Dehradun was forested, and had the tallest trees, silver oak, eucalyptus, sal, but here in Delhi there were planted gardens in the roundabouts, flowers and trees along the roads, and a cleanliness and neatness I had never seen in Dehradun.

Cynthia meanwhile had located a room-kitchen-bathroom unit in Vasant Vihar for us to rent. The whole unit was the size of a garage. The rent was Rs 400 a month. This was high for those days, though today a similar unit could cost ten thousand rupees or more. After getting three months' rent in advance, the landlord was totally uninterested in who we were or in our marital status. He had nine such units at the side of his house, in three levels: ground, first and second floors. Ours was a corner unit on the second floor, and we faced both water and power problems. Just next door, in the middle unit on the same floor, was a similar couple, a foreign woman and an Indian man. Cynthia was attractive, vibrant and charming, but this woman, with her light brown eyes, golden skin, and silky long blonde hair, was just gorgeous. She was tall, at least six inches taller than I, and slender. Cynthia caught me looking at her a few times. 'Are you attracted to her?' she asked.

'No, Cynthia,' I said. 'It is you I am attracted to. But she is beautiful in a different way. I have never seen anyone like her before.' Cynthia smiled and accepted my explanation. And truly, I was not attracted to Gladys, which was the blonde woman's name. She was lovely to look at, but seemed too passive and quiet.

Because of the at least superficial similarities between us, living side by side, we became moderately friendly with them. The man, Manish, worked in a bank. He had first met Gladys in the US, where he had been sent for a meeting. Later, she came to India, and moved in with him.

They too were not married. His parents, he confided in me, knew nothing of the relationship. He could not ever think of marrying her, and, he said, his parents were already in the process of arranging a marriage for him. Gladys knew nothing of this.

I began to think of my parents too then. I hadn't met them before I left, but had informed them through someone who was going to my village, that I was taking up a job in Delhi. I knew they wouldn't mind if I married Cynthia, all they wanted was my happiness. But after the initial thought, I wasn't very keen on marrying her. I liked her, but there was something missing, some spark of passion, or even of love.

In the time before the classes started, I was more or less on my own all day. Cynthia said she wanted to meet old friends and contact people to get them to join the classes. One day I went with her, but felt awkward and out of place. That day we met a woman friend of hers named Laura, who was quite pleasant, but I wasn't able to participate in their laughter and talk. I took to visiting the IIC library and sitting there for most of the day, a wonderful place, though it did not have all I wanted on religion and philosophy. In breaks from the library, I walked in Lodi Gardens and ate from the wandering food-sellers, some spicy chana, or some papri chaat. As it was winter, just outside the gardens I would find barrows selling boiled eggs and roasted sweet potatoes. When I got home in the evening, I was the one who had to cook. Cynthia had begun coming home late. Sometimes she ate what I had made, sometimes she said she had already eaten. It seemed we were drifting apart. I was careful not to add to the problems by talking to Gladys, who stayed home all day, cooking, cleaning, or just sitting on a chair on their balcony, soaking up the sun. Sometimes, sitting there, she sewed or embroidered. I never saw her reading.

Cynthia had paid the rent, and she paid for her personal expenses, but I was paying for the food, and I had very little money left. It was worrying, but I thought with yoga classes starting soon, the amount I had would carry me through. With a little more money, I could enjoy life in Delhi.

Manish and Gladys used to go out together on Sundays. One Sunday evening I went with them to Bengali Market, where I had never been before, and was fascinated by all the food shops there. I ate jalebis after a long time, and then left them, saying I would find my own way home. As I walked towards the main road, I passed a grey stone building—the board on the gate said it was Triveni Kala Sangam—and went inside.

And there I found another haven where I could spend my evenings and even my days. There were dance and music classes going on, held in various rooms, their melodious sounds faintly audible. There were two art galleries, and an attractive café, where one could sit for hours over a low-priced meal. In the smaller gallery, a new art exhibition used to open every third day, with relatively unknown artists. And every time an exhibition opened, tea was served to all visitors, along with cakes and sandwiches. Thus, I began saving some money by eating there on opening days. I learnt something about art too, as I had to walk around and pretend to take an interest in the paintings on display. There was an open-air theatre, where there were occasional dance performances and a daily dance practice.

I often sat on those stairs in the evenings, drinking a hot cup of soup, and watching the Manipuri dance practice, soothed by the sound of the drums, the bright costumes, and the precise movements of the dancers. I would leave around 7.30 p.m., and never failed to buy a paper cone of chana from the old chana seller outside the gate. Sandwiches at an art exhibition, or an early meal in Triveni, or a later one in Bengali Market, prevented the need to cook at home.

It was like a brief vacation. I shut my mind to the future and to the past, and just enjoyed the pale sunshine, the IIC library, Triveni in the evenings, and sometimes in the afternoons too. It was all fascinating for me. Once I went to Kamani auditorium and heard a music performance by Pandit Jasraj. That was glorious! I began to love Delhi.

It was soon the 1st of January 1976.

Two sessions of yoga classes were fixed from 10-11 and 11.30-12.30 every morning. Cynthia accompanied me on the first day. She had insisted on advance payment for one month's classes. The amount for the month was fixed at Rs 300. I felt it was a bit high, that was almost the amount of my month's salary in school, and of one month's rent here! But it did not seem too much for the people of Delhi. Seven students were booked for the first class, and twelve for the second. We collected Rs 5,700 on that day! I couldn't believe it. I struggled for a year to earn that much.

There were three men in the first class and two in the second, the rest were women. Mostly they were well-dressed, well-groomed women, who on the whole were not interested in yoga. There were a couple of exceptions, and the men seemed serious about learning, but these overweight women were just there for, as we say, 'time-pass'. The first day's classes went off smoothly. I paid nineteen hundred rupees to the centre, which left us with Rs 3,800. I felt good, and I suggested to Cynthia that we celebrate together in Bengali Market. I had warm feelings for her once again, and thought I was lucky to have met her. As we reached there, just outside Nathu's shop, she counted out five hundred-rupee notes and gave them to me. 'That's your share, Dev,' she said. It took me a few moments to understand. 'What do you mean, Cynthia?' I said. 'I am the one teaching. You can take a commission, maybe ten or twenty per cent, but the rest of the money should be mine.' Standing there we began to fight. 'I'm the one who has made all the efforts to get you these classes, Dev,' she said. 'I'm paying the rent, and in addition, I'm giving you more than your monthly salary as a schoolteacher.'

'You said you were rich, you had plenty of money,' I answered. 'You persuaded me to leave my job, my home. And now you are exploiting me.'

Cynthia looked furious. 'Okay, Dev,' she said, and she put all the money in my hand. 'Now you are on your own. I am going back to the room and removing my things. I made a terrible mistake when I thought I loved you. Now take care of yourself, run your classes, and do what you like.' I was aghast. 'But Cynthia,' I said, 'you brought me here. How can you leave me like this?' 'Well Dev,' she responded, 'that's up to you now. You either accept my way of doing things, or you manage on your own.' What had made me think of marrying her? What kind of a controlling woman was this? The money was in my hand and I did not want to give it up.

'I think I'll go my own way, Cynthia,' I spoke calmly, though a burning anger was rising in my heart.

'Okay then,' said Cynthia, her face whitening with anger. 'This is where we part. Enjoy your celebratory meal by yourself. You won't see me again.'

I ignored her and entered Nathu's. I ordered two plates of aloo-chaat, and after I had eaten this, two plates of gulab jamuns. One could say I was eating for both of us. I couldn't believe that the day that had started out so well, was ending like this. I took my time over eating, enjoying my food. I had a cup of tea, then another. I was nervous but trying not to think or feel. To earn the money that was now in my pocket, I still had to teach for the rest of the month. From Nathu's I moved on to Triveni, and sat on the theatre steps, warmed by the fading afternoon sun. At 4 p.m. the Manipuri dance practice started on the stage. I remained watching, and left at six-thirty. It was already dark, and I felt totally alone. Taking a meandering bus, I reached home an hour later. We each had a key, and now I unlocked the door and went in.

Cynthia's few belongings were gone. On the table was an envelope with my name on it. I opened it and found a short and pointless note. 'You are a fool, Dev,' I read, 'Goodbye. Cynthia.'

Yes, I was a fool. I lay down in bed trying to think. What was my future? In a flash, it came to me—everything was all right, I had done the right thing. I was already a yoga teacher. I would teach well, improve my practice, study more, and soon, soon, I would achieve my aim of becoming a guru.

***

Nityananda

The fourth part of Dev's story ended here. It seemed he wanted to become a guru both to gain power and money and to share his knowledge of yoga. What would happen next? I went to see him the next day, and he handed over a few more pages.

10. Becoming a Guru

Dev's Story

That night after Cynthia had gone, I slept peacefully and woke early. I wanted to begin my further studies straight away, but I had only two books with me—the *Yoga Sutras* and the *Collected Works of Shakespeare*. I picked up the *Yoga Sutras* and began to read them again. The second sentence, 'yoga-chitta-vritti-nirodhah' on which Sundararaman had spent so much time, and which he explained at length in this book that he had written, reminded me of the need to stay calm. A bath, and a quick breakfast of bread, butter and tea, and I set off for my classes—reached there on time, explained some simple pranayama and asanas, and it all went off fine. I decided to have a snacky lunch in Lodi gardens, and then go to the IIC library, to think, plan and read.

I had first gone to the library with Cynthia, but then later I had been going there practically every day on my own. No one had ever asked me to produce a library card, but that is what happened at the entrance that day. When I said I had been coming there every day, the man allowed me in, but said that next time I came I would have to produce my card. Had Cynthia said something to them? Why were they asking me for a card for the first time that day? Was Cynthia staying at the IIC again? There were questions in my mind, but I decided it did not matter, as I would not go there again. In any case the library did not have a good stock of spiritual books.

I read a few newspapers and left in about an hour. While

leaving I asked one of the librarians if he knew of any libraries with books on religion. He mentioned Bharatiya Vidya Bhavan and gave me directions. It was not far from Bengali Market and I had no problem in getting in there to read their books. And yes, they had a good stock of Sanskrit texts, books on Hinduism, and even books on other religions. The librarian there was extremely helpful and suggested I also look at the Ramakrishna Mission library and the Sahitya Akademi. I visited them over the next few days and felt I could read and study there forever.

My classes too proceeded well. I developed a rapport with my students, and even some sympathy for the over-dressed, over-painted and overweight women. Maybe they were just whiling away their time, but surely yoga was a better way to do so than a kitty party.

It was about a week after Cynthia had left that Manish asked me about her. I told him we had differences and had split up. He confided in me then, telling me that he would soon be leaving to get married. Gladys still knew nothing about it. 'Gladys is the ideal woman,' Manish said. 'She is quiet, patient, cooks, sews, and doesn't ask questions. But my parents will never accept a foreigner.'

'Why don't you try?' I asked. 'They may like her when they meet her. I think such marriages are quite common now.'

I felt that with a little insistence from him, things could have been sorted out, but Manish didn't have the courage. Just three days later, he left, telling Gladys he was going away for a few days for some work. I didn't know whether to tell Gladys or not. She must have suspected something, because after a week she came and asked me if Manish had said anything to me.

I told her the truth. I was afraid she would break down and start crying, but I believed she had a right to know. Strangely, Gladys wasn't too perturbed. 'I didn't want to marry him either,' she said. 'I just wish he had told me himself.'

'Why were you staying with him then? What did you come to India for?'

'I met Manish in the US. I was living with my parents then. I was quite a timid person, and hadn't completed school. I tried taking various jobs, but found it difficult to manage most of them. I worked as a waitress for a while but could not take the diners' orders correctly. Then I got a job in a clothes' shop in a hotel. I'd already made a few errors and the manager had warned me that the next time I would have to leave. One day Manish came in to buy a shirt. He chose one in pale green, but somehow I packed one in pale yellow. The next day Manish returned to complain, and the shop manager shouted at me. Seeing how upset I was, Manish tried to say it did not matter, and that he preferred the pale yellow. I felt he was a kind person, and I had not known much kindness in my life. Then he gave me his card and said to contact him if I ever came to India. I knew nothing of India, had never thought about it, but now an idea was planted in my head. A week later, I made another error at work and had to leave my job. I had saved most of the money I earned. I applied for a passport, and in a few months I reached India. When I landed in India, I met someone who helped me to contact Manish and reach this place. And Manish just let me stay with him. Though he didn't say anything, I knew it was a temporary arrangement. I liked him, but I can't say it was love. I don't know what love is.

'Now, though, I will have to return to the US. And I don't even have the money for my return fare. The rent for this month is paid, I don't think I can stay here longer than that.'

'Well, Gladys,' I said, 'Cynthia has left me as you have probably noticed. So, if you like you can move in with me, at least temporarily, until you figure out what to do.'

And thus, Cynthia was replaced by Gladys. Gladys was a simple person, sweet and generous, but she definitely had an IQ slightly below normal. She had a real difficulty with money, as the smallest sums confused her. I realized she would find working in any job difficult.

Soon it was February. By the third of the month, I had collected the advance payment for the yoga classes. Two people had dropped out and it came to Rs 5,300. I handed over Rs 1,800 to the centre, and that left me with Rs 3,300. That was more than enough for Gladys and me, and I could even save something. Now, I should add that I did not sleep with Gladys. I could see she wasn't keen on it, but would have agreed just to have a place to stay. I felt it would have been like exploiting a child. There was only one room, but I pushed the two beds far apart, and that is how we lived. I went out to my classes, and she took care of the cooking and cleaning. Everything in the room was perfectly kept and organized. After classes, I went to the Bharatiya Vidya Bhavan to pursue my studies. Sometimes I'd come home, have lunch with Gladys, and then we would go together to Bengali Market and Triveni, and spend the afternoons and evenings there. There was so much I learnt in those days.

It was quite amazing that the landlord seemed unconcerned that Cynthia had left, Manish had disappeared without telling him anything, though the advance rent had been paid, and Gladys had moved in with me. It was quite a pleasant life, far better than what I had in Dehradun. One thing I missed though, was having my own garden, though there were beautiful gardens all over Delhi, where one could sit forever if one felt like it.

I could not forget my aim of becoming a guru, but I was not clear how to begin. I decided to start some simple meditation, one of the techniques I had learnt in Enzo's ashram, and to try and think of a plan. Both Enzo and Sundararaman had described meditation techniques to me, and both had also given me a mantra to use with the meditation. I have never revealed these mantras as I was asked not to. I chose the one given by Sundararaman. I began the practice and felt I was making some progress. Just a few days into this, I remembered Peter's Emerald Tablets. No, I wasn't interested in them, they weren't part of my path, but I believed I could set myself up more easily as a guru for foreigners, and could make more money through them too. In that context, I thought it may help me to know more about stuff like the *Tablets*. I had read very little about the Western occult in Enzo's library and I was keen to get into it more deeply, especially as the thought had come to me through meditation.

I queried the librarian at the Bharatiya Vidya Bhavan. Was there any library with books on Western mysticism and religion? He did not know of any, he said, but he did know of a bookshop that stocked books on these. And he directed me to Piccadilly Book Store. It was located in Shankar Market, and I could walk there from my usual haunt in Bengali Market or Triveni. Once I reached there and saw what it contained, I almost gave up visiting

Bharatiya Vidya Bhavan. The dark, dimly lit shop seemed to have books on every aspect of spiritualism, both Indian and Western. I occasionally bought a book or two, but there were chairs placed outside the shop, and the owner did not mind me sitting there for hours, reading. The shop was somewhat like Merlin's cave, piled high with books. I could find nothing there myself, but I just had to mention a topic, and Mr C would pull out some books for me.

I read the Gnostic Gospels, the Akashic records of Jesus' visit to India, texts on Buddhism, on the Cathars, the Knights Templar, the Rosicrucians, Hermes Trismegistus, the Bible Code, the Secret History of the World. I looked at Tarot cards and runes, and I learnt about druids, ovates and bards, black magic and white magic. Then I began to wonder—this was mainly European stuff, what about the rest of the world? There were one or two books on the Mayas, who later became so popular, but nothing on Native Americans, the indigenous people of Australia, or of Africa. I know there are all these traditions about the Mayas being the greatest ever, but as I read more I realized it didn't correspond with history. They made some good monuments but there is no evidence that they were enlightened. I tried to find out more about the Emerald Tablets, but it was several days before Mr C found a small pamphlet on it, and I was able to read a brief account of the Tablets. Meanwhile, I continued my reading. I read about John Dee and Alistair Crowley, and through the White Lodge and Madame Blavatsky, I once again came to nineteenth-century developments in India.

Finally, when I got the Emerald Tablets and read them, I felt the matter was certainly mysterious, but was it ancient? It seemed to be in the style of what I had read by Blavatsky, could it have been written by her, or one of her followers? The ten tablets spoke of reincarnation, magic and power, but were difficult to understand. Later, Mr C gave me a different book on the Emerald Tablet of Hermes, a short and even more mysterious document.

By now, of course, though I wasn't an expert, I knew something about many different religious and philosophical systems. Of all I had read, I felt that the ideas of the Upanishads that I had started my studies with in Enzo's ashram, and Advaita Vedanta based on them, were the closest to the truth, that is, that there is only One Reality, and that the same Reality is within each one of us. I didn't like the concept of 'obedience,' that occurred in the Tablets, or the concept of Masters with superior wisdom. To me it was more acceptable that the true Self within each person is equal to the highest, to have Masters who were intermediaries was a denial of one's individuality and personal power. To cut it short, I could understand the hold the Emerald Tablets had had on Peter; they too, pointed a way forward to the seeker, but somehow they didn't appeal to me. I read through them to gain more knowledge of religions of the East and of the West, and of things beyond and outside traditional religion, I found the words beautiful, but still I felt there was nothing to equal the wisdom of our own texts.

I wanted to be a guru, and I had started reading with that aim, but reading all this was also a joy and a pleasure for me. Immersing myself in these books, my mind was awhirl with thoughts and ideas. Occasionally I thought of visiting Sundararaman and pursuing my yoga studies with him and along with that, continuing to read fascinating and mysterious books like these. But away from the bookshop, my main purpose was almost constant in my heart and mind.

I began to believe that in this aim I was only following my destiny, the one predicted by the swami who blessed me at my birth.

***

Many Europeans visited the bookshop. Some came regularly and greeted me as I sat there reading. Mr C not only charged me nothing for reading there, but even gave me tea and sometimes snacks.

One day he asked me: 'So what is your aim, Devdarshan? Are you seeking enlightenment? These books will not give it to you. They provide outer knowledge, while for that you need an inner search.'

'Enlightenment is far away,' I replied. 'But I already teach yoga. I am studying to become a more broad-based teacher, perhaps a spiritual authority.'

'You want to be a guru then,' he responded and my heart skipped a beat.

'How did you know?' I blurted out.

'I sit amidst all these books, day after day, year after year. I haven't read them all, but I do know something about each of them. Maybe I have imbibed some wisdom from them. But I cannot make you a guru.'

Listening to our conversation was another regular visitor to the bookshop. He raised his head from what he was reading and pronounced, 'There is a very simple first step to becoming a guru. You wear gerua and you change your name.'

'Doesn't a guru need to initiate me?' I thought of the guru living in the mountains near Enzo's ashram. I knew he would never give me diksha, initiation. He knew that I was not spiritual enough.

'I will give you a sort of initiation,' said the unknown man. 'You could say that god has directed me to do so. I can't exactly give you diksha, but I will give you a new name, that will be enough for you to start off with. This is Shankar Market. As you know, Shankar is a name of the god Shiva. And you must also know about that greatest of philosophers, Shankara. Now you are Swami Shankarananda Giri.'

'Giri?' I queried. I knew, of course, that giri meant mountain.

'There are several swami sects,' said he. 'One of them is Giri. You are from the mountains, hence Giri is appropriate for you. Now just begin wearing gerua. Take an inner vow of sannyas if you like. And you are done.'

I liked the sound of it.

'But who are you?' I asked. 'Can I know your name? And how do you know I am from the mountains?'

'I'll tell you someday,' said the man, as he closed his book and walked away. I had seen this man often before, though I had not spoken to him. He was tall and broad-shouldered, with a military bearing, and always sat reading a Sanskrit text. Mr C was impressed. 'You know Dev,' he said, 'all the books say that when you are ready, the guru appears. I think he was a saint in ordinary clothes. A true guru. And now you are one.'

'But who is he?' I asked Mr C.

'I don't know much about him,' said Mr C. 'He has never revealed his name, but when he first starting visiting my shop he had told me he had once been in the army. He had taken part in the 1965 war, and seeing the dead and wounded had horrified him. He did not tell me exactly how, but he left the army, and walked into the mountains.

As you know there are many sannyasis meditating in and wandering through the Himalayas. He began to travel with one of them, but, he said, one day this man just walked into a swirling mist and disappeared. Before he did so, he turned towards him and said a few words: "Adhyayan kijiye. Parishram kijiye" (Study hard. Make an effort). He came down to the plains to do so.'

'Should I follow what he said? Does it make any sense?'

'I don't know if you should or you shouldn't. That is up to you. But he is some sort of a holy man, so it would not be wrong to take his advice.'

Was it so simple? Could I now proclaim I was a guru? Should I start wearing gerua? Inwardly, a kind of excitement arose in me, and I decided to do so. There were innumerable cloth and tailor shops in Shankar Market. Mr C directed me to a shop where I could buy white cloth, get it dyed the right colour, and even get two pairs of kurta-pyjamas made with the material. It took only three days for it to be ready. I added a thick beige sweater and a brown shawl to the outfit.

I took the clothes home and decided to wear them the next day. I put them on and looked in the mirror. I was no longer Devdarshan Mangal, I was now Swami Shankarananda. The change was astounding, and I almost did not recognize myself. Gladys looked up calmly, glanced at me, and carried on sewing. Did she think I was trying on some fancy dress? I was irritated. The next morning I went out wearing my new clothes and she looked confused, but said nothing. I reached the yoga class in my outfit.

All along the way I was impressed by the change in everyone's approach. 'Sit here, Swamiji,' said the bus conductor, as he gave me his own seat in an already crowded bus. He refused the money I offered for the ticket, and remained standing the rest of the way. Almost everyone who got on the bus greeted me with 'Pranam Swamiji,' or 'Namaste Swamiji,' and many of them touched my feet and I blessed them. Some pressed money into my hand, or put it directly into my cloth bag in which I kept my wallet, pen, and a book or two.

Could clothes make such a difference? I was filled with love for all these people and for India. What a wonderful country this was, where such respect was given to gurus and saintly people! The stranger who gave me my new name, maybe he was god himself, descended on earth. Or maybe, I thought, he was the one who had given me my name at birth. Of course, I had hoped for that from the guru who lived in the cave, but that was not intended to be. But surely, there was something mysterious about all this? That morning I felt so blessed, that I vowed not to seek power, but to follow Sundararaman's advice and become a true teacher and a real saint.

I reached my class early, but as the yoga students came in, each one greeted me reverentially, and most touched my feet too. When all seven students had arrived, I told them that I had taken sannyas, and an unknown saint had initiated me. Their attitude towards me too changed markedly once I had made this pronouncement. Some of the women had earlier been quite condescending, perhaps because of their wealth, and also because they believed they belonged to a higher social class. But now there was total respect from everyone. In the second class the same thing happened. And all day I felt blessed, as if I were surrounded by light and grace.

On the way home, the problem of Gladys began to

trouble me. It was true I had not slept with her and had no intention of doing so, but would anyone believe me if she continued to live with me? If others came to know, I would soon be discredited as a sannyasi. Yes, I was naïve and sincere at that time, not as I became later. Should I ask the landlord for a separate room for Gladys? I knew one was available on the ground floor. But then I would have to pay the rent for both.

When I reached my room though, I got a shock. It was locked! Gladys never went anywhere, and I did not have a key with me. I had a fit of panic, thinking that perhaps something had happened to her. Accident? Hospital? As my mind raced, I saw a small piece of paper tucked into the lock. I pulled it out, and found a one-line note. 'Key with Mrs Bhatnagar.' I knew the Bhatnagars lived on the ground floor though I had never spoken to them. I rushed down and rang their bell. Mrs B opened the door. She looked me up and down and said, 'Oh! So that is why she left!'

'What do you mean?' I responded, having forgotten that I was dressed in saffron clothes.

'You have taken sannyas,' she said, and repeated, 'that is why she left.'

My words almost echoed hers. 'What do you mean she left?'

'Well she took a bag with her, so she has left you. And that too with another man.'

'Did Manish return for her?' That seemed a plausible explanation to me. Perhaps he hadn't got married, and had convinced his parents that he would marry Gladys. But Gladys herself wasn't keen on him, so why had she gone? 'Not Manish, Mangalji,' Mrs B's grating voice cut through my thoughts. 'Or should I now call you Swamiji? The other man who visited her everyday.'

A man who visited her every day? I stared at her, speechless.

'Anyway, I am sure you know all about it,' she continued. 'Here's your key'. And she pushed it into my hand, and closed the door in my face. I kept standing there, the key in my hand. I did not know what to think. Slowly I made my way upstairs and unlocked the door. It looked as if all Gladys' things were gone. And on the table was a folded paper. I picked it up. A letter from Gladys.

'Dear Dev,' I read, 'Thanks for your kindness to me. I know you do not love me and you will be quite happy that I have left. I am going away with my friend Sanjay. Sanjay had been helpful to me when I arrived in India, and had brought me to Manish's door. He knew where I stayed and we became good friends after Manish left. When I told him about your new way of dressing, he assured me that now there was no place in your life for me, and it was time to leave you. Affectionately, Gladys.'

I sat down holding the letter. It took me a while to digest. I had thought Gladys was like a child, someone to be protected. But all along, she was a woman, deceiving me with someone else. It was true that the problem of what to do about her had been resolved, but this was not the right way. Were all women deceitful like this? Cynthia, and now Gladys. The sense of beauty and grace I had in the morning, was replaced once again by a burning anger. I made some tea and tried to calm down. The anger ebbed, but still smouldered.

I took off my saffron swami robes and changed into ordinary clothes. Those clothes had led Gladys to leave. They would define my life and make me a prisoner. Right then I decided I could be Swami Shankarananda, a guru and teacher, without wearing them. Yes, it had been wonderful to be greeted by everyone with such reverence. But it placed me in a mould of preconceived ideas, about what I should do, and what I should be. Surely a guru should be unconfined, a free spirit, beyond boundaries?

I left my room in my normal clothes and took a bus to Triveni. There in the café I had a good meal of parathas and raita, and walked to Piccadilly Book Store. I sat in one of the chairs outside, and picked up a book at random.

Mr C came over to me. 'You look depressed,' he commented.

'I need a change,' I responded. 'I want to go away somewhere.' These words came out of me without thinking.

'Wearing gerua did not suit you?'

'I don't think so—it had some plus points, but it was very limiting.'

'Why don't you go abroad and teach there?'

I remembered that this had been one of Cynthia's plans. But without her, how could I go?

I put my question to Mr C.

'It's not difficult,' he replied. 'Apply for a passport. Many foreigners visit this shop. One of them may be ready to help you. Or you could just go as a tourist.'

Sitting there, reading a book on the Cathars, I mulled over the idea. But as I became immersed in the book, I forgot myself and my problems. There was so much to know in the world. After an hour or so, I got up to leave. I had a feeling that no one could understand the divine, if at all it existed. That is why there were so many different religions, and within the religions, so many different sects. God was One, they all believed, yet each sect, or even each group or person, had a different view of what god was, and of the path to the divine. Surely, if god existed, everyone would have the same, or at least, similar, views? That there was such a vast divergence of opinion, was an indication to me of the absence of god, of there being any truth in his existence. I had thought Advaita held the secret to the supreme truth, but what was my reason for thinking that? Was it because both Enzo and Sundararaman had talked about it? Or because of its impeccable logic? All those were part of it, but I think Advaita appealed to me because of its concept of equality. There was no one high or low, no hierarchy, no 'masters', no 'children', no one superior or inferior.

I continued with my classes and thought over this for the next few days. When I first went to the classes after discarding my sannyasi's clothes, I had thought of an explanation to give them. I said that though I was now a sannyasi and I had been given the name Swami Shankarananda, I believed that a true sannyasi should not always reveal himself. He should move through the world unknown, to understand the people and their problems better. They accepted this and continued to treat me with respect.

During those days I went over all I had studied in Enzo's ashram too. I felt god, as we knew it, was a product of the mind, an attempt to explain the inexplicable, the wonders of nature, the seasons, suffering, and death. Each religion tried to search for logical or fanciful reasons for the origin of life and its meaning. The Buddha searched deep into these questions, and whatever answers he found, he refused to speak about them, and never even mentioned god. I had become interested in the Buddha recently, when I came across the *Digha Nikaya* in Piccadilly Book Store. In fact, the *Pasadika Sutta*, which forms part of this, records that he commented on the different beliefs people had, and how each one thought they were right. The Buddha said he would not reveal that which should not be revealed. He just tried to provide guidance for a way of life that would end personal suffering. Perhaps he had discovered the truth, and knew that god did not exist.

But his followers found this unacceptable, and began to invent god and deities and hidden mysteries, pretending these were the Buddha's secret teachings. To some extent, Mahavira's followers did the same. Maybe there was some ultimate source from which this plethora of beliefs emerged. Once again, I came to the conclusion that Advaita made the most sense, at least intellectually, though I had neither explored its concepts fully, nor internalized its ideas. But I could still be a guru, and teach what others before me had taught.

I tried to reassess my feelings and thoughts. I was already a yoga teacher, I had attained one of my aims. Why did I want to be a guru, to assume the persona of Swami Shankarananda, what did I expect to gain? Maybe there were some complex motives that I wasn't fully aware of, but I could analyze some of my reasons.

Firstly, I really wanted to teach and to share my knowledge, and I was already doing that. Secondly, I wanted power. I did not want to be in the helpless position I was in when Gita died. Of course, I was helpless even with Cynthia and Gladys' desertion of me, but I was not so emotionally involved with them. I wanted power over women, and over other people too—I would decide every relationship, I would reject them. No one must ever reject me again. Wearing gerua, I saw how everyone revered me. It was a good feeling, and I believed I could get it as a guru without wearing those formal clothes. Being a guru was far superior to being an English teacher in some small-town school. But beyond these reasons, there were some I just could not fathom or define. There was something in me that said—become a guru, you are a guru. This seemed to be a feeling similar to that which made me feel separate and special from childhood. Once again, I wondered if it had something to do with the swami who gave me my name when I was born, and that unknown man who named me in Shankar Market. Could they have been the same person? Was it my destiny to be a guru? Would I be able to follow Sundararaman's advice and be a true guru? Even then it seemed unlikely to me, though at that time I had done nothing that could be considered wrong, and I did not know what the future held. But when there was within me, both anger and a desire for power, coupled with the lack of belief in god, how could I ever become a true guru? I liked the words from *Invictus*, 'I am the master of my fate, I am the captain of my soul,' and in those days I began to believe that I was.

***

Nityananda

Who was that mysterious man who suggested Dev become a guru? Did Dev ever meet him again? I thought I would go and ask him. Somehow, I had never heard of Piccadilly Book Store, on my next visit to Delhi I would see if it still existed in Shankar Market. And why did he never use all that he read there in his talks? After so many years he still remembered some details.

I visited him in the afternoon. He was lying in bed, propped up with pillows, his breathing was laboured. He looked like an old man, yet according to his story, he was just around fifty-five. Dev managed a smile when he saw me. I knew he was not feeling well, still I posed the question to him. Had he ever again met that man who had named him Shankarananda so long ago in Delhi? Who was he? 'I never met him again, I don't know who he was,' said Dev. 'He was like that unknown guru who named me at birth. I never saw or heard from either of them again.'

Then I asked him my next question. Why had he never used all that he learnt from the books he read at the time? His answer shocked me. 'Of course I used it, Nitya,' he responded. 'That was what I taught my Inner Circle.' The Inner Circle! Dev had told me about this once, I recollected, but I hadn't paid much attention. They were a special group who gathered together when he visited Sparks, or perhaps elsewhere too.

He looked so tired that I let it go and thought I would find out more from Diana. I did not ask him anything more. Yet my mind went back to those two gurus. There are many things mysterious in the world, and certainly, they were a mystery. If these strange men, who perhaps had superior powers, had envisaged Dev's life as a guru, why had they chosen someone so flawed? Did they see some positive aspects in his nature, that should have given him the strength to choose wisely and become a true guru? Was I now veering to the other side and believing he was worse than he was?

I took some more papers he had written, and returned to the ashram.

11. Departure and Arrival

Dev's Story

I continued living in that room for the next few months, and had no more relationships. The yoga classes proceeded with the addition of a few more students. I collected the fees at the beginning of each month, and after giving the centre its share, still had a substantial amount left. I was able to save a few thousand rupees every month. Meanwhile, I applied for a passport. Four months later, the police verification was done, and soon after that I received my first passport.

Now I was on the verge of my new life. Still, I wasn't sure how to proceed. That afternoon, after my classes, I went to Piccadilly Book Store as I often did, and sat there, reading, thinking. I'd made friends with two young Americans, Madge and Bart, who also often came there to read, drink tea, and once in a way, to buy a book. Though they were always together, they had said they were not a couple, but were business partners, they imported brass items from India, and sold them in the US. That day they were there before me, and late afternoon, over a tea-break, I asked them if they knew how I could get to the US. I told them I wanted to open an ashram there. They said they would think it over and find some way for me. I could, of course, go as a tourist, but even to get a tourist visa, I needed to indicate where I was going, and to have some kind of support there.

A few days later we met again and they suggested a solution. I could marry Madge. They said they had discovered it was a simple procedure for an American to marry an Indian, through the international marriage registry office in New Delhi. Then Madge would return to the US, and I could soon follow. In a year or two I would get a green card or even citizenship, after that we would get a divorce, and I would be all set.

I couldn't figure out why they would do all this for me. They went on to explain that this was a business proposal, not an act of kindness. I was never to have any kind of relationship with Madge, except for a formal one. Madge owned some land near Sparks, Nevada, and had a cottage there where they lived in between business trips. They would help me to set up an ashram on her land. I would have to pay them for the marriage, as well as all costs, and once the place started making a profit, hand over 50 per cent of all profits. Bart had a degree in marketing, and he believed he could get me students. Once we reached the US, they would draw up a legal document regarding the financial aspects.

And I thought they were friendly, kind, and trying to help me! I would hardly be able to make a profit, if I first had to pay them such a lot. Internally, I was angry, but I just smiled and said, maybe it would work out. I would think it over and let them know, I said. Meanwhile, a plan was evolving in my head. If they had their way they would turn me into a slave, but I was not going to let that happen. I would marry Madge, I had no desire for a relationship with her, so that was not a problem, but maybe I could get her to fall in love with me? Somehow or the other, once I reached there, I would get Madge to transfer the land to me.

I felt life was guiding me to my true destiny, and I believed I would be able to outsmart them both.

Madge and I were married the next week. The marriage registrar was in Jawaharlal Nehru University, and we just needed two witnesses. Bart was one, and a student on the campus agreed to act as the other. Next, I applied for a resident visa. Madge and Bart returned to the US, while I waited for this to come through. It took around two months, based on my marriage to a US citizen. I had saved enough money for a ticket, and now I bought one on British Airways, from the airline office in the city. The route was via Dubai and London to Los Angeles. From there I had to change planes and airlines to go to Reno, which had the airport nearest to Sparks.

I was nervous. It was not about going to the US, but about the aeroplane. Not only had I never flown before, but I had never even seen a plane on the ground. Planes did not go to Dehradun in those days, and they did not fly overhead either. I had viewed them high up in the air once I began to stay in Delhi, but still they were something mysterious to me. The next day I took a bus to the airport. I wandered around a bit, and was amazed by the size of the planes parked on the ground. I went to the café upstairs, from where I could watch the planes landing and taking off. The noise was deafening. I ordered tomato soup, and as I sipped it, I had my eyes glued to the tarmac. In those days, one could just buy an entry ticket to get inside the airport, the security of later times was unknown.

In just two weeks, I would be flying in one of these planes. I had to wind up my classes and tell Mr Verma, the landlord, that I would be leaving. There was a strange sense of excitement, anxiety and tension. I did not know what the future would bring. I remembered reading India's first prime minister, Jawaharlal Nehru's words when India gained independence: 'The appointed day has come, the day appointed by destiny.' The day before I left, these words played themselves in my head, over and over again. The flight was leaving at 11 p.m. It would reach London at 7 a.m., London time. I had to wait a few hours at Heathrow and then change planes for the flight to Los Angeles. I knew in theory about time differences, but still it was intriguing to discover that I would be going back in time, well to some extent at least, as India was about twelve hours ahead of Los Angeles.

I must have flown a thousand times since then, but I still remember that first flight. The thrill when the plane lifted off the ground, flying above the clouds the next day, the sunlight on white clouds, the lights of the cities below. Flying, I felt, was something like being in heaven.

***

My entry into the US was smooth, there was just a perfunctory glance at my passport and documents, after which the officer asked where my wife was. I said she was getting our house ready at Sparks and would meet me there. He saw I had an onward ticket to Reno International Airport, and stamped and handed back my passport, saying, 'Welcome to the US'. Right then I began thinking about when I would become a US citizen and rid myself of Madge.

I had to wait three hours at Los Angeles airport for the connecting flight to Reno. I leaned back in one of the chairs, marvelling at the fact that I was actually in the US. I would have liked to get a cup of coffee but did not want to spend my dollars. I had applied for foreign exchange and managed to get $200 to take with me, which I had bought with the last of my money. One dollar had cost me ten rupees.

After what seemed like ages, the flight was called, and I was on my way to Reno. As the plane landed, anxiety rose in me again. What awaited me here? As I had already gone through customs and immigration at LA, I only had to walk out of the airport after collecting my suitcase. I found Bart waiting for me. He greeted me, shook my hand, and asked me to wait while he brought his van around. 'Where's Madge?' I asked, as I got into the front seat next to him. 'Madge is supervising some construction work that we are doing, to get the yoga centre started.'

'I have to thank you for all the trouble you are taking. It's great to be here!'

Bart's reply was dry and matter-of-fact. 'It's a business deal, Dev. Don't forget that. We'll be recovering both cost and profit from you.'

Anxiety rose in me again. 'But suppose it doesn't work? Suppose we don't make profits, and I can't repay you?'

'We have worked it all out,' he said. 'I have had a legal contract drawn up, and you can go over it and sign it.'

After an hour's drive, we reached Madge's land on the outskirts of Sparks. The land area was quite large, and there was a small cottage at one end. I could see some construction going on at the far end, but we went straight into the cottage. Madge was waiting for us there at the door. 'I am getting tea ready, Dev,' Madge said, as she ushered me in. 'I know you would love some after your long journey. Have a wash first if you like, Bart will show you to your room.'

The front door led into a large sitting room. The walls were pale grey, and there was a sofa and matching chairs upholstered in bright yellow. The curtains were patterned in grey and yellow. A small high table held a grey and yellow Chinese vase. I guessed the rest of the décor was designed around the vase. The vase was a beautiful one, with muted colours, but the yellow in the room was so bright it hurt my eyes.

Bart showed me my room, which had blue walls, mauve curtains, a single bed with a solid blue bedspread, a bedside table with a lamp and a clock, and another table and chair. It was neat and clean, but once again the colours jarred, the blue too bright. I had a quick wash and joined Bart and Madge in the sitting room. A tea tray was set out, along with a plate of biscuits. 'I made these cookies myself,' said Madge. Cookies? My tired and fuddled brain took a while to remember that Cynthia too called biscuits, 'cookies'. Must be an American thing. Suddenly I was absolutely dropping with tiredness. I finished the tea and ate one biscuit. My eyes were closing. 'You'd better sleep,' Bart said. 'It's jet-lag. Madge is just going to make dinner, we'll talk later.' I didn't know any longer what he was talking about. I got to my room, and just managed to take off my shoes and lie down on the bed, as I fell into a deep, deep, sleep. I didn't wake for dinner. Bart later said he tried to rouse me, but I wouldn't stir. I woke sometime during the night. As I slowly gained consciousness in that dark room, I remembered—I was in the United States! Or was I dreaming that I was there? I put the table-lamp on. The clock told me it was 3.30 a.m. A moments' panic and then a thrill of joy surged through me. I had reached here! Though it was the month of July, I was cold. I had fallen asleep on top of the bedspread, and now still fully dressed, I got under the blankets, dozed and slept again, though not so deeply.

When I woke, I saw that it was almost 8 a.m., and I went to get dressed.

The previous day, along with my room, Bart had showed

me the long tub, shower, and the hot- and cold-water taps. There was no mug or bucket, no way to have a bath the way I was used to, but I managed a shower. Obviously sitting in dirty water in the tub was out of the question. I'd also had to use toilet paper, something I didn't like, but at least I knew about it from my stay in the IIC.

Wearing fresh clothes, and feeling clean and rested, I went into the sitting room. Bart and Madge were sitting close together and talking. There were empty plates and cups in front of them. They broke off their conversation when they saw me, and looked up.

'Welcome, Dev,' said Madge, getting to her feet and dusting off her dressing gown. 'I'll bring you some breakfast,' and she moved towards the kitchen. Bart was still in his pyjamas, unshaven.

Breakfast consisted of toast, butter, peach jam, and orange juice, followed by coffee. I thought soon I would teach Madge to make an Indian breakfast. After breakfast, Bart said he would show me around. He had changed into jeans and a T-shirt, though he still looked unwashed.

Ten rooms in a row were being constructed at one end of the land. They were connected by a corridor in front, and had bathrooms at both ends. A long passage led off from the corridor and opened into a hall, where Bart said I could hold discussions, yoga classes and lectures. He explained that we could not expect many local people to come to learn yoga. 'They are mostly ranch owners and farmers, or shopkeepers, and probably wouldn't be interested,' he said. But, he added, he expected to get a good response from some other areas and cities. He said he would discuss the financial aspects later that day. The buildings would be ready within two weeks. The framework was in place, the electricity and plumbing was almost done. I was amazed to see the tough workmen dressed in shirts and jeans, clothes that looked a lot better than my own outfit. Such a contrast to our skinny, poorly dressed and underfed labourers back in India. And these workmen were speaking English—there wasn't that huge language divide that we had. Later, I learnt that there were different kinds of divides, Hispanics, African-Americans, but on that day it looked idyllic to me.

The type of construction too surprised me. There were no bricks, badarpur, sand, or cement, just some flimsy-looking boards that were being fixed together. 'It's prefabricated,' Bart explained.

As I gazed at it, it seemed promising, even magical, my new land, my new life. But my euphoria only lasted till the evening, when Bart showed me the contract he had drawn up. When I saw it, I was desperate, I felt trapped. The contract said I was in debt to him for $100,000! This would be a large amount at any time, but in the '70s, it was absolutely exorbitant. In India, the maximum I had earned in one month with my yoga classes was Rs 4,000. As a schoolteacher I earned one-tenth of that. One hundred thousand dollars was about ten lakh rupees! This was a lot in those days, and today would amount to fifty lakhs. How would I ever pay him back? I said as much to Bart. I told him I would have to go back to India if that was what he demanded of me, and then I asked him how he reached that figure. He said that $50,000 was Madge's charge for marrying me and providing me documents to enable me to come to the US. And the other 50,000 was for the buildings. I looked again at the document. It said nothing about the ownership of the buildings. I would bring in the money, give them 50 per cent of it, and the land and the buildings would still be theirs. I was almost shaking with shock when he said that in addition, I would have to pay them $5,000 every month for board and lodging. But when I said I would return to India instead, he said that if I tried to do that without paying them what I owed, he and Madge would have me put in jail for illegally entering the US through deception and a fraudulent marriage. If I tried to escape and returned to India without telling them, they would have me extradited!

Maybe it was all bluff, but I was afraid. When I kept quiet and said nothing more, he patted me on the back. 'Don't worry,' he said, 'you will soon make adequate profits. It just seems like a lot to you right now.' I took a few deep breaths. Maybe he was right. Maybe it would all work out.

The next two weeks passed pleasantly enough. Bart took me to a big supermarket, and loaned me money to buy the few things I needed. It was a small addition to what I already owed them.

Finally, the buildings were ready. Furniture, sheets, towels, curtains, and mats for yoga had to be bought. I was to pay an additional amount for all that too. The furniture was very basic, but it all looked neat and clean. And there were six people booked for the very next weekend! Bart explained that he was charging $1,000 per person for a weekend stay, of two days and two nights. That included accommodation, classes and food. A third night with dinner was an extra $300.

The first weekend came. Four people stayed an extra night. That was $7,200 in one week! I felt more cheerful. My classes consisted of simple asanas and pranayama, some lectures and an evening discussion. There was free time in the afternoon. We needed a good library, but at present there was none. Madge cooked and served them food, but refused to give them vegetarian meals, as I requested. 'I know what people will like,' she said. Cleaning, making the beds, and all the other work was done by Bart. Madge and Bart took $500 per person for their weekend work, as they said there was a lot of effort involved. Perhaps that was okay, but in addition they took 50 per cent of the remaining profit. This too was in that dreaded contract, in small print. My share was only $2,100. Bart handed over $450 to me, he said for any expenses I might have. Fifty dollars had been spent earlier on my shopping. And $1,600 was kept towards the first month's payment to them. The month was almost over. I still owed $3,400 for my board and lodging, apart from the basic $100,000 and the expenses on the furniture and curtains. My debts had increased.

The second month seemed much better. In fact, we earned a total of $25,000. With the expenses being $7,500 for Madge/Bart, I expected half of $17,500, that was $8,750. With that I could pay off the boarding and lodging dues, and begin to reduce my huge debt to them. In a few months I could perhaps expect a profit.

But this was not to be. Bart often left on business trips, and came back with bills for things he had bought or ordered, and the cost of all this was added to my existing debt. A well-equipped kitchen was constructed in the yoga centre, and then a laundry room. There were additional building costs, as well as the costs of a dish-washer, clothes washer and dryer, cooking range, coffee maker, plates, dishes, and so much else. Every month there seemed to be something new to buy. I wasn't able to argue with him because if I tried to protest, he immediately revived his threat of putting me in prison. I knew Madge too would be involved if they accused me, but I didn't think I could fight a battle in the US courts. I knew hardly anything about the country, and nor did I know a single person there. I knew from the time we agreed to a deal in New Delhi that they would exploit me, but I hadn't realized the extent to which they would go.

Those were the days before cell phones, and there was just one landline in the main cottage. The next expense was another new room in the yoga centre, next to the guest rooms. This would have an extension phone, and would be the sitting room. It would have a shelf of books too, as well as chairs, a couple of tables, lamps, sofas and a TV.

I carried on with teaching, profits were being made, but I was getting none of it. Five months had passed. Bart gave me 500 dollars every month for my expenses, and this too was added to my debt, along with the boarding and lodging costs and all expenses for the new buildings and fittings. A new residential course was started, a ten-day yoga course, costing $2,500. I did enjoy this and the other classes, but I was in despair about the future. How could this go on? I had read a few Greek myths in my days in Delhi, and now I compared myself with Sisyphus, incessantly trying to climb a mountain, only to slide down to the bottom again.

I thought of confiding in one of my students and asking for help, but I did not know what to say. To them, I was an Indian yoga teacher, married to Madge, with Bart as the administrator. In fact, I was never in close proximity to Madge, while she and Bart shared a room. They lived like a married couple, though legally Madge was married to me. I guessed they were not just business partners, but had a close and intimate association. Yet recently, in the last month or two I had begun to see and sense some changes in their relationship. They used to be quite close, sitting together companionably at meals and in the evenings. While Madge cooked, Bart helped in laying the table, clearing the dishes and in washing up. They worked together in the guest cottages, and I had seen them laughing together, and Bart affectionately putting his arm around her shoulders. But now things were different. Both had stiff faces and were hardly ever together except at meals, and when they retired to their room at night. Sometimes Bart did not appear at all at lunch, saying that he had errands to do in town. On those occasions I found Madge being more friendly. She smiled and talked with me, something she never did if Bart was around. Once she opened a cupboard and gave me a packet of delicious chocolates—'to snack on when you are reading,' she said. Another time she made an apple pie, and when I praised it, she said I could eat more of it whenever I liked, and showed me how to use the microwave to warm it up. One day, on the pretext of looking at my watch, which was just an ordinary one from India, she held my wrist in her hand. I backed away as soon as I found it polite to do so. I wasn't attracted to Madge. She was short and stocky, her brown hair was wispy, and frankly I was afraid of Bart, who seemed to be becoming increasingly sullen.

To keep away from both of them, I began spending more time in the guests' sitting room, where the phone extension had been installed. Looking at the phone, I wondered if I could make a call to India. But who would I call? Hardly anyone in those days had phones in their houses. Mr Gosain did have one, but what would I say to him?

Sometimes I would just pick up that extension phone,

and hold it near my ear. I would imagine that I was talking to someone in India, though I didn't even know if there was a direct dial system from the US to India. Certainly, one could not dial the US from India. In those days one had to book a call, even to another city within the country. Unless one was a government official or held an important position, one could not get a landline easily, if at all. An application for a phone took several years to be granted. For a long-distance call, we waited near a PCO, or at a friend's house, someone who was lucky enough to have a phone. After booking the call, it took several hours to get to speak to someone in another city. Then too, one had to shout at the top of one's voice to be heard at the other end. After three minutes the operator would cut in, and say the call was over, and one would desperately shout, 'please extend, please extend,' trying for another three minutes. Remembering all this, I was nostalgic for my country. Whatever the problems there, it was my home, and I longed to go back.

One day, when there were no students around and I picked up the extension, I heard Bart's voice. I was about to put it down, when I heard him say, 'Oh, he's thoroughly in our power now.' I wondered if he was talking about me, and held on, quietening my breath, so that he would not know I was there. A very familiar female voice responded to Bart. 'That is good, Bart,' it said. 'He is our golden goose, and we'll get all we can from him.'

I knew that voice. It sounded like Cynthia, though I had never heard her on the phone. But could it be? Bart was speaking again. 'The only thing that worries me, Cynthia,' I heard, 'is that I can see Dev is getting desperate. Should I allow him to make profits for a while?'

'No!' Cynthia's voice was hard and cold. 'That won't help us. And in case he starts protesting or trying to contact anyone, you know what we had planned.'

'I don't like that plan, Cynthia. I've told you that. We could get caught. Besides it's not right.'

'We can wait a while more,' Cynthia said, 'but we have to go through with the plan. One day he will lose his inhibitions, confide in someone and create problems for us. We won't get any more profits, and we may even have to pay him back. He could try to take over everything himself. He's not stupid. It is just that he is in a new country and still unsure of himself.'

'He's entered here on a valid passport, Cynthia,' said Bart. 'If he disappears there may be a search for him. And if his body is found here, we will be in trouble.'

'No one will search for him, and his body will never be found. My plan is foolproof. Wait a few months if he is cooperating, or carry out our plan sooner if you suspect he is not.'

'Frankly, Cynthia, the plan is far too dangerous. Maybe if we give him just a small portion of our profits, he will carry on without questioning us. Gradually, we'll all benefit, and it could continue for our lifetime. Are you trying to take revenge on him for the quarrel you once had? I am sure you were never really in love with him.'

'No dark-skinned Indian is ever going to get the better of me,' said Cynthia, and I heard her slam the phone down. Carefully I replaced the receiver though my hand was trembling. I needed to think, but the first thing was to get out of that room, in case Bart suspected I had been listening and came to look for me. I quickly walked down the corridor, entered the yoga hall, sat down in padmasana, and closed my eyes as if in meditation. My mind was racing. Why were they planning to kill me? Could Cynthia have loved me and had I hurt her that deeply by refusing to go along with her plans? But when I had wanted to marry her, she had refused. Cynthia and I had parted ways, and I knew she was furious that I had not given in to her demand to keep most of the profits from the yoga classes for herself, but surely a revenge like this was absurd? What did she mean 'dark-skinned'? I was quite fair! How did Bart know Cynthia? Was their meeting me and offer of marriage planned by her?

Bart entered the room. I held my breath and kept my eyes shut. 'In deep meditation, Dev?' his voice broke through my thoughts. I opened my eyes. Somehow, I was able to speak normally. 'Not deep enough, Bart,' I said. 'I have been sitting here for the last one hour, trying to enter into samadhi, but I haven't succeeded.'

'I just came to tell you to come for lunch in half an hour.'

'Okay,' I said, and smiled at him, though I hardly felt like smiling. Fear was in my heart, my stomach muscles were tense, but I had to control my feelings.

***

After a while I went in for lunch. I should add something about my meals, and way of life in that cottage. As I said earlier, I preferred vegetarian food for myself and the students, but Madge refused to listen. Madge made good bread, biscuits and pies, but the rest of her food was not to my liking. Meals consisted of bread, boiled or roast vegetables, and roast meat. Initially I had tried to suggest that I would cook my own meals, or show her how to cook what I liked, but she would not allow me into the kitchen. Mostly I ate whatever she served, including the meat. I guessed I was eating beef. I was not superstitious, but sometimes I felt all the problems I was facing were because of this, because I was going against my traditions and religion.

Anyway, that day I ate as usual, not wanting to indicate that anything was wrong. It was Friday, and a new batch of students would arrive, some at night, some the next morning, but I had the afternoon to myself. Going into my room, I sat at the table and tried to analyze what I had heard. As Bart himself had said, there would be long-term profits if we continued as partners. What then was the point of depriving me of all money as they were doing, which would ultimately lead to some kind of crisis? What could be the point in killing me, their 'golden goose'? Or was I meant to hear that conversation, feel afraid, and not ask for my share? Rationally, I thought that was the most likely explanation. After all, Bart knew that I often sat in the room where the telephone extension was. But I just couldn't be sure. I also did not know how or why Cynthia was connected. I would have to figure out the relationship between them. It would seem that Bart and Madge's approach to me was planned, that they had been in touch with Cynthia. What had I done to her that was so terrible, to merit this kind of revenge? Or was there another reason for it, some sort of plot to make more money?

Gradually anger replaced my fear. And a thought came to me that I had never had before. They were either planning to kill me, or to scare me into thinking they would. Perhaps I should kill them instead? As this thought entered my head, I welcomed it, feeling a kind of exhilaration. It would solve all my problems, but I had to think about it carefully. How would I kill them, and how would I ensure that no one suspected me? I would also have to destroy that contract, and somehow get hold of this property. Without their presence, I could run this centre in a wonderful way, and make good profits. I already had permission to reside in the US. After some time, as I had planned, I could become a citizen.

Briefly, a memory of Sundararaman flashed through my mind. How shocked he would be at my thoughts! Ahimsa was absolutely the first rule of the principles of Raja Yoga that he had taught me. I knew there was a big difference between wanting to kill someone, and actually doing it. I had to think calmly, forget such ideas, and look at other options. I thought about this over the next few days. What were my options? Again and again I went over them in my head. If I protested and tried to leave, they may put me in jail, as they had threatened, or if they had violent plans, they could kill me. I did not know much about US law, but I did not think that it would support me. There was that contract too to think about. Was it a proper legal document? If so, it may be registered somewhere, and destroying this copy may not help.

Was there someone I could ask for help? I didn't think anyone in India could help me. In the US the only people I had some contact with were my students. I went over each of them in my mind, and I thought of one possibility—Mark. Mark had come three times for weekend courses. He seemed interested in proceeding on the path of yoga, and asked a number of questions. Though he used the name Mark, his real name was Marco, and he was of Italian origin. We had had a few personal conversations and I had told him about Enzo, though he hadn't told me much about himself, except that his parents had emigrated to the US when he was a child, and that he grew up in Brooklyn. Ten days later, Mark was due to come for his fourth course. Could I confide in him? Get his advice? He had said he was an accountant, but he would know some lawyers, or at least something about the law. I thought I would wait for him, and make a decision on what to do after he arrived.

Nothing much happened over the next few days. As the day of his arrival approached, I was more and more sure that he was the only person I could possibly ask. I looked into myself, and felt that even if I went to jail or was threatened with death, it would be difficult, even impossible, for me to kill anyone. Thoughts and actions are not the same. In fact, it would be better to die, than to kill. Having thought that through, I realized there was no harm in telling Mark. He could not do anything worse to me than Madge and Bart could.

But a few days before Mark was to arrive there was a new development. That morning Bart had gone to town as he often did, and as I sat reading in the sitting room in the yoga centre, Madge came inside. This was unprecedented. I got up and faced her as she stood in the doorway. 'I want to talk to you about something, Dev,' she said in a soft and hesitant voice, unlike her usual self. I pulled a chair forward for her and she sank into it, looking worried and tired. I sat facing her and as she remained silent, I asked her what she wanted to talk to me about. Sitting straighter and leaning towards me, she asked, 'Are you happy here Dev?'

'I am', I replied, 'except for my mounting debts. I thought that at least by now most of my debt would have been paid off, instead it is only growing.'

'This is not how we initially planned it, Dev', she

responded. 'We wanted to make money of course, and we planned to benefit more than you, but it was not our plan to totally deprive you of profits. When we met you, Bart and I said we were business partners, but actually we have had a live-in relationship for many years. My marriage to you was only a formality, which would have been dissolved in a year or two. But somehow, though it was a mere formality, Bart felt threatened by it. He did not tell me this at first, and our relationship seemed okay. Around two months ago I came to know that Bart had a relationship with another woman. There were subtle signs—he had been going away a lot on business trips, and asking me to stay behind to take care of the yoga centre. Then there was a strange perfume on his clothes. Finally I asked him and he admitted it, but the person he was having an affair with, came as a shock to me. I think you know Cynthia. He seems to have fallen in love with her. Cynthia is now living in Reno.'

'I know Cynthia, but how do you know her?'

'Cynthia had met us in Delhi. We had all been invited to a function organized by the American embassy, and we met over cocktails and became friendly. In fact, she suggested that we get in touch with you. It had been her plan to bring you to the States and set you up as a yoga teacher, she was sure she could make good money out of you that way, but after your quarrel she couldn't bring herself to contact you again. She told us where you stayed and on one occasion Bart followed you when you left your room. It was a Sunday and you went straight to Triveni and after some time to Piccadilly Book Store. That day Bart sat a little way away reading a book, and later he asked Mr C about you. He learnt that you came there regularly, and we started visiting too. We weren't in any hurry, we were in India for six months, and then you yourself approached us. It was Cynthia who had suggested my marriage to you, and Bart had agreed it was a good idea, an easy way to bring you to the US and get us all started on a profitable venture.'

'But what has that got to do with the financial relationship between us? Why has Bart been exploiting me from the day I came?'

'I got to know the reason only recently. I could not understand it, and tried to reason with him, but he told me I did not understand finance. When I persisted he explained to me that he had huge debts. After we returned from India, but before you arrived, he had made a few trips to Las Vegas, starting gambling in the casinos and lost vast sums of money. The bookies there were threatening him, and he hoped to pay them back from the profits from the yoga centre. I loved Bart and so I went along with what he was doing.

'But even though he was not giving you any money, these profits were not enough. He started asking me to sell part of the land and give him the money. I was ready to do it, till I found out about his relationship with Cynthia. That too started soon after we returned, and she too went with him on those trips to Vegas and gambled in the casinos, but lost only small sums of money that she was able to repay. She lent Bart money to pay part of his debts, but wanted it back. Meanwhile the bookies were threatening Bart, asking for the rest of the amount. When I resisted selling the land, he accused me of having an affair with you. In the last month he has started threatening me, saying that if I don't give him the land, I will regret it.'

My mind grappled with what she was saying. 'What do you think Bart will do?' I asked.

Was she telling me that Bart and Cynthia intended to kill both her and me? The conversation I had overheard on the phone now made a little more sense, it was not just about Cynthia taking her revenge on me. Perhaps she was trying to establish control over Bart. Cynthia would not have been happy about having lent him money. Even though she was wealthy, I had seen in Delhi, how mercenary she was.

'Actually I still love Bart', she replied. 'He seems to think that you and I have more than a fake marriage together. I want you to convince him that there is nothing between us. He may get back with me. If he does that, I don't mind selling some land. I will repay Cynthia and pay off his debts. I won't sell the yoga centre cottages. I'll persuade him to give you a fair deal, and we will all benefit.'

Though, at that moment I couldn't think how I would approach Bart, I began to feel a little more hopeful. At the same time I wasn't sure what to believe. Was she sincere and telling me the truth? Or was it all part of a plan among the three of them? I thought of the chocolates Madge had given me, the apple pie, and of her holding my wrist that afternoon. And now she said she loved Bart! She seemed to read my thoughts, for she continued, 'When I learnt of his relationship with Cynthia, I actually thought of starting one with you. I tried to get friendly, but I couldn't find anything in common with you.'

I told her I would think about how to talk to Bart and what to say to him, but she would need to give me a few days. I thought I would wait for Mark to come and discuss all this with him.

Mark arrived on Friday night, for a weekend course that had twelve people. I told him I wanted to talk to him about a personal matter, and we arranged to meet in the yoga hall, the following afternoon. There was nothing unusual in this, I often met students individually, to answer specific questions or to help them with their problems.

Mark came alone to the hall the next afternoon. We both sat in padmasana, so that it looked like a meditation or pranayama session.

Then I told him the story of my life from the time I met Madge and Bart. I did not go into details of my life before that but briefly mentioned that I had been married, my wife and child had died in childbirth, and that I had then gone to Enzo's ashram. I had to tell him something about Cynthia too as she was relevant to the present story. I explained the fake marriage, how I came to the US, the contract, my increasing debts, and the phone conversation I had overheard. I did tell him that I thought I was meant to overhear it, and not that they, in fact, planned to kill me, as that would not serve any purpose. Then I told him about Madge's conversation with me. What did he think about it? How was I to go to Bart and tell him I was not involved with Madge, when Bart himself had not asked me anything?

I added that I wasn't sure whether to believe her, but even if she had communicated honestly with me, would her plan work? If Bart was in love with Cynthia, I really didn't think that anything I said would change it. Was there some legal way I could get out of the mess I was in? He said he wasn't sure, it looked difficult. But, he added, they, or at least Bart and Cynthia, seemed to be corrupt exploiters and I deserved justice. He didn't know whether or not I should trust Madge. I said that I too felt like that, but what could I do? Could Mark smuggle me out and arrange for my return to India? I would repay him, I said. He said he would think it over and see what could be done. Rather hesitantly he added that he knew certain things that I did not. He would perhaps be able to share them with me tomorrow. Then even more hesitantly, he asked, would I mind if they got killed? If I had nothing to do with it? Without thinking I replied that I would be happy if they ceased to exist. Then I stopped, saying, 'I mean...what I meant was...' Mark smiled. 'It's okay,' he said, 'let's meet again tomorrow.' We arranged to meet the next day at the same time. What could he possibly know that was relevant to my situation? I was curious, and also wished I hadn't blurted out that reply. But still, I felt better for having talked to him.

When we met the following afternoon, Mark began by saying that whether we proceeded further or not, I would have to keep what he was about to tell me, a secret. I should decide if I wanted to hear it or not. If I listened to what he had to say, and then revealed it to anyone, now or in the future, he himself would kill me.

I deeply regretted ever coming to this country. I had thought reaching here would give me money, respect, and a new life, but now it seemed my new life would start only after I had died and been reincarnated! With a sense of fatalism I accepted that my own death was possible, one way or the other, and promised Mark that I would tell no one what he said. Now Mark revealed to me that he was not making several trips here merely to learn yoga. He was a drug dealer, he was part of the mafia, his job as an accountant was a cover. He came here to sell drugs to the yoga students. He said he hoped I knew something about the mafia? I had heard of it, I said, but did not know much.

My head was reeling. I couldn't believe my ears. So the

students weren't coming because of my excellent teaching? They weren't interested in yoga? Seeing the expression on my face, Mark quickly added that only a few of the yoga students bought drugs—not all or even most, of them.

He added that Cynthia too was part of this, and it was she who had suggested he contact Bart, who, she said was desperately in need of money. 'I then came to know of the yoga centre and started learning yoga,' he said. Bart agreed to be a conduit for selling drugs to the yoga students, but as he was new to the trade, he only received a small commission. Cynthia, though, had been in the drug trade for a long time. She was a courier for the mafia, she supplied them with drugs sourced from Nepal and India and was paid highly in return. I had to interrupt, I said Cynthia had told me her life story, and about her marriage, and that it was her father who supplied her with money. Mark said Cynthia was very inventive, and told several different stories. She was an orphan, and though she had been married to Carl, the problems in the marriage arose because of her drug-dealing. All the money she acquired was through that, and not because of some rich father. Though Carl had known her from their teenage days, this was an aspect she had kept secret from him. My state of shock deepened. But I had to interrupt again. What about Enzo? I asked. Yes, he said, Enzo too was a part of it. Cynthia was one of his suppliers, but there were others too, some of them local. Several people who visited his ashram, smuggled the drugs, mainly opium and ganja, back to the US. Profits were made by all. Finally, I asked Mark why he had got into the drug trade. He said that there were a lot of Italian families in Brooklyn, and because they couldn't find jobs, many ended up dealing in drugs. He said he had avoided it, he studied hard, graduated from school, and later qualified as a CPA. He dropped his Italian name, and got a job as an accountant in a well-recognized firm. His problems began after that, he confided. One of the members of the board of directors, known as Paul, was actually Paulo, an Italian, who, he learnt later, was also a key figure in the drug mafia. Paul recruited him through a mixture of threats and enticements. He offered him a senior position in the company in the Texas branch, a salary raise, and of course a high unofficial income if he agreed to cooperate. He threatened to kidnap Mark's sister if he did not agree. Mark said he agreed in desperation, but once he had joined he made friends for the first time in his life. He knew drug-dealing was bad, but wasn't what the politicians were doing in countries across the world, worse? He said he hoped one day to retire from the drug world, and to atone for what he had done through yoga and spirituality.

I didn't know whether to believe him or not, but what choice did I have?

Mark now got to the main point. He said that he was now employed not by Paul, but by another drug lord, whose name he would not tell me. Even the drug trade, he explained, had its code of conduct, and Paul had become more and more exploitative and had been eliminated. If he told his employer that Bart was doing something devious, such as buying drugs himself from another dealer, or threatening to reveal Mark's role, the drug baron would have Bart killed. The killing would not take place here, and it wouldn't be obvious, it would look like an accident. Bart would probably be invited by the drug lord to a special function, and he would be keen to go. He would never return from that trip. But for this to be worthwhile for me, I needed to find the contract and see if it had the stamp of any lawyer or law company, or if it had just been drawn up by them. If it was the latter, I just had to destroy the contract, and there would be no trace of it. If it was registered with a law firm, I needed to give him the details of which firm it was—he would probably be able to get it destroyed, but he needed to know before initiating the plan. I explained that the contract was not as bad as the unwritten agreement by which they were continuously extracting money from me. Mark said I may be right, but the contract stated I had to pay Madge for marrying me, and that could land me in prison. Also, if there was a copy of it somewhere, it might lead to suspicion falling on me. Once I had another look at it, he would proceed with the plan if I wanted him to. What about Madge? I asked. Did he think she could be trusted? As she was closely associated with Bart would she have to be killed too? If Bart was not around, would she run the ashram in a better way, and share the profits with me? Mark said that I needed to decide. Did I think that Madge and I could have a real marriage? If so, she could be spared. A decision had to be made soon, as it wouldn't be possible to wait and see, there couldn't be two accidents one after the other.

I realized that if I said yes, I would be responsible for murder. But I felt trapped, there was no other way out. I felt confused by all he had told me. Paul had been eliminated, Bart could soon be killed, and perhaps Madge too, I could hardly take it in. I stalled and asked Mark what was in it for him? Why would he do this? Would the drug lord have to know about me? I wondered if I was exchanging one set of exploiters for another worse set.

Mark said there were many reasons why he was ready to

do this. The first was that he loved what he had learnt from me. He wanted to go on learning, and he hoped to have a closer association with me in future. Secondly, even though he himself was involved in drug dealing, he believed Bart and Madge, as well as Cynthia, had gone too far, just as Paul had, many years ago. I had done nothing against them and did not deserve this treatment. As for my question, I did not need to be involved in drug dealing, or to meet his employer. What I did need to do, was to turn a blind eye to anything Mark did, if I chose to keep him with me and run the yoga centre on my own once Bart and Madge had been dealt with, as he could not suddenly leave the drug business. 'And that will be your choice,' Mark said. 'You are not compelled to do so. You'll pay me a salary and I'll leave my present job. I'll be your accountant, your bodyguard, your watchdog, your right-hand man. The day you don't want me, I will leave.' After all the exploitative people, I had been associated with, Mark's approach came as a relief. I didn't know if he meant what he said, or what would happen in the future. I couldn't even try to analyze what sort of person he really was. Had he been the cause for Paul's death? Was he a murderer and drug dealer from the start, or was he an innocent, hard-working man, caught up in circumstances beyond his control? I just agreed to what he said, as I felt I had no option. If things went as planned and he worked for me, I would have to accept that he would continue his drug dealing, and perhaps other illegal businesses too. There was no written agreement this time, how could there be? 'We are partners now,' Mark said, and we shook hands. 'Partners in crime,' I thought to myself. Mark gave me a phone number where I could contact him, but he said to use it only in an emergency. He asked me to remember it and not write it down anywhere, and I did so.

He left on Sunday night, after the weekend course got over. Eleven students were arriving on Wednesday for a ten-day course, there were two free days in between. My first task was to have another look at that contract. After Madge's talk with me, she showed no signs of friendship, and seemed to be avoiding me. She made sure she was never alone in the same room with me. Bart too was spending more time at home, and had stopped his town trips. I felt the best way to see the contract was the simplest. I would ask Bart if I could see it again, or even if I could have a copy. I could not go looking through their cupboards, as one of them was always around. I thought it was a reasonable request, and I made it on Monday morning. Bart was reading the newspaper. He lifted his head and stared at me. 'Why do you need to see it?' he asked.

'I've forgotten exactly what it said,' I replied. 'I need a copy of it so that I can focus on how to pay you back.'

'Okay,' he said, 'I'll get you a copy tomorrow,' and went back to his newspaper.

He was so casual about it, I started to think that all my fears were imaginary. I had to remind myself that I had actually heard that phone call. But in the middle of the night, I got a scare. I heard some sounds around midnight. I was lying in bed, but not asleep, worrying about the future. I got up and looked out of the window. I saw Bart in the back garden, he was busy digging, while Madge was standing near him. She was saying something but I couldn't hear. Somehow, I was afraid. What could they be digging at this time? It looked like a flowerbed. Why would they dig a flowerbed in the middle of the night? Or was it a grave? I got goosebumps, and felt shivery cold.

I crept out of my room and reached the sitting room. As silently as possible, I lifted the receiver and dialled the number Mark had given me. Frozen with fear, I thought this was surely an emergency. The number connected, and Mark picked up the phone almost immediately. In a whisper I told him what I had seen. Mark listened, and thought for a minute. Then he told me to go out and call them, to tell them I had woken up after hearing the phone ringing, that Mark was on the line, and wanted to speak to them urgently. Then I should return to my room and bolt the door. I did as he said. I switched on the light in the sitting room and opened the back door. Bart stood up, framed in the light of the door, a pick still in his hand. Madge looked startled. I gave them the message and quickly returned to my room. I heard Bart enter and go to the phone, while Madge tried to open my door, but I had already locked it. After a couple of minutes, I heard Bart say something to Madge, and she moved away from the door.

I took a deep breath. Yes, what they had been digging looked like a grave. Was it only to scare me? Or was it to bury me there? But surely, if that had been the plan, they should have killed me first, and dug the grave later? And why was Madge there? Had she decided that the way to win back Bart's love was to join him in a plot to kill me? Anyway, the night's actions had made it clear that I could not trust her.

***

Nothing further happened that night. I began to have paranoid thoughts about Mark being in collusion with them. I couldn't sleep at all, and rose early to bathe and dress. At 7 a.m. I heard a car pull into the drive. I couldn't see the front of the house from my room, but after a few moments I heard Mark's voice in the sitting room. I stepped out of my room. If all three were in it together, I thought, this was my last hour on earth. Somehow, I didn't care any longer, anything was better than living in fear, with the additional burden of a huge debt. There was another aspect too. It was almost in my subconscious, but I was dimly aware of it. I wanted to be saved from becoming a murderer and a criminal. And at this point, only death could save me. But death passed me by, death let me live.

As I entered Bart said, 'Mark has returned here instead of heading home to Austin. That's what he phoned last night to tell us. His car broke down, and he has given it for repair at Las Vegas. He hired a car there to come here, and will pick his own up on his way home.'

'Yes,' said Mark, before I could speak. 'I checked into a motel, but could not get to sleep. Then I thought, why not spend a couple more days with my yoga guru? I decided to drive back in the middle of the night, and phoned before I started, just to check that you were not already full. Bart said you would find space for me, so I told him I'd be here by morning.'

'It's good to have you back, Mark,' I said. I still did not know if I could trust him, though he had responded to my call, and he had come. Madge brought in some tea and biscuits, and Bart said he had got a room ready for Mark. I asked Mark if he would like some extra classes, as the students for the ten-day course would arrive at night and the following morning. He said he would like a class in the afternoon, but he wanted to rest in the morning, as the night had been exhausting.

I walked with him to his room. 'Whatever they had

planned, they will do nothing while I am here,' he said, 'so don't worry.' As I looked into his eyes, I knew Mark was a friend.

What had Bart and Madge planned? I still could not understand it, or why Madge had again joined forces with him. I avoided them in the morning, and remained in the yoga centre, though we all met at lunch. In the afternoon we had a genuine yoga class, and I taught Mark some new techniques. Bart looked in while the class was going on.

Four students were due to arrive that night, and seven the next morning. When no one turned up at night, it confirmed my suspicions, that something was definitely wrong. Mark said there was no danger to both of us that night, as Bart and Madge knew who employed him, and knew what the consequences would be if any harm came to him on their premises. But he suggested I stay in a room next to him in the yoga centre at night, and not in the cottage with them.

By morning it was clear that there was some plot or plan, as not a single student had arrived. Bart had no explanation for this. He said he didn't know why, perhaps the roads were bad, though he knew that many came by air. He hadn't gone to the airport either to fetch them from the early morning flight, as he generally did. When I asked him about this, he said all had said they would be driving down. I doubted that. There were students even from New York and Chicago, who would want to drive from there for just a ten-day course?

We had breakfast together. Mark asked me in front of them if I would like to accompany him on a trip to town, as he needed to buy a few things. I said yes, and we set off in his hired car. On the way he said it was time to deal with Bart, but I should confirm what I wanted done about Madge. She may have been pressured by Bart, and might not have had any role in his plans. I took a while thinking this over, though in retrospect I can say I was not in a rational state that day. I had gone through too much stress, too many worries over the past few months, and ever since I had seen that grave being dug I was consumed by fear. Finally, I told Mark that I did not trust Madge. I did not want to see either of them again. When we reached town, he made a lengthy call from a pay phone. Then he told me that there was a three-day fundraiser taking place in New York, in which his boss had a role. He had spoken to his boss about inviting Bart and Madge. Soon his boss would make a call to Bart, and invite them to the fundraiser in New York. Air tickets would be delivered to them, and they would leave in the evening. Bart and Madge would be put up in a hotel and would attend a number of programmes. Mark said that his boss trusted him, and if he told him they were buying from another dealer and double-crossing him, he would have them eliminated. But before that, he would himself talk to Bart and Madge. He would tell them that he knew about Bart's unfair dealings with me, and would see if Bart offered a solution or promised to change. If that was the case they could return home, if not he would inform his boss against them.

We got back in time for lunch. Madge had made no vegetables, once again there was only roast beef. It just confirmed my feeling that Madge did not care for me at all. I vowed I was eating it for the very last time. I thought that soon this would be a pure vegetarian centre and I hoped they would never return.

It was halfway through lunch that Bart said they had

an invitation to go to New York, and would be leaving in the evening. They said they hoped I would be okay on my own, after Mark left, and they would be back in a few days. I said I would be fine but I regretted that there were no students. In the evening, a taxi came for them, and they left for the airport, each carrying a small overnight bag. Mark suggested I phone each of the students who were supposed to come, ask why they hadn't, and offer a discount if they were still able to reach here, a day or two late. I started with one of the women, Patsy, whom I knew slightly as she had attended a weekend course some time ago.

'Oh Dev,' she said, as soon as I had told her who I was. 'What happened? Was your trip cancelled?' I told her there must have been some misunderstanding, as I had not been going on any trip, and I offered 25 per cent off, if she could still make it for the course. She said she would try, and perhaps could come by Friday. As I phoned the rest of the students, I learnt about Bart's call to each of them, telling them I was going to India. While Patsy thought it was a visit, most of the others had got the impression that I would not be returning to the US. Out of the eleven students, seven agreed to come. One would reach the next day, and the others on Friday. Mark said he would leave after they arrived. Later, he would phone and let me know what had been decided. He would not say anything directly, but we would use a code. If Madge and Bart were not returning, Mark would thank me for the extra class. If they were, he would ask me a question on the *Yoga Sutras* that we had been studying.

After his call, if they were not returning, I should move all my things into the room shared by Madge and Bart, and Bart's things into mine. It should look as if Madge and I had a genuine marriage, and Bart was just the administrator. But, as I pointed out, a flaw in this was that Bart and Madge had gone to New York together. How would I explain that? Mark said that in case I was questioned about this, I would have to say that I did not know why they had gone, but that they had some commitments in which I was not involved. I was to show grief at the loss of Madge, and also indicate that I had full trust in her. I listened to all Mark's instructions. As they made sense, I was determined to follow them.

Meanwhile, Mark said he would help me to locate the contract. He said most probably it was in their safe, and as he knew the combination, it would not be difficult to open it. He had watched them opening it once, and had memorized the numbers. It did not take long, and we found the contract. He looked at it closely, and said that it did not seem to be the work of a law firm. Probably Mark had drawn it up himself. I had signed it; thus it was just an agreement between two people. It had not even been witnessed by anyone. He asked me if I had signed a second copy. I said no, I had a clear recollection of signing only one. In the safe was also our marriage certificate, and I took it out and kept it with me. We left the safe open, and did not immediately destroy the agreement. Mark said I should wait for his call. He again assured me that before telling his boss they were double-crossing him, he would speak to them, and try and gauge if they were ready to change their approach to me. If Madge and Bart were returning, it meant there was still scope to work with them, and their intentions were not entirely evil. In that case, I should return the documents to the safe, and reset the same combination, which he showed me how to do.

If they were not returning, I should close the safe, destroy the agreement, and keep the marriage document with me.

The next day, Thursday, one student arrived. All seven had reached by Friday, and Mark left in the afternoon. The ten-day course would continue till the next weekend. Mark had helped me to get the rooms ready. We had also bought sufficient supplies from the town. He said I should explain to the students that while Madge and Bart were away, we would take turns cooking, dish-washing, etc. He said it was a good opportunity for me to see how to run the centre on my own. I replied that as there were only seven students I could easily do the cooking and washing up myself, though I could ask some of them if they wanted to help.

On Friday night I made a simple Indian meal for my students, palak paneer, chana dal, potato raita, and phulkas. They loved it, and did all the washing and clearing themselves. I did get a few puzzled looks and questions. They had been told by Bart that I was going to India, but I was still here, and instead Bart and Madge were not around. I answered truthfully, saying I had no idea why Bart had thought I was returning to India, and that they had suddenly been called to New York for a fundraiser.

The course continued smoothly. I cooked Indian vegetarian food for my students, with their help. Everyone liked it, though I had to tone down the spices a bit.

***

On Monday morning I received a phone call from Mark. 'Thank you for those extra classes, Dev,' he said. 'I greatly benefitted from them.'

My heart leapt. So it was as I thought—their intentions towards me had not been right, and they would not be returning. Mark added that he'd had to leave suddenly and was already in Italy as his grandmother was ill, and would contact me when he returned. That left me a little worried. We hadn't discussed that possibility. What if I needed him? He seemed to be telling me that he wouldn't be available for a while. I did all that he had instructed, destroyed the agreement, kept the marriage certificate with me, and moved my stuff into Madge's room, and Bart's into mine. To be extra careful, I had never let the students into the cottage, all the cooking had been done in the yoga-centre kitchen.

Tuesday morning, a police car drew up at the house. I was in the yoga hall with the students, but I saw the car through the window, and sent one of them to find out why they had come, and asked the others to continue with the class. Two police officers soon walked in, surveying the scene. Finding everyone in odd postures, they looked bemused. I got out of mayur asana, stood up, and asked them if they wanted anything. Perhaps, seeing I was an Indian, they did not respond to me, but addressed the rest of the class instead. After all these years I seem to have forgotten their names, hence I will just refer to them as A and B. Officer A, who was taller and seemed to be in charge, said there had been an accident, and asked if there was anyone here related to Madge or Bart.

Once again I spoke to them. 'What sort of accident? I am related. I am Madge's husband.' I have to say the policemen looked shocked, astounded. Without responding to my question, policeman A asked what my relationship was with Bart. 'He is the administrator of this institute,' I replied. Next, he asked my name, and when I said Devdarshan Mangal, they exchanged glances. Policeman B then spoke. 'We would like to speak to you in private, Mr Monkey.'

'The name's Mangal,' I said as I went out of the hall with them, and guided them to the sitting room. Could they really not pronounce it, or was it a deliberate mispronunciation? We remained standing, as I asked, 'What has happened? Is it a bad accident? How is my wife?'

'I am sorry to tell you,' said Policeman A, 'that the car they were travelling in, collided with a truck. Both suffered serious injuries. Your wife did not survive, while Bart is on life support.'

I stared at them in silence. I hope I looked suitably shocked. They too kept silent. Then I mumbled: 'That can't be. She will be back today.' I closed my eyes and let my body drop to the ground in a faint. The thing is, I couldn't face them, I thought they would read the expression on my face. By now I had been doing asanas and practising pranayama for more than a year. As officer A bent over me, I let out my breath, and held it out. I knew I could manage this for a few minutes. The officer put his hand near my nose, and found I was not breathing. He felt for my pulse, but I had slowed it down immensely. Soon he was calling on his walkie-talkie for an ambulance. I had to breathe, so I took a deep breath, called out 'Madge!,' on the out breath, and then held it out again. 'He's coming around,' said the officer, and I slowly allowed my breathing to return to normal, but kept my eyes shut. 'Are you all right? How do you feel?' I heard the questions, but did not answer. I wanted to seem grief-stricken. I thought back to the early days and the death of my newborn son, and managed to get a few tears in my eyes. I think the faint, combined with the tears, convinced the officers that my grief was genuine. I was helped to my feet, and taken into the cottage to lie down in my bed—that had, until recently, been Bart's.

The ambulance arrived, along with a doctor, who seemed to think it was not necessary to send me to hospital. He gave me an injection of something, and I slept.

I awoke a couple of hours later. One of the students was sitting near me. He told me to just relax, not to think, and added that at least Bart was still alive, there may be some hope.

I was afraid. What if he recovered? I sat up. 'I must visit him,' I said, though I wasn't sure what I could do. Mark could not even be contacted. Did he know about this? 'Bart's in New York,' said the student. 'You aren't fit to travel.' A few more students came into the room, offered their condolences, and asked how I was feeling. A cup of coffee was brought for me. I drank it, still looking and feeling dazed. I remembered once again that similar scene, when Gita and my boy had died, that cup of sweet tea...and again tears filled my eyes.

As I thought of Bart, still alive, my tears dried. I just had to hope that Mark knew about it, and some action was being taken. If I didn't hear anything more, I would try to get to New York myself. Maybe I could smother him? These were my thoughts, as I lay in bed looking miserable, a blanket pulled up to my chin. The phone rang, and Jake, one of the students, went to answer it. I couldn't hear what he said, but he was back in a few minutes. 'It was the police,' he announced, looking at me anxiously. 'There is more bad news. Bart has succumbed to his injuries.'

I hid my face in my hands, so that no one would see how relieved I was. Now I was free, and I would be able to run the centre in my own way. As soon as I thought that, though, I realized, that there was a lot standing in my way. The centre, the land, the cottage, were not mine. Nor was there any document to show how much I had spent out of my earnings on the buildings. Why hadn't I thought of this earlier, and why hadn't Mark pointed it out? I was free of them, but my dream of having a yoga institute of my own, was still far away. I wondered if Madge had left a Will, and who her property would go to.

Jake's voice intruded on my thoughts. 'The police want to know if you will be able to answer a few questions.'

I removed my hands from my face, rubbing my eyes, so that they looked red. I looked up briefly, and then closed my eyes and lay back against the pillows. Trying to compose my features to look sorrowful and distressed, I weakly said that they could come, I'd answer their questions. Jake and Patsy sat near my bed, while the others drifted out.

One policeman arrived in about half an hour. He was a different one from the earlier two, perhaps more senior. He introduced himself as Sergeant Thompson, and I responded with my name, which he pronounced correctly, offering his condolences. He then asked me about how I had met Madge, when I had got married, and how long I had been in the US. I answered those questions truthfully, and knew they could check existing records to confirm most of what I said. Of course, I did not reveal that the marriage had just been a convenient arrangement. Then he asked about my relationship with Madge, and whether I had been happy with her. I said yes, I was happy on the whole, though there were a few problems caused by cultural differences. Could I give him an example? I told him about Madge cooking meat, particularly beef, when I did not like to eat it, and about her having a bath in the evening, and that too not every day. He looked a bit baffled at my second example, but did not comment. Then he asked about Bart. He said he had heard he was my manager, but he wanted to know more about my relationship with him, and also about his equation with Madge, and whether that had created a problem for me.

I explained in some detail, that Bart and Madge had known each other even when they were in India, but had not been very close. When Madge and I decided to get married, Bart seemed happy about the decision, and congratulated us. I didn't know anyone except them when I reached the US, and when Madge suggested Bart become the manager and administrator, I agreed. I said I got on well with Bart on the whole, though at times we disagreed. As far as I knew, Bart and Madge always had a professional relationship, nothing more. In that case, he queried, why had they gone together to New York without me? I said they had told me that the group who had invited them for the fundraiser, did not know about me. The invitation arrived at the last minute, and there was no time to contact the organizers to include me, or to replace Bart with me. Anyway, I said, I did not know much about these events, or about what I would have to do there, and had not wanted to go. Then he wanted to know why the current course I was teaching had been cancelled and then reinstituted. I realized he must have already spoken to the students, to find out whatever he could. I said I had had a tentative plan to go to India, but then decided against it. Bart must have cancelled the classes, thinking I would be going. As I hadn't gone anywhere, I phoned the students and asked them to come.

Thompson wandered around and returned with more questions. He wanted to know about the newly dug land at the back, I said I thought they were planning a flowerbed, but I did not know for sure. Then he asked me who owned the land, and I said that Madge owned it, but some of the buildings and the money for running the institute were paid for by me. Next, he enquired whether there was any legal document indicating my contribution, and when I said I did not think so, his next question was on whether Madge had left a Will, and again I had to admit I did not know. I did know that Madge had no other close relatives, and I told him so. He said yes, he already knew that, and that Bart's sister had been informed. I didn't know anything about his sister. I felt totally exhausted. I think he could see that, and after asking if I needed a doctor, he left. I continued to feel exhausted, I just did not want to think or face life. The course had been interrupted, but considering the circumstances, no one requested a refund. The next day, four of the students left. Three still stayed on, looking after the cooking, cleaning, and me. I let them do everything, remaining in a kind of cocoon. The days passed, and soon it was time for them to leave too. The last to leave was Jake, who had taken care of everything. He assured me that if I felt I could not manage, he would return. I was grateful to Jake, but just as he was leaving he told me of a conversation he had overheard between the first two policemen, who were convinced of my shock and grief. One of them, he said, remarked, 'Poor fellow, I wonder what he will do now,' and the other, less sympathetic, responded, 'He will probably return to his own country, which is a good thing, one less of them here.' I did wonder why Jake reported that last sentence. He seemed helpful and concerned, but did he feel the same? At that moment, I longed to be back in India, it was the only thing I wanted. I didn't care about yoga, being a guru, or running an ashram. I wished I had just escaped and gone home before all these happenings.

Thompson came again the day Jake was leaving. He asked about others who had been here recently, and I gave him the names of the students who had come for the last couple of classes. I included Mark's name with them, and he did not ask me anything else.

12. A New Life Begins

Dev's Story

Finally, I was alone. I ached for someone to talk to. I knew there was no way to contact Mark at present, but he was the only person I considered my friend.

It was odd, but I was so alone that I even missed the presence of Bart and Madge. I did not know what I needed to do. Should I go to a lawyer? Should I just return to India? I did not even have enough money for a ticket. All I had with me were the fees of the last interrupted course. Could I go on staying here and organize another course? Madge and Bart's bodies had not yet been brought back for the cremation. And, of course, they would be buried, not cremated. First the police had to perform an autopsy, what we usually called a post mortem, something I had refused for Gita and my son. Even after that it would seem that they kept the body in a mortuary, and one had to book a day in advance for the funeral.

Somehow, my mind was in turmoil, I could not calm down. And there was another big problem that I hadn't thought of while the students were around. I did not know how to get food or any other items that I needed. The smallest village in India would have a grocery store one could walk to. I think every town too would have a shop not too far away, or at least some means of transport. But in Sparks and the other small towns and cities of the US, there was no public transport and no market centre that was walking distance. Later I realized that there may have been taxis available but I did not think of it at the time. In addition, Madge's place was well outside Sparks. And the people here were odd. In India, everyone in the vicinity and beyond would arrive at one's doorstep in case of a death. Even those whom one did not know, would be there waiting, offering help. I remembered how crowds had gathered when Gita and my son had died.

Here houses had wide spaces in between. Walking on the road outside Madge's place, one may not see anyone at all.

Bart's van was still parked in the garage, but of course, I did not know how to drive. While I was wondering how to get some supplies, the funeral-to-be brought me a visitor, one I had never seen before. He was the pastor of the church to which Madge belonged. In all the time I had been there, Madge had not visited any church, but the priest, Mr Harold, said he knew her, and she would be buried in their graveyard. He told me that Bart's sister would be taking his body to their hometown in Pittsburgh, Pennsylvania. When I told him my problem, he proved helpful and promised to bring back some groceries the next day. I had money with me to pay him, but how long would it last?

I was still feeling despondent, but somehow, that was my lucky day. Late afternoon, I saw a police car draw up, and Thompson stepped out. I saw him coming to the cottage door, and opened it as he reached it. He came in and sat down, but refused my offer of tea.

'What are your plans now?' he asked, after enquiring how I was. I think I looked as miserable as I felt. 'I don't know,' I said. 'Maybe I will return to India, though I don't think I have enough for the ticket.' He looked at me quizzically. 'But you have been here for seven months, you must have made a lot of money since then.'

'No,' I said, 'I did make money but all the profits went into the buildings that were constructed.'

'And you said you are not even the owner of the buildings?'

'Nothing had been worked out legally,' I said. 'Maybe it would have been in future, but we did not expect everything to end so tragically.' As I said this there were tears in my eyes. Of course, it wasn't at the loss of Madge, but at the loss of all my hopes and dreams.

'I believe you did not know that Madge had left a Will?'

'No,' I replied, wondering who all these buildings would now go to.

'The Will was registered with a local attorney,' Thompson continued. 'Would you like to know its contents?'

'I don't suppose it has any relevance to me,' I said. 'I'm not interested.'

'On the contrary,' said Thompson. 'It has every relevance to you. By her Will, Madge has left almost everything she owned to you.'

I was struck dumb. This time, I thought I would genuinely faint. How could that be possible? Why and when had she done that? Was she then genuine? And I had got her killed! Thompson fished a paper out of his pocket and gave it to me, saying, 'Here is a copy of the Will.' I took it with trembling hands. It was brief and short. The first bequest was simple—it said, 'To my beloved husband, Devdarshan Mangal, all my land and properties, in their entirety.' Beloved husband? Land and properties? I didn't understand. Was it a joke? I looked up, bewildered, and almost asked him that, but then stayed silent.

'There are a few things I can tell you, that Madge confided in her lawyer,' he continued. 'Bart had some kind of a hold on her, and she evidently felt threatened by him. She then went to J.V. Legal Firm, and had a will made in your favour, witnessed and registered. This cancelled a previous Will, in which everything was left to Bart. She told the lawyer that in case anything happened to her, she did not want Bart to get her property. Had she confided in you at all about Bart?'

Of course, Madge had confided in me, but I thought it best not to reveal this. 'No,' I said, 'I knew nothing of this. They always seemed to get on well together.'

My mind was slowly grappling with these new developments. I was certainly not her 'beloved husband'. She had told me that she felt threatened by Bart, but also that she loved him. She must have made her Will before that night when they dug that grave, perhaps as a safeguard or even a threat. Perhaps she told him about it, and promised to cancel it and again leave everything to him if he returned to her, and also to sell part of the land. Had he tested her by asking her to join him in planning my murder and digging a grave for me, to prove her loyalty to him? Thompson was watching me. I stopped my thoughts and told him that the Will was quite a shock for me. Then I asked him what I needed to do next. Thompson said I would need to contact a lawyer to look at the legalities of the Will, and to get the land and buildings transferred to me. He told me that there had been some suspicions of me because I hadn't been long in the country, and particularly after they learnt that I benefitted from Madge's Will, but after a thorough investigation they realized that it was just an unfortunate accident. As I stood at the door to see him off I felt a miracle had occurred. Even the light outside seemed brighter. My mind had suddenly taken a leap of joy—my dreams were coming true! The euphoria didn't last long, but I did feel better.

The next day Harold brought the groceries, and I paid him from the money I had. Then I told him about the Will, and asked him if he knew of a lawyer who could help me, whom I could pay later, as I had hardly anything with me now. Harold said he knew just the person to help me, a young law student. He would explain my difficulties to him, and he was sure he would accept a delayed payment.

David, the law student, came the next day. He took the copy of the Will that I had, and said he would find out what needed to be done. The next day he was back, and returned my copy, having made one for himself. He said he had started working on the property transfer, and it would not be much of a problem. Harold and David also helped me to open a bank account, where I deposited the cash I had with me. I knew I would soon be able to earn more, but I wanted all legalities completed and a decent interval to pass before I started holding classes once again. I was also waiting for Mark to return.

Meanwhile David became a new friend, and was a great help. He took me to town whenever I needed anything, and also started teaching me to drive. Slowly I began understanding the new country. Petrol was called gas here, and was sold in gallons! The old measurement systems of miles, ounces and pounds were still used here, while India had switched over to the decimal system in the '50s.

Earlier, I had hardly bothered to find out anything about Nevada, but now I made a few discoveries. Of course, Las Vegas was its most famous city, and though I had never visited it, it had already played a part in my life. There, in the many casinos, Bart had lost money, leading him to change his approach to me. I learnt that Nevada meant snowy, and was mountainous, but though it had a number of rivers, it was a dry area. Sparks was in the Washoe County of Nevada, and the Washoe were Native Americans. About 100 kilometres from Nevada was Frenchman Flat where nuclear bombs were tested. I began wondering how almost an entire population in a country could be replaced, as had been done in the US. The British had ruled India, but they hadn't attempted to eliminate and replace the people. I went for long walks, exploring the countryside. As I walked near the Truckee river, I felt homesick for the rushing, icy Ganga.

Everything was going smoothly now, but within myself I was not at peace. Until then, I had not been responsible for the tragedies that had taken place in my life, for Gita's death, for Cynthia's and Glady's betrayal, but even if I had not physically killed them, I was responsible for the deaths of Madge and Bart. I had not expected the huge burden of guilt, the terrible sense of darkness in my mind and heart, that increased whenever I remembered Madge's Will, clouding the relief and joy, I had felt earlier when I learned that I had been freed of my captors and had inherited the property. Madge seemed to have been a victim herself. But I felt bad even about Bart's death. I wished I had been murdered instead, or that I had gone to jail for life. Anything would have been better than this feeling within me. I was no longer myself, I could never dream again, never hope for joy. I thought of Sundararaman and how disappointed he would have been in me. I remembered the old yogi in the mountain cave. But even as I thought of them, I knew that I could not have lived a life like theirs. Something in me was just not ready for it. Even so, surely

I need not have been responsible for murder? What can I say? Life somehow led me on this path. Did I have free will, could I have refused to walk on it? I do not know.

David and Harold continued to visit, and I was glad of their company, and their help. My driving lessons were progressing. I kept my fears and despair to myself, though I know they showed on my face. I thought that was not a bad thing, further proof of my grief at what had happened. Thus, there were two parallel streams of thoughts and emotions. I wanted to die, to go to jail, to confess what I had done. At the same time, I wanted to live, to be free, and to enjoy my life. And there was a third part of me too, that watched myself, unable to understand these contradictions.

Gradually, the second stream became dominant. It was all destined, I told myself. I was fated to be a great guru and yoga teacher. I had just followed the path set for me. Thus, I convinced myself, and began to feel almost normal.

***

In just one month since I had a copy of the Will in my hand, the property was transferred to my name. Madge's funeral had already taken place, where I was the chief mourner. Not many people came, there were just a few members of her church.

The following month I resumed the yoga courses. The fees were reduced slightly, and for the ten-day courses the students took turns doing the chores, as we had done at Enzo's ashram. For the weekend courses, David helped out and I paid him 10 per cent of the fees. In two months, I was able to pay David's legal fees, and add to my own bank balance.

Soon after that, Mark returned. He had heard about the

Will while he was away. He had also found out something about Cynthia, both from a close friend of hers, and from the lawyer who had become Madge's confidant. Putting both versions together, Mark confirmed the story that Madge had told me, and added a few details. After the marriage to me, things changed. Bart felt alienated, got close to Cynthia, and then they went to Vegas where he lost huge sums of money. Initially, Madge was unaware of the amount Bart had decided I should pay. When she got to know the details, she did not like it, and wondered why Bart was following whatever Cynthia asked him to do. When Bart told her about the debts she accepted what he was doing, but then when she realized they were having an affair she was desperate to win him back. She made the Will in my favour, and told him about it, only as a ploy to win him back. She told him she would change the Will back in his favour, if he ended his relationship with Cynthia. But when Bart instead began to threaten her, she backed down, and said that she had not yet made the Will, but planned to do so. Pushed by Cynthia, Bart decided to kill me to eliminate that threat. As she was afraid, Madge cooperated with him, and said nothing more. She even began to make statements against me, and increasingly cooked the sort of food I did not like, in order to make him less suspicious and reduce the threat to her. She had conveyed all this to her lawyer, who had told the police about it, something Madge had asked him to do in case of her untimely death, but as Bart had died along with her, no suspicion could fall on him. The general conclusion was that it must have been an accident. The whole sequence of events began to make sense. Regarding Cynthia's role, Mark had discovered through her friend that her idea of getting me to the US and starting a yoga centre, was initially to have a legitimate business as a front for her drug profits. She herself had not lost much money in Vegas, and though she could afford to, she did not want to repay Bart's debts. Probably he wanted to sell the land so that he could both repay the money to the bookies, and remain independent. Obviously the friend knew nothing of Cynthia's role in the plan to murder me.

At that time Mark and I puzzled over it, but much later he had met Cynthia and asked her about it. She said it was not about taking revenge on me, she put forward the idea of killing me to stop Bart from constantly asking her for money.

She knew about Madge's threats to change her Will, and she believed Madge had already done so. She believed that if I was killed, it would serve two purposes—Madge would be afraid and give Bart the money he needed, and Bart would be in her power, as she could threaten to reveal his secret. Of course, the original plan had been to make money through me and the yoga centre, but this was just not making enough. And she could see that if I began to question their exploitation, they could all be in trouble.

If I had wound up dead, it would not have bothered her, she said, but she was rather happy that Bart had died. She had got tired of him. Cynthia, said Mark, was a person without morals or a conscience. She had far too much money, and the capriciousness of a child.

And so a whole saga of events had led to the death of Bart and Madge—my marriage to Madge, Bart's uneasiness with this, his relationship with Cynthia, and most important, his gambling debts that he could not repay. If he hadn't been killed by the drug lord, said Mark, he would anyway have been killed by the bookies if he couldn't pay up. At times I could forget about or justify Bart's death, but my regret at the death of Madge always remained with me, even though I had benefitted from her Will, and through that fulfilled my dream of becoming a guru.

I asked Mark if he would become my administrator and manager, and he agreed. I believed he would be an asset in case of any future problems, and he was. He helped me in every way, and always stood by me. Gradually, there were more employees. The institute received its present name, Shri Shankarananda's Yoga Centre. It flourished and people came to it from all over the US, and even from other countries. Soon other ashrams and institutes too were founded, in all parts of the world.

I continued my yoga practice, and perfected the most difficult asanas and pranayama. Not only the students, but even other yoga teachers respected and admired me.

But the first two stages of Raja Yoga, and the last four, became impossible for me. A darkness haunted me. Much of the time I was not aware of it, but I could never again get any peace through meditation, even though I encouraged everyone to meditate, initiated them, gave them mantras. From my own experience, I think that meditation is not for everyone, but only for those who have already overcome their problems and hidden emotions. The peaceful states, chakras and hidden lights revealed through meditation, and even the powers, all that I had tried so hard to attain in Enzo's ashram, seemed forever out of reach. When I sat in meditation, one of two things occurred. If I watched my breath and tried to still my mind, darkness and depression soon overwhelmed me. I was gripped by fear, almost terror, accompanied by a deep unbearable sorrow.

I turned to women for comfort, to forget. If I chanted

any of the mantras I knew, deep, dark, insatiable desires would rise in me, and I would call one of the many women in love with me, there were always so many around, so many wanting the sacred touch of Swamiji. And I persuaded those who were reluctant, I was the guru, wasn't I, surrendering to the guru was the same as surrendering to god; I was using a sacred method to rid them of their monstrous egos. I was providing them with the most sacred of initiations, through tantric rites. They were the chosen ones. How would they find god if they refused? Besides they'd have to leave the ashram, and where would they go? Sex with the guru became a privilege. In my favour, I would say that I never ever thought of using physical force on anyone, even though I had been accused of it. Persuasion and words were my only weapons. Sometimes, when my despair was too great, Mark provided me with drugs, though I was not an addict. Mark always told me to forget and move on, that he had committed innumerable deeds far worse, but I could not. I remembered that Sundararaman had warned me of this, of walking on the wrong path, and where it would take me.

For many years after that, there were no overt problems. The institute ran smoothly, and was famous. Money was plentiful, and gradually I opened ashrams in other parts of USA and Europe. I opened one in India too, in Rishikesh, and I bought a house nearby for myself. But after Serina filed a case against me, everything began to fall apart. Somehow, I spoke to god for the first time in my life, he saved me once again from jail, and I returned to my homeland. And now my life is ending.

Well, I think I have finished my story. At least as much as I am able to write, I could not go into every detail. I will hand it over to Nitya when he comes next—perhaps it will help him to understand me, though I am not sure I understand myself. But that is the way things were, that is how it all happened. I remember some words from a song in that musical, *Jesus Christ Superstar*: 'Could we start again please, could we start again.' I wish I could start again, though I don't know if I could have done anything differently.

***

Nitya hasn't come for quite a few days. It is night now, and I am hoping he comes tomorrow. Diana seemed in a pensive mood this evening, strange for her, perhaps she is being affected by Sophie's attitude. As we sat in the fading light, she began a conversation that shook me.

'Dev,' she said, 'do you think I did wrong supporting you against Lydia? And in that final case filed by Serina?'

'How can you say that, Diana? Of course, you did right. Did you want me to go to prison?'

'But I told a lot of lies.'

'So what? The lies were in a good cause. To save me, an enlightened being, from a scheming person.'

She looked at me, silent for a while. Then she said: 'I don't think Lydia was a scheming person. She was just too sensitive and intense. Everything affected her too deeply. And Serina—of course she was stronger than Lydia, but she was just so young.'

'Look, Diana,' I said, repeating my stock line that I'd convinced people with, so many times before. 'As an enlightened being I know what is right and what will help each person grow. Whatever befell Lydia was only to enable her to destroy her monstrous ego. I've told you often enough, the small conditioned mind is not competent to judge the unconditioned. You were right to support me. Lydia suffered from the effects of her own bad karma. She suffered for refusing to trust me, her guru, and for refusing to surrender completely. When she died she was to some extent cleansed of her bad karma. She brought that terrible karma, of being shot dead, of dying an untimely death on herself, for accusing me, whom she should have revered and worshipped. You know that she called me a fake guru, and that she said she would expose me as one to the world. And you know that she was mistaken, that those were lies.'

Diana looked confused. For a moment I thought she was going to ask if I had anything to do with Lydia's death. Instead she said, 'So Dev, what's your bad karma that you got AIDS? You say you were doing everything for the good of your disciples, what did you do wrong? And Serina too accused you, how is it that nothing bad happened to her?'

'My bad karma? Wrong? An enlightened guru, my dear Diana, has no karma and can never do wrong. Out of the love and compassion of my heart, I've only taken on some of the bad karma of my disciples. As for Serina—as you said, she is young. Her karma will catch up with her someday.'

Diana gave me a sceptical glance, but said nothing more. Perhaps she could see how I was dropping with tiredness. I thought back to Lydia's death. I was never sure if Mark was responsible for it, or for other deaths that had taken place. He may have believed he was protecting me. I neither asked him nor accused him, but at the time of Serina's case, I suggested that the time had come for us to part. I told him that I was now withdrawing from my role as guru and returning to India. Mark said he would be available whenever I needed him, but he too was thinking of retiring and going to Italy.

He did not mean just retiring from working with me, but from the whole drug business that he had continued with all along. He had made more than enough money, he said, and he did not need to continue.

It was a real effort now to go on with that guru spiel, I'd done it long enough without believing in a word I said. Strange then how they all believed me! Perhaps that is the power of the Word. I'll think about this more when I can. For the present, I wish I could drop it all, all the pretence, the false self I presented ever since I left Enzo's ashram. It served me well, I had pleasures, money, all the luxuries of life, but wasn't there something I missed? In my early life, in my school and college days, my life with Gita, I had a kind of purity of heart, an inner joy. Perhaps I could have regained it with Sharada or someone else, or even by myself, but I got onto a different path. I'd like to be myself again. That's why I write here, revealing my truth. I wish I had the courage in these last days to reveal it to the world. But at least, by handing over what I have written to him, I will reveal it to one person, to Nitya.

13. Can There Be Peace?

Nityananda

I went to see Dev the day after he wrote that seventh section. Later I read what he had written, including his conversation with Diana.

Dev said that meditation led him into depression or aroused desires in him. Obviously, he was practising the wrong sort, because I used meditation to calm down and remove all desire. Or perhaps he was right, unless one had a certain purity and goodness, unless one followed an ethical path, meditation could lead to a worse state of mind.

In his time in the ashram he learnt so fast, he seemed to have a brilliant mind. As a guru, he did convey his learning, but was that sufficient? He betrayed and destroyed so many. Still I was impressed by his knowledge, by all he still remembered of what he had read so long ago. And when I read the words 'Could we start again...' I was flooded with love and pity.

Yet there were a few things in his story that really puzzled me. He could have returned to India, particularly after he had confided in Mark. Mark would have loaned him the money and could have smuggled him out when Bart and Madge were away in New York. Would Bart really have gone to the trouble of trying to extradite him, accusing him of a false marriage and putting him in jail, knowing that that would indict Madge—and himself—as well? And was his account of the sequence of events true? I decided to ask him, even though he was so weak and ill. He insisted that whatever he had written was true, it was exactly as it happened. Still, I pressed him further. Why didn't he return to India? Was he aware of Madge's Will, and was that the reason he agreed to allow them to be murdered? Why was Mark so willing to help him?

He was silent for some time. His mind seemed to travel back to those early days in Sparks. Finally, he said, 'I did not know about Madge's Will. Yes, I could certainly have returned after they died, if not before. But that would have been the end of my dream of becoming a guru, of being rich, and even more important to me, of being powerful.

'I made a mistake though. I attained my dream but never again did I have peace in my heart and soul. I had lost myself. How could I then ever seek that inner light that you have glimpsed at times? But regrets are of no use now.

'As for Mark, I thought he was helping me, but whatever he did was to his advantage. He had me in his power, he could extend his drug empire, and attain the wealth he wanted. I don't know if his story of being forced into the drug trade was true. He was like a spider at the centre of a web containing all my ashrams. He gave me plenty of money and encouraged me to start new ashrams, but placed his drug dealers in almost every one of them.'

'How is it there were none in Oshkosh?' I asked. 'It was a new ashram when I sent you there,' replied Dev. 'I persuaded Mark to allow one ashram in the US to be exactly as it should be. I said that your honesty was palpable and would come in handy. And so it was.'

It was really terribly depressing. This was the man I had revered as a guru. Dev too had pondered over what makes a person good and ethical, or not good at all. What was the process by which one made choices? Did life just carry us along? Why did he choose this path, that gave him his dream, but finally caused him so much trauma?

His last days approached, and he was not able to write any more.

In those days I tried to be kind to Dev as I would to any ordinary person filled with his confusions. In myself, I remain unhappy with his life and actions, in fact unhappy is too mild a word. I have an abhorrence for what he had done, the word 'evil' comes to my mind, yet yesterday as I sat in meditation or rather contemplation, a somewhat different perspective came to me. I tried to analyze my own feelings regarding the world. It's not just Dev, I've always had a lot of agony at the way people behave—with their bombs, wars and mass destruction, or at a lesser level in their daily lives. I'm troubled by the fact that while each person has the power to protect and help, they choose instead to hurt and destroy. Thus, they cut a beautiful tree because it temporarily blocks their sun, eat meat to satisfy their appetites though they know they are depriving a living creature of life, or injure an animal just because they consider it harmful, irritating, or even irrelevant. And, of course, there is so much else, greed, lust and all those so-called 'deadly sins'.

Sometimes I see a future world where no such people remain. There would only be a few who live unobtrusively in friendship with the plants, birds, animals and reptiles.

Once again, yesterday, to console myself for the defects of reality, I conjured up in my mind this beautiful world. But as I began to look at this world more closely, I saw that animals too have their conflicts with each other. It may be on a lower scale, but they too have angers, fears, needs, a desire to protect their territory, they too kill, injure, hurt. They could be better than humans, the scale of their violence could never be so grand, their greed for the treasures of the earth did not exist, still, they weren't perfect. Yet, when a tiger killed a deer, or a cat a mouse, I couldn't blame the animal. It was part of their nature, they were made that way.

With these thoughts, a revelation came to me. People were no different. One condemned them because one believed they were capable of choice, but in actuality, they weren't. In the process of evolution or development, they'd been handed a whole lot of additional abilities, along with additional needs and desires. Unsure of what to do with all this, they acted in a blind, selfish, confused way. Philosophies and philosophers, thinkers and prophets, and creative visionaries emerged out of all this, but only a few could see that people were part of evolution, and not some ideal being. As I saw people as just a stage in animal development, as helpless in their actions as the tiger and the cat, pure love and compassion arose in my heart. Once again, I had a fleeting glimpse of the love that emanates from within, that makes one whole, that Nachiketa reminded me of, and that I had seen in that cave in my heart. Who was I to condemn Dev, who too was a divine being following the path given to him, in confusion, blindly and unthinkingly?

Out of my meditation I was judgemental again, but still, love had touched me, and I could direct some part of it at him when we met again.

***

When I went to see Dev, he was extremely weak and knew his last days were near. He could not write any more, but holding my hand he told me in a rasping voice, 'Last night

I had a beautiful dream. I crossed the ancient river, the separator between life and death, and there on the other side I saw her—my dream woman. She was not Gita, she was not Sharada, she was the one who existed in my heart, whom I had always known, and for the second time in my life, I saw her clearly—black hair, a pale face, a white sari—before I could come any closer, before I could reach her, she disappeared into a rising mist.'

He had referred to this dream woman before, and I asked if she was the same as the one he had first glimpsed when he was in Enzo's ashram. He said he was not sure, she looked the same, but the woman in his heart had a different quality, she was not sensual, but comforting, even motherly, and at the same time like a friend and companion. I wondered if he realized his description was similar to Gita's of Varun. Had Gita totally invented it, or had she half-believed in it out of the need for an imaginary friend? I listened patiently without commenting, and told him a story in turn—a Celtic tale, that I had read long ago. Once, I narrated, there was a warrior named Oenghus, who dreamed every night of a mythical woman, and in his longing for her, he grew thin and pale. He searched for her everywhere, and he found that she was not just a dream, she did exist and her name was Caer. But Caer, the daughter of a god, had magical powers, and one of these was that she could change into a bird. When Oenghus found her, she was a swan, on a lake with 150 other swans. She said she would accept Oenghus' love if he too became a swan, and so he did, and they lived happily ever after.

Dev thought it was a beautiful story. 'Maybe,' he said, 'I too will become a swan when I die, a hamsa.' Yes, in our texts, a hamsa is a sacred bird, one who can separate milk from water, that is, the pure from the impure, and hamsa was also the name of the highest category of rishis, purified by the chant 'ham-sa,' 'I am He' or 'I am That,' the whole universe, the source of all, the sustainer, the breath of life.

Dev too remembered Gita, and added that her story of Pururava and Urvashi was somewhat similar. 'There is so much to learn in life, but now it is too late,' he said. He continued, almost to himself, 'Would I be able to study and read in the other world? Or would I live in darkness, in some sort of numbing hell? Perhaps I wouldn't be conscious at all, perhaps this was the final end, I'd never know anything, never exist again.'

There was nothing I could find to say. I sat there for a while in the fading light. Dev's breathing grew shallow and as he slipped into sleep, I left.

14. An End and a Beginning

Nityananda

The next day I thought I must talk to Dev again.

As a historian specialized in ancient Indian history, I was already aware of most of the texts of ancient India, but it was only when I joined Dev that I began to study some of them from a religious and spiritual point of view.

I started with the Bhagavad Gita, and that remains my favourite text. I had to set aside the historical interpretations I had learnt of the Gita being a product of its times, a reflection of class struggle, and a means to preserve the caste system. Perhaps all that was true, but it still didn't detract from what I began to see as the eternal spiritual truths of the text. Through me, Nachiketa too began to love this text. I went on to study the major Upanishads, the *Vedanta Sutra*, and the *Bhagavatam*. Because of my background in history I never went overboard with blind belief.

Now I tried to think over all I had learnt, and to take from it a few key principles to discuss with Dev. Dev knew these texts better than I did. He often quoted from them, but did they mean something to him, had they influenced his life?

I set out from the ashram in the jeep, instead of walking to his house. I don't know why I suddenly felt time was of the essence. I brushed aside Diana who was trying to stop me and reached Dev's bedside. He was half sitting, propped against pillows, his eyes shut, his breathing heavy. 'Dev,' I said, and he opened his eyes and smiled. It was a gentle and beautiful smile. I had never seen him smile that way before. I felt his end was near, and I hesitated.

'Ask me whatever you want,' he said, 'I can see that look in your eyes.' For the last time I approached him as a student to a teacher. And he showed no sign of weakness as he entered into a fierce debate with me.

I took a deep breath and began. 'Dev,' I said 'I know there is only One reality, which we call Brahman. There is no second. That is what the mahavakyas, the great statements in the Upanishads say. That is the essence of Advaita. Brahman is not created but has always existed. It can never be destroyed or polluted. But does this theory make the actions of a person irrelevant? Can a person do wrong, as you have done, and then say that it does not matter?'

'Nitya,' he replied, 'I am sure you understand. The purity of the Universal Self, the Atman, is identical with Brahman. It is the same in me and the same in you. It cannot be affected by anything I have done or not done.' He quoted from the Bhagavad Gita: '"What is unreal can never exist; what is real always exists. This Reality can be seen only by those who can see the true"'. (2.16)

He added: 'What you are seeing and condemning as my actions is part of unreality. There is only One reality. The rest is maya, a play, an illusion. I played with life as all must do. Diana gave me a book by Ramanna. He too says the same.'

Somehow I was getting angry. 'I can give you another quote from the Bhagavad Gita,' I said.

'"The unwise have no vision, but speak flowery words. Full of desires, with heaven as their goal, they have prayers for pleasures and power, the reward for which is earthly rebirth."(2.42-43) You are one of those, Dev. You have not reached the indestructible Self within you. You were a false guru.'

And suddenly he crumbled.

'Don't get angry with me, Nitya,' he pleaded. 'It may be the last day of my life, and still I am just playing around with words. I know I have done several wrong things in my life, I began my life as a guru through murder, and later I betrayed and exploited many people. At the same time I helped and provided knowledge to many. I know I have not reached the indestructible true Self within. And I have not understood the relationship of my individual self with Brahman. I know I will be reborn, and I hope I can do better in the next life. But what do you think? Will I suffer after death? Will there be a dreadful period of suffering before I am reborn?'

His fear was pitiable, and I gave up on my accusations. Who was I to judge, when I too had almost been complicit in all he did? If suffering awaited him, what awaited me?

'I don't think anyone knows what happens after death,' I said. 'In fact I have been reading a few things that indicate that there are no simple answers'.

'Tell me what you have read.'

'Recently I have been reading Sri Aurobindo. If I have understood him rightly, he says there is no karma as we understand it, no divine accountant distributing reward and punishment. Ignorance is the reason for all one does wrong, and life provides lessons that help one to overcome ignorance. There is no retribution, only guidance to move towards the divine.'

Dev responded, 'Of course Aurobindo's ideas about ignorance derive from the concept of avidya, that you are familiar with. As you know, in both Advaita and in Buddhism, avidya represents cosmic ignorance, the ignorance that prevents us from seeing the Truth.'

'Yes,' I said, 'but Aurobindo has related the concept to our daily life. And his ideas on karma are different.'

'Thanks for reminding me about avidya, Nitya. I will think over that. Though it is a humbling thought that I, the great guru, worshipped and revered by so many, have only been acting out of ignorance all my life! And as for his ideas on karma—I can't see in what way I was guided by the events in my life to follow a spiritual path. Rather they took me on a downward spiral.'

After a bit he added, 'As I have told you earlier, in my younger days I knew a lot of the Bible. A verse from there comes to my mind: "The Lord does not deal with us according to our sins, nor repay us according to our inequities" (Psalm 103.10.).'

'Yes,' I said, 'and the Bible also has something about "he makes the rain fall on the just and the unjust". And there are many stories of hope in our texts too. Don't you know the story of Ajamila, the man from a good family, who sank into depravity? When he was dying, he called out to his son, Narayana. And as he took the name of god in his last moments, Yama's messengers couldn't take him away. He went to Vaikuntha, Lord Vishnu's abode.'

Dev seemed to have cheered up a bit. I too was calm now. He just said, 'Nitya, have I sunk into depravity? Is that what you think?'

'I don't know what I think,' I replied. 'I too am far from my true self. I am confused and bewildered by what I have come to know about you, but at the same time all the indications were there earlier. I just did not want to register or think about those possibilities.'

He stretched his hand out and I held it. Love and compassion arose in my heart, for him, for me, for everyone. We read, studied, meditated, saw visions perhaps, and still none of us knew the answers. Had anyone ever in the past truly known?

'Dev,' I said, 'I remember a story I had read about the Buddha. One of his disciples asked him, do you know all there is to be known? In return, the Buddha asked him to sweep up the dry leaves in the forest and bring them to him. The disciple brought baskets and baskets, but obviously there were many more, and he gave up. The Buddha then said that in the same way, no one person could know everything.'

'That's right, Nitya,' he said. 'No one knows everything. Or perhaps no one knows anything.'

I left him then.

***

Back in the ashram, I sat in my rocking chair near the window, re-reading one of my old favourites, Gibbon's *Decline and Fall of the Roman Empire*. In the background, I could hear the birds calling. When I lifted my eyes from the book, I could see the grass outside, a few rose bushes, and one or two pink roses. I needed these few peaceful, quiet moments. Nachiketa too was reading some book or the other, but he was restless, I was aware that he kept glancing at me. 'Baba,' he said, 'you keep reading all this history, but how does the past matter? I'm reading in this book that one should always live in the present.'

Irritation stirred in me. 'It's some new-age writer you're reading then,' I said. 'They hardly know what they are writing about. Any cat or dog can live in the present and enjoy the present moment without the burden of time. As I see it, a human is a higher stage in evolution, who has reached a more complex state, enabling one to look beyond the immediate present of one's own life. In fact, the present is extremely vast. It includes not only us in this room, but all that is happening in the world. It includes wars and battles, death and suffering. Only a person can understand all this, and not live a limited life, confined to his own personal present. A person has the vision to look into the past and plan the future. Awareness of the whole, has led to great creations; unless one has this awareness, creating a better future is impossible. Of course, many, because of their limited knowledge and focus on mundane things, continue to act in a blind, instinctive way. But there are other options too. You know, Nachiketa, those who talk of living in the present, they are trying to provide a way out from pain. I feel one shouldn't seek this simplistic way out, creating one's own little pleasant moment. One should be aware of the world's pain, hold it, absorb it, and then try and subsume it. I've been thinking about this a lot. I am going to try to absorb the pain of all those I know who have suffered in the past and the present, I'll try to hold it within me, then sit in meditation, pour healing white light on their pain. That too is not enough. I'll try to think, what can I do in practical terms? I'm constantly thinking this lately.'

'But right now, you're sitting and reading Gibbon.'

'I need a break sometimes. It doesn't mean I'm living in the present and forgetting the past.'

'You can't cure the whole world, can you?'

'No, Nachiketa. I can try doing something in a very limited sphere. I want to do something for the women

Swamiji harmed. Provide them with some counselling, some money. A few of them have children. If they're unwanted, we'll take them into our ashram. I don't know, these are just thoughts. I'll ask Sharada what she thinks. I feel responsible, Nachiketa, some of them came to me and complained, but I refused to believe them. Anita and Lucy committed suicide...Lydia was shot, I don't know by whom. I can't live in the present and forget them.'

'Don't you think god looks after everyone?'

'No, I don't. I think god created us to take care of each other, to take care of the earth, the plants and animals. So far we have failed.'

'What about the theory that their suffering is only part of their own karma?'

'I don't believe that either. Plants suffer. Innocent animals suffer. I don't believe they have a karma, they are evolving beings with limited freedom of choice. All who are not fully developed suffer.

'For instance, I'm suffering because I loved, I trusted and believed, when I should not have. Because I did not use my mind, my wisdom and rationality. These too are god-given gifts, but following tradition, I neglected them. I'm suffering because I had not developed and used all my faculties. Others suffer because of their desires, and these desires exist once again because such people are not developed, have not grown to their fullest potential.

'That's how I see life today. One has to strive for perfection. In perfection, one causes no suffering to others, one gains a certain peace.'

'But not happiness?'

'Those who strive for personal happiness may achieve it. I believe the higher soul can never do so, can never leave the suffering world behind.'

'Aren't you going against what our texts say?'

'Our texts have great words, the words of living saints. They contain the truth, but truth cannot be contained. It is more vast, it goes beyond texts.'

'And you think you have found it?'

'No, Nachiketa, of course not. I'm only using the limited faculties I have, trying to develop them further. My thoughts anyway are not new. Even these have been thought before, explained through the Bodhisattva concept, discussed in Aurobindo. Nothing I am saying is new. I'm only departing from the tradition in which I was trained, allowing myself the freedom to think.'

***

I thought Dev would not last the night, but in fact when I went to see him in the morning, he looked better. I told him some of my thoughts of the previous day.

After thinking for a while, he said, 'You know, Nitya, I don't know about the higher soul, but definitely, the gods don't care, neither about us, nor about anything that happens in the world.'

'What do you mean? You yourself said you had contacted god and he saved you from jail.'

'Yes, I tried to speak to god. But now I don't know whether I contacted anyone or not. Look at my life. I was a good person to start with. But did god help me? He hindered me at every point and turned me into a different person, a bad person, or at least, one who was not good.'

'I think you had a choice. No one forced you to do what you did.'

'Just think of my circumstances. What choice did I have? I even wanted to die...But I was led to commit that first wrong act.'

'But what led you to commit the other wrong acts? And the first wrong act was not planning that murder, or allowing them to be murdered. Your first wrong act was entering into a fake marriage with Madge. If you think back to your life, till that point, your life had conspired to send you on a spiritual path. You were blessed and named by a holy man soon after your birth. You received a good education. You always had a sense of being different. Even Gita and your son's deaths had a positive role, as through them you went to Enzo's ashram and learnt so much. Then Sundararaman arrived to give you guidance and direct you on the right path. Cynthia appeared to make you a yoga teacher. And another unknown teacher gave you a new name and you became a guru. The other day you said that life conspired to send you on a downward spiral. On the contrary, life had conspired to place you on a spiritual path, and to make you a guru.'

'But is a fake marriage so wrong?'

'Perhaps not for an ordinary person. But you were on a spiritual path! Once you get on that path, I think that any wrong action has huge consequences.'

'You may be right, Nitya. Perhaps others commit murder and feel nothing, it does not affect their lives unless they are caught. I was wrong in marrying Madge, and instead of rectifying it, I made things worse. Once one does something that is wrong, it is very difficult to get back to the right path. And it may be because I was already on a spiritual path, that I was aware that I had lost my purity, my innocence. I couldn't face myself. I could never relax, never be at peace. I tried to meditate to find that lost source of goodness, but I told you what happened. Either darkness or waves of sexual desire rose in me. You've read my story, I had never earlier been someone focused on sex.'

'It could be that the meditation you were doing was wrong. You said you tried watching your breath and alternatively focusing on various mantras given by Sundararaman and Enzo. If you jump from one thing to another, meditation will have no results. Or else perhaps no meditation would work once you stepped on the wrong path. I use meditation to gain a state of desirelessness—if not something more. And sometimes I get a sense of truth, and a glimpse of the white light.'

'I feel sad that I have never seen that light. What about rousing the kundalini? Doesn't one type of meditation arouse it and take the sexual power up to the brain? Could that have been happening to me?'

'I think this whole question of kundalini is a mystery that is still not revealed. As I told you earlier, another theory is that kundalini descends from above. And in that case it kills sex, it does not generate it.'

'And where did you learn that, Nitya?'

'In a book. And the meditation I use too is from a book.'

'But...I initiated you. I gave you a mantra.'

'I was not comfortable with it.'

Dev tried a different tack. 'Well you know that sahaja is a path to enlightenment. And sahaja indicates all that is natural, including sex.'

'If sahaja is the way to enlightenment, every animal would be enlightened, as they all live a sahaja life, with natural sex.'

Dev was silent, leaning back against the pillows, he looked tired. I thought perhaps he needed to rest for some time and sat near him quietly.

***

I began to think over what we had discussed, and to ponder again over the question of free will. Did people have free will? Was there ever a choice, or was everything predetermined? Philosophies had examined these questions for centuries but they could not agree. Dev seemed to have had a choice in his marriage to Madge, but was that really so? Given his desire to go abroad, Madge too would have seemed like part of some divine plan. I started wondering whether the individual self has any entity or existence on its own. Can it acquire power and do things by its will, or is it always subject to something else, usually termed god? A person may be rich, famous, a guru, a rishi, a sage, yet the world can be knocked out beneath him. It is the individual's lack of power that maintains him always in a state of fear. 'God' is the being ultimately feared, though one may call it by other names, such as 'fate'. Can a person, an individual, gain power and exist independently of god? If so, god, the creator of all, cannot exist, because if one is the creator, then the power to destroy one's creation also exists.

If a person cannot exist as an individual, without the benediction of a so-called god, then the person is nothing, is irrelevant, is always inferior to another being. Such a person cannot get a sense of peace, except as they say by 'surrender' or by setting aside the individual identity, by ceasing to have desires, by making one's desires subservient to those of a higher power. Finally, peace is achieved by merging with that higher entity, or remaining in devotional surrender to it.

The whole of society, the way it is structured, reinforces these ideas. A person who goes against social norms has a tough time, unless certain avenues are followed that allow for freedom within them. Thus, being a sannyasi gives freedom, but is also part of an institution, a way of life. Being an artist, also gives a person a certain license denied to others. Being rich, or in a position of power, does the same.

Yet all these categories of people are vulnerable. Death comes to all, they can be killed, murdered, raped, fall prey to disease, accidents, suffer personal loss. Through all this the ark that carries one through is belief in God, or surrender to a higher power, which cannot be comprehended.

Can one at least challenge this idea? Can a person exist as an independent individual supreme in his/her own power? Wasn't that Nietzsche's idea? God is dead, long live the superman? But ideas are not reality, and Nietzsche could never achieve his ideal. He was just forty-four when he lost his powers of reason, and his will.

Perhaps one had to proceed slowly, gradually establish oneself as an individual. If Dev had refused to marry Madge, that may have been the beginning of him as an independent entity. I would ask Dev what he thought. Obviously, he believed in a kind of determinism, but even now there was time to discuss and learn.

When I looked at him, I found he was sleeping. Then I looked again. A sudden fear gripped me. Was his sleep too deep? Was this the end? His face was peaceful, almost beautiful. I called out in panic to Diana and she rushed into the room. Other people came in, there was confusion and many voices. I stood on one side. I knew that Dev, my friend and guru, of whom I had been so critical, was no more. I felt a deep, aching, sense of loss. There was no one else in the world that I was close to. Of course, there was Nachiketa, but he, after all, was a child, or at least still too young. Who would I talk to now? With whom would

I share my ideas? And how would I proceed towards the truth?

Diana interrupted my thoughts. 'We need a doctor,' she said, pulling on my sleeve.

Yes, I thought. We needed a doctor to certify death. There had been a doctor coming to see him now and then. I asked Diana to phone him. Feeling numb I went and sat in the next room. Half an hour passed before the doctor came. A temporary death certificate was made out. The official one would have to be applied for later.

The question arose, what were we to do with him? His concerns came to my mind. Could he be placed in samadhi? I hesitated. I had been angry and upset when I first heard of his illness. But was he a bad person? Hadn't he proved a good guide to many? Wasn't he excellent at the physical aspects of yoga? He could even stop breathing for up to five minutes, and slow down his pulse to almost nothing. But then somehow, in the odd way the mind wanders, I thought of bears. Any bear could do more than him. In some parts of the world, bears hibernate for seven months of the year without eating, drinking or excreting. Their pulse rate drops to eight per minute to conserve heat. Yet their brains are somewhat alert. If faced with a threat they can awaken. So, what was so great about controlling one's breath and slowing one's pulse? I even thought about Siberian salamanders. They stayed frozen for years and woke up fine. Better than any yogi.

And I remembered Lydia, Gudiya, Serina.

Diana was still standing in front of me, asking what had to be done next. It was already 4 p.m. 'He will be cremated,' I said. 'It is already evening, I will make arrangements for it tomorrow.' Telling them I would return shortly, I went back to the ashram to give Nachiketa the news, and to get some help from the nearby gurukul. Nachiketa took the news calmly. 'He will move on to another body,' he said.

'Do you really believe that, Nachiketa?'

'Yes,' he said.

I didn't know what I believed any more, but it wasn't the time to get into a discussion with him. I went to the gurukul and asked for two of the boys to join me in the night-long vigil near Dev's body, and arranged for the prayers for the cremation the next day.

Then I returned to Dev's house with Nachiketa and two gurukul boys. Dev was bathed, dressed in fresh white clothes, and laid on a mat on the ground. Oil diyas were lit and placed at five points round the body. Mantras were chanted and then we sat near his body. Early morning, the pandits, teachers and boys of the gurukul arrived, and the body was covered in flowers, laid on a bier and loaded in an ambulance to be taken to the cremation grounds at Hardwar. Diana, Sophie, and a few others followed the ambulance in two cars. From the night onwards villagers had started gathering outside his house. They did not care what his illness was, to them he was still god. They had organized trucks to take them to the cremation ground, and crammed with people, the trucks followed the cars. More trucks joined in along the way, and when we reached the cremation grounds there seemed to be thousands of people. Some members of the gurukul had already reached and had got the pyre ready. It wasn't possible to allow them all to pay their last respects, it would have taken hours. Dev's body was placed on the pyre, smeared with ghee and camphor, and more logs placed on top. Then I performed the task of the son, walking around the pyre with a ghara filled with water trickling out through a hole, and breaking it near the head. A burning log was handed to me, I paid my last obeisances, and circling the pyre three times, set it alight. The flames caught and gradually blazed. I stepped aside. Most of the people remained for an hour or so, and then began to disperse. I avoided the kapala kriya, the traditional breaking of the skull with a bamboo pole. This kriya was to help the soul to leave the body, and to prevent tantrics from using the skull for wrong purposes. These tantrics with long matted hair generally hover around the cremation ground and are said to be able to gain control of the spirit of the dead person, if they find an intact skull. I had performed this kriya for my wife, my father, and my mother, but I could not do it for Dev. When the pandit urged me, I said he was a holy man, he did not require it. Immediately my mind asked why I had said that, but somehow I could not do it. Nachiketa, Diana, Sophie, some of the gurukul people, staff from the ashram and I remained there till the flames died down, then we returned. Before leaving we threw green leaves behind us over the head, a symbol of his new life to follow. We informed the pandit that we would ourselves collect the bones and ashes from the pyre on the third day, and he assured me he would leave them untouched till we came.

As we reached the ashram, I was aware of my exhaustion and emptiness. After a wash outside we went in to bathe and change our clothes, then I retired to my room, closed the door and lay on my bed. I did not want to see anyone, not even Nachiketa. As I lay down, an unlikely sleep overtook me, but then I had a nightmare. A typical matted-hair tantric stood in the doorway, and was sucking my life away. In my sleep I chanted Om, Om, and held up my hand to ward him off, and he backed away and disappeared. I woke in a cold sweat.

As I calmed down I started thinking about death and the eternal and non-eternal self. Dev had acknowledged that he had not reached Brahman or that eternal self. But what relationship does the eternal unchanging Self described in Advaita have with the personal self that we know? This too, had been analyzed in philosophical texts of Vedanta, but I hadn't read and understood them all. Perhaps, I thought, the brain represents this self. It creates all kinds of thoughts, emotions, dreams. But when the brain dies, there is no trace of the eternal or the personal self. No self comes forward to speak in Alzheimer's. What then is the self? It needs the body and brain to function. In 'near death experiences' or NDEs people claim they float above the body, hear everything going on, see beautiful lights, etc. It should be noted though, that many NDEs are also horrifying. Anyway, all NDEs are revealed only when the person wakes, through the brain, speech, and other body mechanisms. Angels or other-worldly experiences, as well as hallucinations and everything else that happens, are experienced through the brain and body. People say they can contact other formless beings, or those who have died. Yet only the living person reveals these details, can make these contacts.

Being alive is an adventure in which one can experience or imagine all kinds of things. No one knows what being dead is like. Unless suicidal or deeply spiritual and philosophical, every living being fears death. What are the indications of life after death, what could suggest that there is such life?

Then I remembered the three-day rule.

In Hinduism, and I think in several other cultures across the world, a ceremony for the dead is held on the third or fourth day. The soul leaves the earth on that day. I was touched when I read that animals too sometimes stay with their dead, particularly young ones, for three days, before moving on. And I had seen mother cats—if they lose their kittens they cry and howl for exactly three days. If even the animal world follows this, there must be something in it. It is the only true indication I could find of life after death.

In fact, that reminded me that the collection of bones on the third day would have to be done early tomorrow. After my dream of the tantric I had woken too early and hadn't had enough sleep. The day passed in a daze, there was a sort of hollowness in me. I hardly ate, but drank a few cups of tea.

The next morning Nachiketa, Bholu and I set off again for Hardwar to collect the bones and ashes. The self-effacing and ever helpful Bholu had returned from his village a few days ago. He had briefly met Dev as soon as he had returned, but overcome with grief, had not wanted to attend the cremation. Now he was composed enough to participate in the last rites. For him, Dev was the best person in the world, who had given him and his ram shelter, and all these years provided everything he needed. Dev also hadn't objected when Bholu added two stray dogs and one injured cat to the animals in the ashram.

I had asked others not to come, as somehow I wanted privacy in my last moments with his remains. We took everything required, including five nails, and a roll of thick thread, five paan leaves, five sweets, diyas, fruits, and fresh cow's milk. Whenever milk for this purpose is requested, it is never charged for. In any case, the gurukul had several cows, and provided us with the milk.

We reached after a drive of half an hour, and the pandit took us to the site where Dev's body had been, and where now just a pile of ashes remained. He stayed with us, chanting shlokas, as we completed the rituals. Three nails were hammered into the ground beyond where the head had been, and two beyond the feet. Then the thread was wrapped around these nails, creating a space around Dev's ashes. Next, the five paan leaves were placed, with one sweet in each, and the five diyas were lit and placed around the space. After that we searched for the bones in the heap of ashes. They must have been very fragile, for there were not many whole pieces. As I searched, I was startled to see a tiny lizard dart out from under my hand. I had a weird thought—was Dev already reborn as a lizard? Then I told myself not to be foolish.

Meanwhile I was internally reciting the Gayatri mantra, followed by *Tryambakam yajamahe*, and at the same time wondering how there could be so many parallel thoughts in my head. A bucket had been half-filled with pure Ganga jal mixed with the fresh milk, and now the bones I had collected were washed in this, and given to me in a small cloth bag. The rest of the ashes were heaped into a gunny sack, and we carried these two bags barefoot to the van. Nachiketa held them in his lap, while I drove to a place I knew, a serene archway facing the Ganga, where I guessed there would not be many people. 'Go, my friend, flow to the river, be reborn again, whole and new,' I prayed, as I poured the bones and then the ashes in the river.

***

Traditionally, we would leave the bags on the river bank or throw them into the water, but Nachiketa had been reading about preserving the environment. He hadn't been keen on polluting the river with the bones and ashes, but it was our age-old tradition, what else could I do? Now I humoured him, and we took the two empty bags with us, and later put them in a garbage bin—an act that would be shocking to many. Before that we went to one of the ghats and distributed new clothes to eleven pandits, and fed them puris and aloo. Then I washed in the river while Nachiketa watched from the bank. Why was he resisting all this? I was too tired to think, and after a hot cup of tea we drove back to the ashram. We didn't talk on the return journey, and when we got back, I bathed and went to my room. A lot had been accomplished, though it was still only 11 a.m. There was an odd emptiness in me. I couldn't sleep, I tried to meditate, but I was just too tired and even close to tears.

The days passed and I tried to get back to normal. I paid a visit to Diana and Sophie, asked them about their plans and told them that I would be withdrawing from Dev's organization. Both said they would return to the main ashram in Sparks, Nevada, and then think about what to do. Diana said she understood why I wanted to withdraw, but she was happy that I had retained my affection for Dev, despite what I had learned about him.

'As his personal assistant you must have known all about his activities?' I could not help asking.

'Perhaps not everything,' she replied, 'but I was aware of quite a lot.'

'So what did you think of it? Why did you continue to support him?'

Diana reflected, and replied: 'Initially, I believed all he said. I thought he knew what was right, and did not question him. As you know I even had a relationship with him. Later, as he moved from one woman to another, I realized that he was not the guru I had thought he was. But I decided to stay on, and just look at it as a job. With me, he was always courteous, and I had a hefty salary. Then when he got ill, I began to feel sorry for him, I wanted to take care of him.'

'You were part of his Inner Circle,' I said. 'What did he teach there?' Diana looked at me with pity. 'You may as well know now, Nitya,' she said. 'The Inner Circle was not a fixed group. They were just people Dev called to a special meeting from time to time. He said that every guru, prophet or spiritual leader of the past, conveyed the highest truths to specially chosen disciples. Usually seven people, plus Dev, would be in these meetings. He would start with some genuine occult teaching, or at least it seemed like that to me, I am neither learned nor knowledgeable. His story or account would end with how union with god began with physical union on earth. And then we would choose our partners and have sex.'

I was stunned. So, though he had been shocked and angry at the experiments with the five Ms in Enzo's ashram, he had started a somewhat similar practice. Still, I queried further—did he speak about tantra? Who attended these meetings? Diana did not seem familiar with the word tantra. 'I do remember something about a Druid priest, and on another occasion about a Cathar priest, though I hardly listened to what he was saying, it was usually something he read out from a book, and I just waited for the end,' she responded. 'No Indians were ever present, the reading or talk was only about Western sects.'

My disillusionment was almost complete, but there was more to come.

I asked if there were any more of Dev's writings that she had, and whether she would give them to me. I said I would like to make sure that people did not misuse his work. Did she have any of his poems, or manuscripts of his published or unpublished books?

Diana hesitated. I thought she looked embarrassed. Then she said she did have a thick file of his poems, and would like to give them to me. She also had the 'Weirdo' file. I looked blank. The Weirdo file, was what Dev called it himself, she explained. It did not have any of his own writings, but contained letters from those he referred to as Weirdos. There were hand-written and typed letters, all with some kind of request or accusation. She would give it to me, she said, but I should keep in mind that most of them were untrue.

There must be manuscripts of his books too, I said, since he never used a computer himself. Or did he dictate the many books he had written?

'Nitya,' said Diana, 'I thought you at least would know. Dev did not write any books, nor did he dictate them.'

'What do you mean? There are so many books by him.'

'Other people in the ashrams wrote those books. He only affixed his name to them.'

This was a further shock; I had at least thought him knowledgeable and learned. Was that too a myth? When he wrote his life story, he revealed he had both knowledge and a good memory. Even his talks were quite erudite and profound. Why couldn't he write his books himself? I said as much to Diana. 'Writing a book requires a sustained effort. He was always travelling, always interacting with people. Some of his talks are recorded, but they are not enough to make a book. He used to mainly repeat the same thing, or read out of the books he claimed to be his own. I think his life story may be the only thing he ever wrote.'

Then I remembered that at the beginning of his story Dev had mentioned that all he had written in life was his poems, yet I had presumed that he was referring to creative writing, not to the learned books published under his name.

'But why didn't the real authors complain? Why did they allow it?'

'He paid them well for their work,' said Diana. 'And he convinced them that they were achieving divine grace by offering it to the guru. It was only Sharada who did not allow him to use her work, and left the ashram.'

'But Sharada was not a writer.'

'No, but don't you remember him displaying a portfolio of exquisite nature paintings? That was Sharada's work. When she found him claiming they were his own, she initially said nothing. She planned carefully, removed all her paintings and left the ashram. Mark suggested that he get them back, but Dev said to let her go.'

I did remember, it was an incident I had forgotten. But Dev never referred to it and always seemed to miss Sharada. Even his recent writings indicate that she had a special place in his heart.

He had not admitted all this in his life story. Perhaps he had not had sufficient time, death reached him before he could record everything. Or perhaps he had glossed over many truths in his life story? In fact, I began to wonder, was there any truth in anything he had written? If the stories of his early life and studies were true, how had he reached this point? Could anyone ever fully know or understand another?

Diana gave me the two files she had, and I took them with me to go through later.

***

Within a week several heads of Dev's ashrams from different parts of the world arrived. There was Paul, from his first ashram in Sparks, Nevada, who had replaced Bidyut a few years ago; Gregory from Florida; Christian from Germany; Vidyananda from Italy, and Franz from Switzerland. I was amused to realize that every one of them had come to claim to be Dev's true successor, to get overall control of his ashrams and properties, and to challenge me, who they believed would succeed him, unless they could displace me. Dev had not named a successor, but they knew that I had been his favourite.

I called them to the ashram for a discussion. When they came in the evening, they were in for a surprise, as I told them I had renounced sannyas, and also renounced my association with any ashram. My son Nachiketa and I would be leaving, as soon as I was able to rent a house in Dehradun. I would also be closing the ashram I had been running in Wisconsin. They could therefore decide among themselves about Dev's successor, and the control of his properties. I asked them not to forget that he had left the USA under a cloud. They should think about whether they wanted to carry on his legacy. I said that though I did not want to reveal too much at present, I had come to know it was a tainted legacy. They should consider this before taking a decision.

On that day I lost all faith in spiritual leaders. For all that the five of them could think of, was money and power. All were relieved that I was out of the picture. I did not know the outcome then, but a year later after fierce fights, each took control independently of their own ashrams. The organization built up by Dev no longer existed. Vidyananda was an Italian renamed by Dev, but soon each of the others too, became a swami with a new Indian name! But I had nothing more to do with them. Nor did I follow a fleeting thought I had about getting the ashrams investigated to end their illegal activities, or putting the police on their track. I realized I lacked the courage for this, my nature was one that wanted to withdraw, to shut my eyes to all that was wrong and carry on with my own life, just as I had done in the past. I saw I had done this throughout my association with Dev, but even now, I could not get myself to change.

That night I had a dream: I had to go on a journey up a mountain, and it had been decided by someone (not me) that though there were easier ways, the fastest way for me would be to use a mule or go on foot. The idea didn't appeal to me, but it seemed I had no option. The mule, which may have been there at the start of the journey was left behind at some point. I was walking up a steep, sandy slope. There was someone else too, a guide of sorts to show the way, but not helping me in the ascent. A shadow fell temporarily on the mountain, and I realized it would soon grow dark and cold. I hadn't even brought a sweater with me. How comforting it would have been to have a thick, warm sweater to wear.

Then the sunlight was back on the sandy slopes. I realized the guide had begun to run upwards. It was essential to reach before dark. I'd never been good at running—how could I run up a sandy slippery slope? Still I tried. It was tough but it didn't take long. Suddenly I reached a ridge which was the top. I realized I had reached the roof of the world. Below there was the whole world in a valley. 'This is the roof of the world,' I said, with some excitement. 'Yes,' said the guide. There was no great thrill to it, but I had arrived.

I remembered the dream clearly in the morning. Who was my guide? Was it Dev? Could even a fake person be a guide? That was something new to think about. I remembered the vast number of Dev's followers, the thousands who had gathered for his funeral, thousands more across the world. I thought of the honest and sincere Bholu, who had loved and revered him. The reasons for people following a guru remained a mystery, even though I had tried to understand and analyze it.

***

There is not much more to tell. Nachiketa and I bought a house in Dehradun. The house wasn't large, but it had three bedrooms, and the garden was quite big. There was an outhouse at the back, and as I had decided to invite Bholu to join us, it was ideal, as his animals too could be accommodated. The other workers at the ashram remained there for the time being. It seemed likely that Vidyananda would take over the Rishikesh ashram, and I thought he may not like Bholu's animals. Bholu was happy to come with us, and wanted to bring a family of cobras too, but this I had to refuse. The cobras lived near a big banyan tree in the ashram, and I explained to Bholu that they may not like to be relocated. The cat, dogs, and Hari the ram joined us.

I now had time to ask Bholu who had stayed in the ashram over the last year, if he knew anything about

Madhav's land. He corroborated what Dev had said, that Vidyananda and Mark had been there, but he did not know anything about the land. I got in touch with Mr and Mrs Bharadwaj, and my old friend Vijay. Vijay was in a poor state, almost an alcoholic, and I had to think of how to help him. Mrs Bharadwaj who still had a deep sense of injustice over Dr Shanti and the nurse, had been proactive. The police refused to take another look at the case, which was too old for them, so she contacted the media. The local newspaper wrote about the events, and a TV channel suggested that Dr Shanti was responsible for several deaths. That was when the police agreed to investigate, and meanwhile Dr Shanti's image suffered, I heard that patients stopped going to her, and her neighbours refused to talk to her.

Mrs Bharadwaj had also found out more about Madhav's land and those involved in the financial scams. She said that Madhav's wife and others confirmed that they were two foreigners, one in sannyasi's clothes, and some Indians. Now it seemed as if it could have been Vidyananda and Mark. Mark was nowhere around, but Vidyananda was still staying in a hotel in Rishikesh and I decided to go and meet him. I confronted him, and he denied any knowledge of murder, but admitted that he and Mark had bought land for a new ashram, and also raised money for its construction. He said there was no fraud involved, but they had a temporary financial crunch, and soon they would pay back the investments with interest. He also said that all this was done on Dev's instructions. Dev, of course, had refuted this, and had even written in his account that he hoped I would find out more. Had they been acting without his knowledge, or was Dev evading the truth? I told Vidyananda that if the money was not returned I would inform the police, though I knew that if he left the country there was little I would be able to do. And I was not even sure if I intended to do anything.

All along I kept mulling over what I had learned of Dev's life, and thinking about spirituality, god, and the true path. I read his poems to try and discover more about him, but there was nothing much in them. About ten of them described his dream woman, and those at least were original, though not great poetry. How could a man who loved Shakespeare write so poorly? The rest were short poems, of no value. I provide a sample here:

'Live life to the full;
You only live once.
Or do you live twice?
Or do you live many times?
O friend, live life to the full.'

When I got to the Weirdo file, I saw that what Diana had said was true. Many of the letters there seemed to be of disturbed people, claiming that Dev had visited them in his astral body, or entered their house through the ceiling with a host of angels, or something similar. Some, however, were genuine, anguished appeals, from women who claimed he was the father of their children. Were they true or invented? I had never heard of those women, they were not the ones I knew about. I was determined to make amends for my own lack of concern earlier, and, as I had said to Nachiketa, to do something for the women affected by him. I had already noted down the names I knew, and I added the letters that seemed genuine, to investigate further.

I could identify two main ways of looking at the world, and one could summarize them into the ways of the East and of the West, or to be more precise, the non-monotheistic and monotheistic religions. The Buddhist, Hindu and Jain way was to learn to ignore the world which was, they believed, either unreal or following its own trajectory of successive eras, in which the individual had little role. The Judaic, Christian and Islamic was to emphasize the importance of the individual, and to seek to change the world. This was a rather simplistic summary, but not incorrect, though I needed to think, study and understand more. Though I was a Hindu, and closest to the Hindu way of life, I did not want to detach myself from the world, but to set it right.

Could I somehow combine the two approaches, was there one path that fitted both world views? There were a lot of changes I needed to make in my own self, a self that I now recognized as one that was too detached, perhaps somewhat weak, content to ignore the faults of the world. I was able to take some action in Dr Shanti's case, probably only because I was not directly involved. Would study help me to be a better person? I planned to begin a systematic course in Indian philosophy—just for myself and Nachiketa, and perhaps Bholu if he was interested. I would read everything I could find on the topic, and then simplify it for them, and this process would help my learning.

I would think about life too. Studying philosophy was an intellectual quest, but from the heart I wanted to try to understand sorrow—the sorrow that existed everywhere, throughout the world. I know, others had tried before me, but their answers had not satisfied me. Wasn't there joy and happiness too in the world? There was, but for me at least, an underlying sorrow always existed. Wasn't it the same with Dev too? Wasn't sorrow the ultimate cause of all that he did?

Love was another great mystery that needed to be explored. There was sexual love, driven by desire, romantic love, closely linked to sorrow and joy, to despair and ecstacy, and then there was bhakti, the love of god, and also the compassionate love of the white light, seen in the cave of the heart.

And so I resolved that I had to translate my learning and thoughts into practical terms, to find answers for myself, and to find ways to help others, those I already knew about, and those whom I still did not know.

There was a long journey ahead, for us all, a journey that I knew would contain both shadow and light as it had in the past, but one that I hoped would lead to a better understanding of that eternal question, the reason for birth and for death, and for life in all its aspects.

Acknowledgements

Among the people I would like to thank are: my first readers, my brother Ardeshir Dalal, and my long-time friend Randal Joy Thompson, who provided encouragement and advice; my editor Renuka Chatterjee of Speaking Tiger who believed in the book from the start; Nandita Aggarwal who contributed to the editing; others at Speaking Tiger involved in the production and design.

I would also like to thank Subhadra Mitra Channa, professor of anthropology, who responded to my questions on the Jads, and whose research I have used for background information on the community. Her work includes *The Inner and Outer Selves* (Oxford University Press, 2013).